KING'S DAUGHTER

A Lost Pharaoh Chronicles Complement, Book II

LAUREN LEE MEREWETHER

LLMBOOKS PUBLISHING

ISBN-13: 979-8643872405

DISCLAIMER

While the author has gone to great lengths to ensure sensitive subject matters are dealt with in a compassionate and respectful manner, they may be troubling for some readers. This book contains violence and adult themes.

King's Daughter will contain spoilers for the following books:

- *Salvation in the Sun* (The Lost Pharaoh Chronicles, Book I)
- *Secrets in the Sand* (The Lost Pharaoh Chronicles, Book II)
- *The Mitanni Princess* (Prequel, Free Novella) and its Free Bonus Ending
- *Paaten's War* (Prequel, Book III)

Her future is pending.

The Mitanni Princess Tadukhipa weighs her options: happiness in exile and poverty, death in prison, or a luxurious life of loneliness.

Cursed to love a servant and practice a servant's trade, Tadukhipa rebels against her father, the King, for a chance to change her destiny.

The Mitanni Princess follows the young girl assumed to be the historical Mitanni bride, Tadukhipa, to Amenhotep III and given the pet name "Kiya" by Akhenaten.

THE LOST PHARAOH CHRONICLES TIMELINE

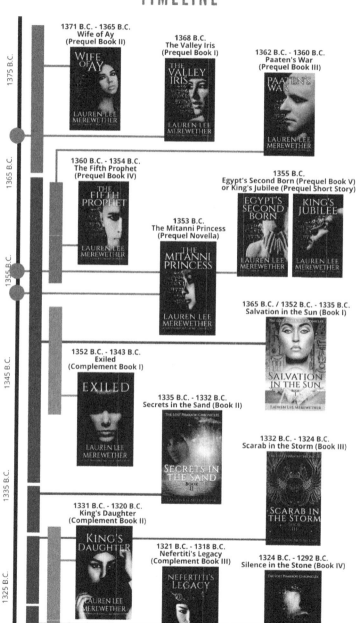

1371 B.C. - 1365 B.C.
Wife of Ay
(Prequel Book II)

1368 B.C.
The Valley Iris
(Prequel Book I)

1362 B.C. - 1360 B.C.
Paaten's War
(Prequel Book III)

1360 B.C. - 1354 B.C.
The Fifth Prophet
(Prequel Book IV)

1355 B.C.
Egypt's Second Born (Prequel Book V)
or **King's Jubilee** (Prequel Short Story)

1353 B.C.
The Mitanni Princess
(Prequel Novella)

1365 B.C. / 1352 B.C. - 1335 B.C.
Salvation in the Sun (Book I)

1352 B.C. - 1343 B.C.
Exiled
(Complement Book I)

1335 B.C. - 1332 B.C.
Secrets in the Sand (Book II)

1332 B.C. - 1324 B.C.
Scarab in the Storm (Book III)

1331 B.C. - 1320 B.C.
King's Daughter
(Complement Book II)

1321 B.C. - 1318 B.C.
Nefertiti's Legacy
(Complement Book III)

1324 B.C. - 1292 B.C.
Silence in the Stone (Book IV)

1375 B.C.

1365 B.C.

1355 B.C.

1345 B.C.

1335 B.C.

1325 B.C.

THE LOST PHARAOH CHRONICLES COMPLEMENT COLLECTION

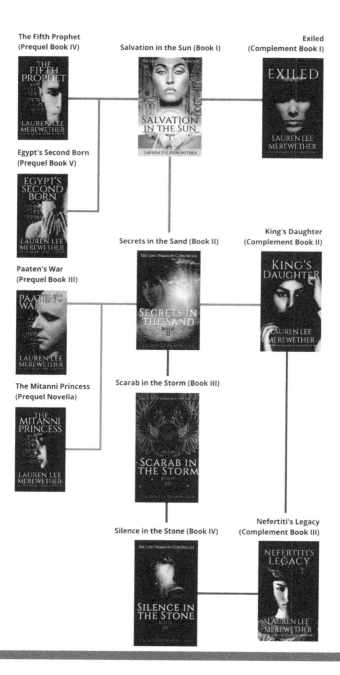

The Fifth Prophet
(Prequel Book IV)

Salvation in the Sun (Book I)

Exiled
(Complement Book I)

Egypt's Second Born
(Prequel Book V)

Paaten's War
(Prequel Book III)

Secrets in the Sand (Book II)

King's Daughter
(Complement Book II)

The Mitanni Princess
(Prequel Novella)

Scarab in the Storm (Book III)

Silence in the Stone (Book IV)

Nefertiti's Legacy
(Complement Book III)

GLOSSARY

CONCEPTS / ITEMS

1. Amphora – a ceramic container usually holding wine or other liquid
2. Ba – a person's personality; takes the form of a human-headed falcon after death
3. Captain of the Troop – one military officer rank of Pharaoh's Army above Greatest of Two Hundred Fifty
4. Commander – military officer; one rank below General
5. Deben – weight of measure equal to about 91 grams
6. Decan – week in Egypt (ten-day period); one month consists of three decans
7. General – military officer; highest military rank
8. "Gone to Re" – a form of the traditional

phrase used to speak about someone's death; another variant is "journeyed west"

9. Governor (Hittite) – appointed warlord of the King
10. Greatest of Two Hundred Fifty – second-lowest-ranking officer of Pharaoh's Army
11. Hin - a jar measuring about half a liter
12. Hekat - a barrel measuring ten hin or about five liters
13. Ka – the spirit or life force of a person
14. Khopesh – a standard military-issued sickle-shaped sword made of bronze
15. Medjay – police or policeman
16. Natron – perfumed soda ash soap that scented bath water for cleansing
17. Nomarch – a governor-type official who oversaw an entire province
18. Pharaoh – the modern title for an ancient Egyptian King
19. Season – three seasons made up the 360-day calendar; each season had 120 days
20. "Set up a house" – a phrase used to speak of marriage
21. Shat – weight of measure; twelve shat equaled one deben
22. Shendyt – apron / skirt; a royal shendyt worn by Pharaoh was pleated and lined with gold
23. Steward – main person in charge of a

noble's estate or care of a royal; position held by a man or a literate woman

24. Susinum – a popular perfume based on lily, myrrh, and cinnamon
25. Troop Commander – military officer; two ranks below Commander

GODS

1. Ammit – goddess and demoness; "Devourer of Hearts"
2. Amun – premier god of Egypt in the Middle Kingdom
3. Amun-Re – name given to show the duality of Amun and Re (the hidden god and the sun, respectively) to appease both priesthoods during the early part of the New Kingdom
4. Anhur – god of war; protector of the military
5. Aten – sun-disc god of Egypt (referred to as "the Aten"); a minor aspect of the sun god Re
6. Bastet - cat goddess and protector of the home, women, women's secrets and children
7. Bes – god of childbirth and of dreams
8. Hathor - goddess of joy, women's health, and childbirth, among other aspects of life
9. Horus the Great – god of the sky and sun

10. Nun – oldest god, who represented the waters of chaos from which creation began
11. Pakhet – wildcat goddess of war
12. Ptah – god of creation, art, and fertility
13. Re – premier god of Egypt in the Old Kingdom; the sun god; the New Kingdom Pharaohs began to associate with Re rather than Amun
14. Shu – god of air; symbolized by fog and clouds
15. Tefnut – goddess of moisture, mists, dew, and rain

PLACES

1. Aketaten – city of modern-day area of El'Amarna
2. Azzati – modern-day port city of Gaza; name taken from an Amarna letter reference
3. Berytus – modern-day city of Beirut; a Canaanite city-state under Egyptian control at the time of this story
4. Damaski – modern-day city of Damascus; a Canaanite city-state under Egyptian control at the time of this story
5. Goshen – Hebrew name for the Eastern Nile Delta
6. Hut-Waret – modern-day city of Avaris
7. Kubna – modern-day city of Byblos; a

Canaanite city-state under Hittite control at the time of this story

8. Land of Hatti – Hittite empire; name taken from an Amarna letter reference
9. Malkata – palace of Pharaoh Amenhotep III
10. Makedo – Canaanite city-state of Megiddo
11. Men-nefer – city of Memphis; located south of modern-day Cairo
12. Per-Amun – modern-day port city of Pelusium

PEOPLE

1. Aitye – female head steward to Nefertiti
2. Akhenaten – prior Pharaoh; father of Nefe, Ankhesenpaaten and Tut
3. Alashiya – King of Cyprus
4. Ankhesenpaaten – Chief Royal Wife to Tut; daughter of Akhenaten and Nefertiti; sister to Nefe
5. Atinuk – Canaanite
6. Ay – Overseer of Pharaoh's Horses; father to Nefertiti
7. Ebana – Captain of the Troop
8. Horemheb – Commander
9. Imhotep – comrade of Paaten
10. Jabari – Chief Royal Guard
11. Kalli – son of Pulli

12. Neferneferuaten (Nefertiti) – Pharaoh;
    mother of Ankhesenpaaten and Nefe
13. Neferneferuaten Tasherit (Nefe) –
    daughter of Akhenaten and Nefertiti;
    sister to Ankhesenpaaten
14. Niwa – wife of Paaten
15. Mai – comrade of Paaten
16. Paaten – General of Pharaoh's Armies
17. Pulli – Hittite governor
18. Senenmut – Greatest of Two Hundred
    Fifty
19. Smenkare – prior Pharaoh; uncle to Nefe
20. Suppiluliuma – Hittite King
21. Tadukhipa (Kiya) – Mitanni Princess
    (deceased); daughter of King Tustratta
22. Tutankhaten (Tut) – Coregent to Pharaoh
    Neferneferuaten; son of Akhenaten;
    husband to Ankhesenpaaten
23. Tuwattaziti – Hittite guard
24. Washuba – Hittite man
25. Zuzulli – son of Pulli

PROLOGUE
DAMASKI, 1355 B.C.

He had promised his wife he would come back to her. Per the command of Pharaoh Amenhotep III, Commander Paaten had put the Hittite traitors to rest in the tributary state of Kubna and traveled with his legions to Damaski. His heart was almost giddy at the thought of seeing his secret Hittite wife once more. His memory pulled her touch and her scent of honey, oil and wine to the forefront of his mind. His lip curled up into a smile as he remembered her long brown hair and eyes of jade from his nightly dreams of her. But the old man Danel's words came back to him in an instant: *Do not leave her at all. She may not be the same woman when you return.*

He gulped down the small fear. He had prayed to Bes every day that he would be released from his oath if he diligently executed Pharaoh's every command. His oath to the gods would then be fulfilled, and he could return to her. He prayed to Bes to send her dreams of his return if that day should come. He had given her leave of their marriage if she found another man, and if he came back and saw she was with another, he would do as he said: he would see her happiness and leave. If that happened, it meant Bes had not sent her dreams as compelling as his; it meant he would never return to her; and it meant the gods would never absolve him from his oath to Pharaoh.

That outcome unsettled his stomach on the bumpy chariot ride.

From her perspective, it had been five years with no word from him.

The giddiness in his heart turned to dread. What if he lost her? He had given her a means to escape marriage to him. He had said to take lamb's blood and present it to the city elders as proof of his death. It would allow her to marry someone else.

The recent rumors of Hittite sympathizers and traitors would have endangered her. What if the people of Damaski stoned her for her Hittite heritage? He doubted she would have returned her loyalty to the land that had treated her so harshly, but did anyone else know that? What if she had returned her loyalty? Had she been killed?

The chariot bounced along the lush gravel plains as he thought. With the salt from the sea no longer in the air, he knew the city upon the hill on the edge of the river was Damaski. He would find out what became of his wife before the sun set that day.

The Egyptian army took to the main city of Damaski where the young men came yelling and pointing fingers in every direction.

"Egypt has come to Damaski's aid!" they yelled while the city elders sat at the gates.

He remembered two of the elders' faces; they had been there when the old man Danel adopted him as his brother so he could marry Niwa. And when Danel passed, it sealed Danel's assets for Niwa. Marriage to him kept her safe from anyone who may have forced her into marriage.

Paaten held out his hand to silence the crowds. He spoke in the language of the Canaanites: Akkadian. "The great and mighty Lord of the Two Lands, Pharaoh Amenhotep III, has heard there are Hittite conspirators here in the land of Damaski. In return for your tribute, he has sent his legions to smite the enemy."

"A Hittite woman lives outside of town!" a man yelled out and pointed in the direction of Niwa's estate.

Paaten's heart skipped a beat—his wife was alive.

"Yes, let us arrest her and burn her with the rest of the traitors!" another yelled.

One of the two city elders Paaten remembered stood up, and, at the action, the young men silenced. "The Hittite woman is Niwa, widow of Danel, married to Danel's brother, Paaten."

"Paaten is no longer here. He gave up his brother's inheritance, or Niwa killed him, as no one has seen or heard from him in years," another man offered up for discussion.

Paaten sensed the stir in his men's chariots. He could feel their eyes shifting to him. He knew their thoughts: Was their Commander this Paaten? Paaten was an Egyptian name. He had been in the land of Hatti for two years, and there was a Hittite woman in question.

He had to act fast, or else a mob would march to Niwa's, and he would have to reveal his secret to his men. If they refused to listen to reason, it could mean potential execution for the both of them—he, a traitor in their eyes, and she, a Hittite sympathizer.

So he bellowed out over the Damaski men's uproar, "I, the Commander of Pharaoh's Armies, will go to this woman and determine if she is a Hittite sympathizer or not." His soldiers stood at the ready, daring the Damaski citizens to move. "Round up the rest of the Hittite traitors for questioning." He gestured to a Troop Commander to oversee the questioning of the suspected traitors.

The crowd dispersed to fulfill what Paaten ordered.

"It may be unwise for you to go by yourself, Commander," a nearby Troop Commander cautioned in a whisper. "You should bring at least two men in case the woman is a sympathizer and has Hittite soldiers or spies on her land."

Paaten agreed, to not arouse suspicion.

"Imhotep and Mai"—he pointed to two heartily

built foot soldiers—"come with me. We will make sure this Hittite woman is not a sympathizer to the land of Hatti."

They came upon the estate. The house he had built for Niwa still stood. It looked like servants lived there, based on their dress—all women, he noticed, and quite a few of them. His eyes fell upon Danel's old home, his home, the home where he had married Niwa; the home he had left her in, alone.

It has been five years.

His heart plummeted into his stomach. What would he say? What would she say? Had she fallen in love with another? Had she been faithful? Had Bes sent the dreams? Was he to return to her one day to live out the rest of their lives?

"Stay here; be alert," he commanded the two soldiers, Imhotep and Mai, at the edge of the grand estate.

He walked up to the door of the home and knocked.

Pigat, Niwa's inherited head steward from Danel, answered it. Pigat bowed and moved from the door. "Master Egyptian," she said to acknowledge him, but seemed not to recognize him.

He looked around the home—not much had changed since he had left. With the door still open, he thought he should keep up his appearance. "I am the Commander of the Egyptian army. We suspect a Hittite woman lives in this house and is a sympathizer to the land of Hatti. Who is the Master here?" He stepped inside.

"Our Master has been away for five years, but his wife remains in his place. I shall bring her to you." Pigat bowed once more before shutting the door behind him.

His heart quickened. Was he still the Master of the estate? Had Niwa not fallen in love with another man?

He heard a slosh of water in the back bedroom of the house, where he had gifted Niwa a bath well before he had left. A memory of Niwa's ethereal singing entered his mind as he followed Pigat to the back room from whence the sound of water came.

Pigat opened the door to slip inside. At the open door, he expected to see Niwa bathing, but instead, a dripping wet, naked toddler ran out into the room and in between his legs, giggling and screaming.

Niwa appeared behind the toddler and grabbed her arm, pulling her into her chest. Niwa's back bowed over the child, her head faced down toward the ground.

"Commander of Pharaoh's Armies, I heard your inquiry." Her voice wavered; a Hittite accent accompanied her Akkadian speech. "I am the wife of the Master of this estate. I was born a Hittite, but I am not a sympathizer to the land of Hatti! I disown the land of Hatti. Damaski is my home. Have mercy on my daughter and me!"

Paaten could only stare at the child peering up at

him from underneath Niwa's body with eyes made of a perfect blend of jade and brown. He was mute, trying to determine the child's age. Was he the father? Was this his child? Had he left Niwa alone in a foreign land pregnant to rear a child on her own?

His thoughts drifted.

Did she find love with another man and have a child during these past five years? That thought stabbed his heart, but it was what he had sanctioned for her to do when he left. If she was happy with another man, that was what he wanted for her.

But right then, he did not want her to be frightened.

He knelt down and lifted her chin, lifting her gaze to his eyes.

She was as beautiful as he remembered. As with Pigat, Niwa appeared not to recognize him with his wig on his head, kohl lining his eyes, and the bronze and leather attire of an Egyptian Commander on his person.

"Please, Commander, have mercy on my house. My heart will never be with the land of Hatti." Her jade eyes grew greener with the tears that almost overcame them.

He looked to her lips, hoping and wishing those lips had not tasted another. But at his gaze, he saw the tension in her shoulders immediately spring up, as it had the first day he spoke to her. Fear of being forced to bed by a Hittite man of wealth from her life in the land of Hatti flooded her eyes.

"I will never hurt the woman who saved me," he whispered in the Hittite tongue, returning his gaze to her eyes.

She stared at him for a moment as the tension crept away from her body. "Paaten?" Her whisper was almost inaudible. Her mouth fell slightly ajar.

Pigat visibly shifted on her feet upon hearing Niwa's realization and bowed her head. "Master," she said.

He swallowed, afraid to ask the question about the child. The question again resurfaced: Had he left her alone and pregnant in the land of Damaski? The child did not appear to be four or five years old—perhaps only two or three? Had she been forced to bed in his absence by wayward wanderers? Was this a love child between her and a man who did not want to marry her? Had she simply adopted an orphaned girl?

"You came back?" Again her whisper was almost inaudible.

He nodded. "I told you I would come back as often as I could."

Could he stay? he asked himself. No; he had to return. His dreams had not been fulfilled. Every night he thought about returning to Niwa, the same horrible, compelling dream came to him: *"Remember your promise, General,"* a woman Pharaoh called out to him. It seemed to him that until the dream came true, his oath to the gods forced him to stay in Egypt.

He pushed the dream away as he caressed Niwa's

cheek, wanting to kiss her, but afraid of the origins of the child.

"Egyptian troops are at the front of the estate. I must return to them. We are rounding up Hittite sympathizers and traitors to Egypt. We will stay in Damaski for a month or so, but I cannot *stay* as I want to."

Her mouth closed. "I see." She pushed his hand away and stood up. Her daughter stood behind her leg, peering out at him.

Paaten stood up as well. Niwa's eyes were ever so green. His heart quickened as she said, "Pigat, please take Anat outside. No one may enter until I step from the main house."

Pigat nodded her head and took the girl named Anat by the hand, leaving Niwa and Paaten alone. They stepped into the back room and closed the door. She spun around to face him, her arms crossed over her chest.

"Are you going to ask me if the child is yours?" Her voice strained.

He had hoped this would not be the welcome. His jaw tightened; he wanted to know the answer but also dreaded to know the answer for many reasons, his child or not.

Her eyes searched his as he thought.

He finally mustered the courage to ask, "Is the child mine?"

"No." The answer came out cold and sharp like a

dagger to the heart. It picked apart an old wound for it to freshly bleed again.

He wanted to crumple over, but he stood firm. He gripped his jaw to appease the ache from clenching it. Letting his hand fall after a moment, he asked, "Whose child is she?"

"Another man's." A coolness lay behind her eyes.

Paaten sensed deceit, or did he only want to sense deceit?

She studied him, as if looking for a reaction. Paaten's brow furrowed; something seemed off. She had said the girl was her daughter; she had said he was not the father—rather, another man. Was the girl an orphan? Was she only mad at him for leaving, rightly so, and therefore trying to hurt him?

At his continued silence, she finally spoke again with a wavering voice. "I did as you said I could do. I have fallen in love with another."

Paaten dropped his head; his life fled his body. Perhaps that was the deceit he was sensing: a reluctance to tell him the truth. He took a moment to steady his broken heart.

His words came out fragmented. "I wish you happiness, Niwa. As I promised, I will leave you with the man you love." He turned to go but stopped when she spoke.

"Is that all?" Her voice shook.

He clenched his hands into fists. "What is all?"

"You are not going to fight for me?"

He spun around to find her with tears welling in

her eyes. *Why is she crying? She is the one who loves another.*

"You made your decision. You had a child with another man. I have been faithful to you, Niwa, all this time, as I promised you. You are my wife; you are the only woman I love. For some reason, probably to do with the estate, you have not proven my death so you can marry this other—"

"You were gone, Paaten!" she screamed. Her chest filled with a trembling breath. "I thought you were not coming back, but I had these dreams about us . . . together . . . growing old . . . having children. They were so real, and every time I thought about releasing you from this marriage, a dream came to me." She shook, and her voice broke. "But . . . even though you are here today, you still have not come back."

Paaten stood in a daze. Had he heard her correctly? Had Bes answered him? Was he to return forever one day? Perhaps this other man was temporary? Maybe she still loved him? Or did she see him as a burden? Had Bes, in answering his prayers, caused him to be a burden to a wife who wanted nothing more than to move on and leave him? He had never asked her if she wanted this life—only that if she found another, he provided a means to end their marriage.

"You are right, Niwa. I left you for five years, and I will leave you again. I cannot tell you when I will be back, but one day I can return to you and stay." He saw a tear roll down her cheek at his confession. "I have been selfish. I desire nothing more than your happiness. You deserve every happiness in this life. You deserve a man who will protect you and love you and be here with you and your daughter—"

"If I told you this child was yours, would you stay?" A longing held in her eyes as she cut him off.

Paaten remembered the same plea—the same question—from the day he left her. He again sensed a deception in her voice. "She is not mine, as you told me?" he said more as a question of confirmation than a statement.

"Answer my question. You at least owe me an answer." Her arms tightened across her chest as she took a few steps to stand in front of him.

"I cannot stay, Niwa." He untied three pouches on his belt. "I have earned much gold and copper that I brought for you to help with whatever it is you need. Give it to your child."

"I do not need or want your trade goods, Paaten."

"Take them. Tell your lover it is a gift to wish you both the best in your life together." He tossed the pouches of copper and gold on the table. "I love you, Niwa, and I always will. May your life be blessed with your—"

"Stop saying that!" Niwa shook her head and slapped him across the cheek. "You do not love me." Her finger pointed in his face. "I was just a bed warmer for you while you took a hiatus from Pharaoh's Army!"

"That is a lie, Niwa!" He grabbed her wrist to

keep her from hitting him again. The scent of honey and wine refreshed his memory. He choked on his next words, hating himself if she had believed such a thing for the last five years.

"I have never loved anyone as dearly or as deeply as I have you." He traced a finger down her face. "I only regret the oaths I made that keep me from you and that have now pushed you into the arms of another man."

A grimace covered his pallid face.

"I see you in my dreams, Niwa, but I cannot get to you. The gods want me to fulfill my oath to them for saving me in the land of Hatti. When that is accomplished, I will come back to you forever. That was my promise to you. That is the promise I intend to keep, but"—he pressed his forehead to hers—"you love another. You had his child."

Despite his heartache at the betrayal he had caused and even sanctioned before his departure, he still wanted nothing more than to kiss her, to be with her, to love her and have her love in return. His lips hovered over hers.

"Are you going to kiss me?" Her whisper of a question came hot on his lips. Did she want him to? Did she still love him? But the child . . .

Tears welled in her eyes and also in his. "I cannot."

"I am still your wife. We are still married." Her free hand smoothed over his large bicep, and the other, in his loose grip of her wrist, feathered away some braids of his wig. Was this some nostalgic moment for her? Did she pity him? Why was she doing this?

Her lips grazed his, and he stilled his breath. He missed her touch. If she loved another, why was she acting this way with him? He cupped her cheek, but still, he refrained from kissing her.

"I cannot be with you when you do not love me," he whispered, knowing the strain it would have on his heart when he walked away forever, knowing she would think it to be a sham encounter.

"Paaten," she whispered without the prior angst in her voice. A tear escaped down her cheek. Her eyes no longer held deception; peace dwelt there instead. What had changed?

She continued in a whisper as she caressed his cheek. "I needed to know your true feelings for me."

What? A stirring gripped his heart. "Had I not shown—"

"You left me, Paaten. You said you would return, and now that you have, I see how you respond to me. I see now that I was never just another woman to you."

"You have never been just—"

"I know; I am certain of it now." She pushed a finger to his lips. "I have let you believe something that is not true. I have lied to you."

He blinked, and his mouth parted. He lifted his head from her forehead. "How have you lied? What is not true?"

"There is no other man. The child is not mine. I said she was my daughter for fear Pharaoh's Army would take her from her true mother." She pulled him closer to her body.

The realization of her confession sank into his stomach, securing him to the ground as his heart leapt in joy. There was no other man. She had no child from another.

"But if she were your daughter, would you stay?" The question came again, this time with an urging.

His heart yelled out, *"Even with no child, I will never leave you!"* But his lips spoke the reality: "I cannot stay, Niwa, but I will always return to you."

Another tear rolled down her cheek.

He wiped it away with a thumb. "This is what I can do. I will return to you as much as I can, or if you do not want me in your life, I will not be in it. I will stay away and live a relatively empty life in servitude to my King, as I pledged before I knew you." He kissed her forehead. It was time to ask her what she wanted for her life. He should have asked her five years ago.

"Will you accept me as your husband now, like in this current life, or do you want me to leave and never return, knowing you will never have to wonder if I am alive or dead or when I will come back to you?"

A long silence filled the space between them. Should her answer be "Leave," he would depart a broken man. He would fulfill his oath to Pharaoh, live a life of solitude aligned with the principles of Ma'at, and travel to the fields of Re at the end of his life. There would never be another woman as Niwa was to him. In the last five years, he had been able to excel in Pharaoh's Army, knowing one day he might return to her if he fulfilled his oath in excellence. But if he knew that day would never come, he questioned how he would wake each morning.

An answer did not come; instead, she looked into his eyes and softly said, "I needed you, Paaten, and you left me."

"No, Niwa." He shook his head. "You are a strong woman with a warrior heart; it is one of the reasons why I love you. You have never needed me. You only wanted me. It is I who have needed you . . . much more than you know."

She lifted her chin; her eyes searched his. "You have never lied in what you promised me, Paaten. That I know now. That I trust. If I must go years in between seeing you, then so be it. I want a life with you, no matter how little time we may share."

A small laugh of relief escaped him as a smile stretched from ear to ear. He placed his parted mouth upon her eager lips. Her hands slid up his neck and onto his smooth head, knocking his wig to the floor. It was then he wished for his long hair for her to tug as she once did. One day it might happen again. The day he would stay would come; otherwise, Bes would not be sending her dreams of his return. The thought lifted his heart even more, and he kissed her harder, feeling her soft moan on his lips. His hands began to roam over her body but stopped when his fingers brushed her belly. . . . The child—Niwa had said she feared Pharaoh's Army would take the girl from her true mother. Why?

He stopped. The unresolved question beat against his mind. She looked into his eyes, wondering why his hands paused and why he had lifted his head.

"Then whose child is Anat?" he asked.

She chuckled and shook her head. "I pledge my love to you, and you only wonder about a child I have already told you is not mine?" Niwa took his hand and guided him backward into their cot on the floor. "She is the daughter of a woman whom we saved from the land of Hatti."

He nodded in acceptance, and her neck again drew his lips. His chest drew her hands upon it. Her scent intoxicated him as his hands got lost in her tresses, and his gaze was caught in her pools of jade. His armor came off, but her answer replayed in his mind . . . *the daughter of a woman whom we saved from the land of Hatti* . . .

"Wait." He paused his hands and his lips as his mind tried to think.

Was this the source of the Hittite sympathizer rumors? He pulled his head back to keep himself from kissing her.

"Who is *we*?"

She grinned, shaking her head. "Five *years, you* and *I* have waited, Paaten." She kissed his mouth. "I will tell you everything that has happened later." Her finger ran from his lips down his strong jaw, defined chest and stomach.

"Now, love your faithful wife," she whispered with green eyes ablaze. Her body pressed against him, and he obliged her request and his desire, thinking no more on her answer.

CHAPTER 1
ESCAPE FROM AMBUSH
AKETATEN, 1331 B.C.

THE TORCHLIGHT FROM THE ROYAL HAREM'S HALL flooded the bedchamber. Nefe stirred in her bed at the sudden stab of light, but at the hushed command, "Princess, get up. You are in danger," her eyes popped open. A pair of hands pulled her upright, and a linen dress was thrust over her shoulders.

"What? Why? What has happened?" Nefe stammered, trying to discern if she was dreaming.

A belt appeared in her hand.

Nefe tried to see who was dressing her out of one eye as she rubbed sleep from the other eye.

"The people have risen up. Pharaoh orders you to the council room," the hushed voice came again. A wig plopped on her head as Nefe girded her waist with the belt. The silhouette of the figure dressing her moved quickly and dropped Nefe's gold-encrusted sandals at her feet. Nefe blinked a few times as she shuffled into her sandals.

The voice sounded familiar.

The people have risen up?

The night's lull almost caused her to close her eyes yet again and brush off the happenings around her as one of her dreams.

A hard yank on her shoulder pulled her awake. "We must go now," the voice said again.

Nefe realized she held an end of her belt in each hand as she was being prodded toward the door. *This certainly does not feel like a dream.*

The light from the door grew bigger as she approached it. A tendril of panic arose in her chest.

If this is not a dream, where is my sister? Is she in danger too?

The thought caused her to turn around to the shadow figure and blurt out, "What about Ankhesenpaaten?"

"I am here, Nefe," her sister whispered behind her. She spun her around to face her. Ankhesenpaaten tied Nefe's belt for her since Nefe was taking too long and then ushered her toward the door.

"Wait! My—" Nefe reached toward her empyreal vulture headdress on its stand by her bed: the symbol of her birthright as a royal woman.

"Leave it," the hushed voice came again and pushed both sisters out of the room.

General Paaten stood at the corridor's end with his khopesh drawn, alert and ready to defend. Nefe turned to look at her sister to ask "What happened?"

but saw her mother's steward, Aitye, next to Ankhesenpaaten.

If Aitye is here, where is Mother? What is going on? What happened?

A chill passed over her as she remembered the hushed whisper that woke her: *The people have risen up; you are in danger.*

Nefe grabbed her sister's hand without another word, and the three women flew down the torchlit corridor. The light from the alabaster torches cast their long shadows against the decorated walls depicting the Aten and her late father's greatness.

They fell into General Paaten's shadow as he led them to Pharaoh's council room. Nefe expected to hear screams, yells, and the clash of bronze weapon against weapon, but the palace was eerily quiet; nothing seemed out of the ordinary. She watched General Paaten's head swivel, and, at one point, he stopped and strained to listen to something.

Perhaps he thinks as I do. But if that is so, why is Aitye here?

Just as they all turned the corner of the palace corridor, the pounding of feet reached Nefe's ears. Chief Royal Guard Jabari and Pharaoh Neferneferuaten ran toward them.

The weight in Nefe's stomach lifted at seeing her mother alive. *Mother! She is alive! She is safe! She must have sent the General and her steward to get us.*

They all met at the council room doors.

The bleary-eyed General growled at Jabari, "Why was I not notified of the attack? I have sent one of your royal guards to tell Ay and Horemheb."

Nefe looked between the two chiefs. *General Paaten was not told of the attack? He is the General. Neither grandfather nor Commander Horemheb were told either?*

A creeping discomfort slithered around her legs and up her back.

"It all came about very suddenly. I sent a messenger to all three of you, but perhaps he was detained," Jabari spouted off, throwing open the door and hurrying the women inside first.

As soon as Ankhesenpaaten stepped foot in the council room, Nefe opened her mouth to ask the question on her mind, but her sister asked her question for her.

"Why are we in the council room? There is no means of escape," Ankhesenpaaten said, her voice trembling. The moonlight barely showed through the almost-completed ceiling, leaving little light to make out the figures in the room.

Nefe held her sister's hand. Ankhesenpaaten was two years older than she and the last living sister she had. If they were going to be murdered in the council room, at least they would be together. An eerie dread overcame her senses, and she shivered at the thought of living without any of her sisters. After losing Royal Wife Kiya, who was like a mother to her, in the plague, along with four of her five sisters, Nefe squeezed Ankhesenpaaten's hand, not bearing the thought of being alone if something happened to Ankhesenpaaten.

I cannot lose you too.

"Is there a torch in here we can light?" her mother asked over Nefe.

Jabari closed the door. "No. We do not light anything, for the rebels may see the light through the unfinished roof."

Nefe's eyes strained to adjust from the brightly torchlit corridor to the dim moonlight.

"You suggest we hide," General Paaten asked him as he hooked his khopesh to his belt, "like cowards?"

"I suggest we take Pharaoh and her family to safety, away from this place. The people have killed the Hittite Prince Zannanza on his journey here, and, one way or another, she will abdicate," Jabari said with a head nod to the leader of the Pharaoh's Armies.

Nefe saw something move in the corner, but she assumed her eyes were playing tricks on her. *Who would be in the council room at this hour?* She squinted, trying to confirm that no one was hiding in the dark.

"Why was I not informed of the Hittite's death?" General Paaten asked his subordinate as he pushed his shoulder. "Why am I the last to know any of this?"

Nothing else stirred in the dark. The cold chill in her spine returned despite her confirmation they were alone in the council room. She glanced to Jabari and heard his response.

"As I said, General, it came about so suddenly. The messenger I sent you . . . he must have been detained." Jabari regained his composure. "There is a secret way out of the council room . . ." He moved his hands along the wall, feeling for the tiny burst of air. "Ah, here it is." He pressed on one of the stones and opened a half-door leading to a dark tunnel.

A thin veil of sand blew in from the night breeze in the tunnel.

"I did not know there was an escape passageway in here," her mother said. "Why did I not know of this?"

Nefe glanced around the room once more.

Something seems . . . not quite right.

Her gaze landed on the dark gaping hole in the wall; it seemed to suck away any light that fell into the council room. An uneasy wave of nausea passed over her stomach the more she stared into the abyss.

"This was a design for the royal guard, in case we needed to get Pharaoh to safety if he were injured in battle. They are all over the palace. The doors only open from the inside. Once it is closed, no one can open it from the other side." Jabari stood and dusted his hands on his legs. "You must always have an escape route in your fortress," he added as a note of sage advice.

He drew Nefe's intense stare. "So, what now?"

Nefe asked, knowing the last thing she wanted to do was step into the dark tunnel with Jabari.

His voice has a certain strain to it, and his story seems off. Why would the night be so quiet and tranquil if rebels were clamoring at the gates?

"You leave." Jabari placed his hands on Nefertiti's shoulders. "Probably never to return, for your own sake."

Nefe let out an audible gasp at the Chief Royal Guard's touching of Pharaoh.

Her mother wrenched back from his grip. Ankhesenpaaten let go of Nefe's hand and grabbed Nefertiti's arm.

"Mother, what about Tut? He will be killed!" Ankhesenpaaten asked with obvious concern for her friend and husband.

Nefe's eyes darted between her mother and sister. *Do they think Jabari is telling the truth?* Her gaze fell upon General Paaten's shadowy silhouette. *Does General Paaten?*

The silence lingered until her mother spoke:

"We are not going anywhere until I know the threat is real." She looked over to Jabari. "Where do your loyalties lie, Chief Royal Guard?"

Ankhesenpaaten, seemingly at her mother's sudden doubt, crossed her arms and looked toward Jabari's silhouette. Nefe did the same, realizing she was not the only one who questioned the account of events. General Paaten puffed up his chest and stood behind Pharaoh.

The moonlight did not penetrate the room enough for them to make out Jabari's reaction, but his voice was clear and forthright: "My loyalties are with Pharaoh."

Silence lingered in the room, and something caused General Paaten to stir.

"Jabari, light a torch," her mother ordered.

"But, my Pharaoh, the rebels will see the light and come to attack," Jabari reasoned.

"I did not hear any rebels," Nefertiti snapped.

"Neither did I." General Paaten's hand fell to his dagger.

Nor did I, Nefe thought, but something moved in the corner again. She was almost sure of it. Her gaze fell from Jabari to whatever it was that seemed to move in the dark.

"Believe what you will, but I was told the Hittite Prince was slain—killed by the very riot that tears down the gates of the palace." The moonlight silhouetted Jabari's hand gestures as he spoke.

"I do not know . . . something does not seem right." General Paaten voiced Nefe's concerns as he walked toward a sound that caused her hairs to stand on end. He turned to her mother and whispered, "I do not think we are alone in here."

Nefe's eyes widened in the dark, but before she could scream out, something bounded toward the Chief Royal Guard.

A glint in the moonlight—and Jabari went down.

Ankhesenpaaten screamed; warm blood splattered her face. Nefe's voice caught in her throat. A hard grip latched onto her upper arm. The abyss drew closer. Her feet shuffled underneath her as her mother pushed her and Ankhesenpaaten into the escape tunnel. She fell through its black gaping mouth and landed firmly on her belly.

"General, remember your promise!" Her mother's voice bounced off the stone walls as the moonlight glowed brighter in the room.

Nefe rolled to her back and propped herself up with her elbows and watched the scene unfold; she was frozen where she lay.

Aitye screamed as she jumped away from a dark figure who wounded her arm. Nefe's mother grabbed the torch, thrust it into Aitye's arms and pushed her into the escape tunnel with the two sisters. Ankhesenpaaten jumped up and reached for their mother.

General Paaten drew his khopesh and dagger and slashed at the air in front of him, defending himself while his old eyes adjusted. He slowly backed to the entrance of the tunnel, waiting for Nefertiti to go inside. But out of the darkness, a kick to his chest sent him flying into the tunnel before her. Ankhesenpaaten screamed, "Mother!" and her fingers just brushed her mother's hand before Pharaoh was yanked away.

General Paaten was up fairly quickly for his age,

but not before someone in the council room slammed the door shut. He banged on the hidden door constructed in the stone wall, perhaps throwing his shoulder into it as well. Nefe could not tell; darkness encased them. She could only assume as much by the grunts of the large, solidly built General. There were neither cracks nor holes for enough light to enter to be of any use.

"Light the torch so I can see!" he yelled to Aitye.

Nefe still stared in the pitch blackness as she lay on the tunnel floor, propped up by her elbows.

What just happened? The scene that had unfurled before her flashed in an instant through her mind. *Where is Mother? Did Mother make it out of the council room? Where is Mother?*

"I am t-trying," Aitye cried. She had been trying to light it since she got into the tunnel; finally, using the flint that attached to its base, she was able to get a spark, and the torch lit.

The stone tunnel lit up. *A sand floor, maybe.* Nefe's fingers dug into the sand by her side. *A sand-covered stone floor.* Her gaze stayed on the door.

The grunts. The yells. The sand. The stone. They shook the fiber of her reality. They jarred her soul in the most nonsensical way.

General Paaten grabbed the torch and pressed his hand against the wall, trying to find some sort of weakness, a handle, or anything to re-open it.

Aitye pulled Nefe up.

Nefe's gaze fell to her sister, to the General, to Aitye . . . *What just happened? Where is Mother?*

General Paaten took a sad step back from the heavy door and dropped his head. His chest caved. He turned to look at the two remaining daughters of Pharaoh and her servant.

A sadness leached into his words, though his voice remained firm and deep.

"Your mother wanted me to take you to safety. She wanted you to live a life of anonymity, where no one will know you are royalty, so you can be safe. Follow me."

Nefe could not command her tongue to argue. With her body in a fluidlike daze, she let Aitye lead her after General Paaten's footsteps. But her sister's yell behind her made her stop and turn around: "We are to do nothing?"

General Paaten stopped and looked back as well. "We cannot do anything more. I made Pharaoh a promise that if anything should happen to her, I was to save you."

"What about Tut?" The tremble in Ankhesenpaaten's voice told Nefe she feared the worst.

"If they came after Pharaoh, they probably have come after him too. He is a much easier target." General Paaten's grimace signaled he wished he could take back his last sentence. The firelight danced on Ankhesenpaaten's horrified expression. "Come now. We need to cover much ground."

He turned and began his brisk walk once again; Nefe and Aitye followed closely behind the light of the torch.

He is probably right, Sister. I am too numb to feel anything right now, but I know your heart breaks. Nefe looked around. *Where is Mother?* Her lips dared not speak what she knew was truth, and she only repeated *Where is Mother?* in her mind.

They had walked for a while until a noise and screams came from behind them. General Paaten turned back, telling them to wait there. The torchlight grew faint, and Nefe grabbed Aitye's hand as they stood in the pitch dark. *Where is Ankhesenpaaten? At least, she is alive; at least, we will be together.* The thought made her stomach churn because she knew her mother would not be. She pushed it away and again asked herself: *Where is Mother?*

But after repeating the question a few more times, Nefe realized she could not force herself to believe the false hope anymore. The truth punched her in the belly as she sucked in the stale air around her. Ankhesenpaaten's cries and screams for their Mother echoed in the tunnel: "He is killing her! Pawah is *killing* her! General, help her!"

Tears burned Nefe's eyes and rolled down her cheeks in an endless succession as she listened to Ankhesenpaaten.

Mother is gone.

Aitye squeezed her hand as General Paaten came

back with Ankhesenpaaten thrown over his shoulder. He set Ankhesenpaaten down next to Nefe and crouched next to them.

"My ladies of the two lands," he whispered as he gathered the daughters of Pharaoh close. "These are dark times." He looked specifically to Ankhesenpaaten. "Your mother knew this was a possibility and made me promise her that I would take her daughters to safety—perhaps even beyond Egypt's borders. I have carried on my person at all times gold for barter, from the treasury, at her command, should the day ever spring upon us. As it has today."

Ankhesenpaaten dropped her head and sobbed. Nefe rubbed her sister's arm helplessly, wondering how much their mother had kept from them.

"King's Daughter, Ankhesenpaaten," he whispered. "Your mother will live through you."

Then he touched Nefe's cheek. "And through you."

His arms wrapped around them as a father's would his daughters. Nefe's father had never embraced her like that, but she had seen her grandfather do so with her mother . . . *Mother. She is gone.*

General Paaten pulled Nefe and Ankhesenpaaten close. Nefe pushed the thought of her mother away and thought of her own father, the great Pharaoh Akhenaten, who had traveled to the afterlife only three years prior. He had embraced her maybe once in her life before he became one with the Aten-disc, or as her mother had told her in recent years, not the Aten but with Re . . . *Mother. She is gone.*

Nefe rested her cheek on General Paaten's golden collar; his bronze armor poked her chest as he squeezed them.

My sister and I . . . we are orphans. The thought chilled her in the light breeze that swept through the tunnel. Tears rolled down her cheeks, but they were not as the sobs of her sister.

I will wake up, and this will all be a dream.

The sobs were not fading.

This is all a dream.

She clutched General Paaten's neck and pressed her cheek further into his collar.

Wake up.

The beads from General Paaten's collar imprinted upon her cheek.

This is no dream.

Ankhesenpaaten's sobs quieted, and he ended their embrace when they had fully subsided. He whispered, "We must go."

AS SOON AS THEY EXITED THE TUNNEL BY WAY OF another hidden door at the tunnel's end, a dark figure appeared in front of them; soft, scattered light emerged in the predawn sky behind him. General Paaten stopped in his tracks. Nefe's heart raced as

Aitye pulled both of the young royal women behind her.

The figure of a man with a hooded cloak was silhouetted against the dusk sky. Reaching up, the man uncovered his head. His black hair nearly blended in with the predawn sky, and the fire of Paaten's torchlight danced in his big brown eyes under full black eyebrows. The shadows of the light emphasized his hard jawline and straight nose.

"You are not Egyptian," General Paaten said, drawing his dagger.

"No, I am not Egyptian but a friend to Pharaoh Neferneferuaten," he said with a bow of his head. A slight Akkadian accent clung to each word. "There is no need for a weapon, General Paaten." He lifted his hands to show they were empty. "My name is Atinuk. Come with me."

"Pharaoh never mentioned a friend named Atinuk to me," General Paaten said, lowering his dagger just a fraction.

Nefe looked at the bow and quiver of arrows strapped over Atinuk's shoulder. She shrank closer to her sister as he responded.

"She did not know me."

General Paaten raised his dagger again, debating whether or not to trust this foreign stranger. "Then how are you a friend?"

"I loved the one known to you as Royal Wife Kiya," he answered as he swished his cloak to reveal his Canaanite attire.

General Paaten's face warmed, seemingly at the memory of such a sweet woman. He let his defense drop, but the women behind him continued to eye the stranger. Kiya had been like a mother to Nefe and Ankhesenpaaten, and yet she had never mentioned a man named Atinuk before she passed eight years earlier.

But Kiya was Mitanni. This man is a Canaanite. How did he love her or even know her? Has he stayed here for eight years alone?

"Her last request of me was to look after the daughters of Nefertiti . . . your Pharaoh Neferneferuaten. With the riots and rebellions," his voice tottered, "I knew it was only a matter of time before I honored her wish."

Nefe's gaze drifted to General Paaten, who stood ready to defend or attack.

Riots and rebellions . . . like the one tonight? Tonight when my mother . . . Nefe froze.

Atinuk gestured to the northeast. "I have land in Canaan. The daughters of Pharaoh will be safe there. The sun is about to rise, and we shall do well to leave now under the cover of darkness."

General Paaten narrowed his eyes at the stranger and pursed his lips, keeping his dagger unsheathed. The silence knocked Nefe into the present. She looked back at the abyss of a tunnel from whence they came, then at her sister.

There is nothing for us back there. I do not trust this man, but we do not have many options.

Nefe grabbed Ankhesenpaaten's hand, but her sister looked off toward the royal harem where Tut remained.

"Agreed," General Paaten finally said, and they followed Atinuk out. Ankhesenpaaten's hand slipped from Nefe's as they ran across the stone courtyard.

At least, my sister is with me.

CHAPTER 2
ESCAPE FROM THE SUN CITY

HER FEET PLOPPED INTO THE SAND OUTSIDE THE palace wall, and she froze amid the warm dawn breeze whipping about her. A swirling wave of nausea caused a shrill ring in her ear and a blur of her vision. Nefe had only left the palace once in her lifetime, and now she was about to leave it forever.

The man who called himself Atinuk stood in front of her, holding out his hand as if he wanted her to take it. He was speaking, but she heard nothing but that shrill ring.

A heavy presence landed next to her. The warmth from his body made her shudder. She waited for one more plop, but it never came. Instead, she realized her feet were shuffling underneath her; General Paaten had a hold on her arm and was running with her in tow. Her vision cleared as her gaze darted among the faces: General Paaten, Atinuk and Aitye, who ran a few lengths behind her.

Something is wrong. Someone is missing.

She yanked her arm out of General Paaten's grip. "Stop!" Her chest heaved, and she looked at her three companions.

There should be a fourth.

"What is it, Daughter of the King?" General Paaten's stare bore into hers. His question attempted to deceive her. He knew what was wrong; his eyes betrayed him. He did not want to tell her, she assumed, and an inability to think swept over her small frame.

"What is it?" he asked again at her silence.

"Where is Ankhesenpaaten?" The question slid off of her tongue in its raw form: no titles, no formality of speech, only the question for which she dreaded to hear the answer.

His brows knitted as he lowered his face to hers. "She decided to stay," he whispered quickly, as if pulling plaster off of an open wound. "We must go—"

"No." Nefe shook her head, denying her sister's choice.

How could she do that to me? She chose Tut over me? She left me alone! Alone! Mother is gone and she leaves me to be killed? I cannot do this. I cannot be without her. She knows this. Why would she leave me?

Her tongue could not keep up with the questions in her mind. "No. Why? Why—"

"We must keep moving, Daughter of the King." General Paaten cut her off and slowly grabbed her arm again. "You are no longer safe here. I must keep my oath to your mother." His grip hardened on her arm as he turned to run again.

"No." Nefe pulled back, but her small frame did nothing to hold back the man of war.

"It will help our escape if we keep quiet," he whispered. His taut jawline strained into his neck as he moved.

Was he lying? Did he leave her?

The question in her mind became an accusation on her tongue.

"You left her. You left her alone to fend for herself." Nefe tried to pry his fingers off of her arm.

He spun her around in front of him and knelt so that he looked up to her. "My Princess, she chose to stay. My orders were clear: Take Pharaoh's remaining daughters, those who are willing, and leave Egypt. Protect them always." His grip loosened. "She stayed for her husband," he whispered.

His thumb brushed an errant tear on her cheek.

Such a gentle, inappropriate thing for him to do, she thought, but after the events of the morning, she welcomed his touch once again. His dark eyes seemed almost soulful; she had never seen him as anything but a hardened warrior devoid of feeling. Yet, here he knelt before her, brushing her tear from her eye as if she were his granddaughter.

His voice held firm and deep like always, but there was a sense of empathy behind his words.

"Please. She made her choice. Now, make yours. If your sister's fate is that of your mother's, you will be the last of Pharaoh Neferneferuaten's line. If you return to the palace, you will not live as you once did, should you survive. If you choose to go to Canaan and start anew, you will live a simple life away from the political turmoil and paranoia that has so plagued your mother ever since she married your father. However, you will no longer be a Daughter of the King."

Her heart nearly beat out of her chest at the choice before her.

Her mother had been right to be paranoid, it seemed now. She had planned for something like this to happen to her; she had tasked General Paaten, the leader of Pharaoh's Armies, to save Nefe and Ankhesenpaaten. She had distanced them from the true depth of corruption that led to her life being taken. She had orchestrated all of it to keep her safe, alive and happy. Yet, Ankhesenpaaten turned back for their half-brother Tut.

Is Mother to die in vain?

Paaten's dark eyes grew soft as he watched her with a patience she had not seen or expected from the daunting warrior.

Atinuk ducked his head. "Your majesty, you need to make a decision quickly. The sun will not be on our side." He gestured to the dawn in the east. His eyes ran over her face, and the warmth of his encouraging-yet-pressed smile seemed familiar, as if she reminded him of someone.

Nefe glanced up at the stone walls of the mighty

palace, white and dazzling in the glowing streaks of dawn that heralded the coming day.

Ankhesenpaaten, I hate you. Why did you stay and face certain death? Why would you leave me alone?

Aitye stood silent, but she caught Nefe's eye. She gave Nefe a slight nod and mouthed the word "live."

My name is Neferneferuaten Tasherit. I am my mother's namesake. I will live for her; I am the last Daughter of the King. Nefe drew a deep breath, wiped her tears, and nodded to General Paaten.

"Start anew," she whispered with a brave face.

A slow smile appeared on his lips, and his grip upon her arm lessened as he stood, towering over her.

"Then we must make haste." Paaten's hand slid down her arm and took her hand. "I will ensure you are safe and live a good life, Daughter of the King."

He locked eyes with her, and she knew he would keep his word.

Leaving this life will be worth the journey. It will be worth the risk to live.

They took off along the riverside palace, headed north toward the docks.

THE LAP OF THE NILE'S WATERS AGAINST THE STONE piers calmed Nefe's heartbeat as the small group approached the dock.

"Wait here," General Paaten ordered, pressing two hands down. He alone went to speak to the men of Pharaoh's Fleet who stood guard at the dock.

Atinuk stood as straight as the stone corner he peered around to watch General Paaten. Aitye leaned her back against the large square pillar and pressed a hand over the dagger wound she had received on her arm in the council room. Her breath shook as it left her mouth, causing Atinuk and Nefe to look at her.

Nefe had forgotten Aitye had been injured during the escape. Her eyes dropped, remembering the brush of her mother's hand against Ankhesenpaaten's fingers before she was wrested back into the council room. Her body became eerily still as the scene replayed in her mind.

She only slightly perceived what was happening in front of her.

"Your arm," Atinuk whispered to Aitye, taking note of her. He pulled a strip of linen from his sling, wiped her hand first to rid it of blood, and then gingerly wrapped her wound. He took a step toward her, and his gaze stayed on her face.

"I have trade goods we can barter with for honey and castor oil in Men-nefer." He applied a slight pressure to the wrapping's tight knot over the wound to stop the bleeding. He reached his other hand for Aitye's shoulder but pulled it back, resting it on her wound dressing as well.

She never lifted her eyes but simply nodded. Nefe noticed the kohl around her eyes was smudged from her tears and was sure hers looked the same.

Nefe watched the two of them before looking back at the North Palace, which she had called home all of her life. Her gaze fell to the calm streets as the morning sun flittered in the clouds behind the dark outline of the palace.

It had all been a lie. There were no rebels. No one was coming to kill my mother. It was only Pawah and Jabari . . .

Her mind stopped thinking—numbed, rather—as the recollection took over yet again. Ankhesenpaaten's scream filled her senses, causing a sudden jolt in her heart: *"He is killing her! Pawah is killing her! General, help her!"*

It had all happened so fast: her mother grabbing her and pushing her to the wall, being thrown into the small corridor, and realizing she stood in the pitch-dark passageway hearing Ankhesenpaaten scream for their mother.

A lump grew thick in her throat, and she forced herself to swallow. *How can Mother be killed on a beautiful morning such as this? How can . . .* A small whimper came from the depths of her throat while her eyes burned with tears. *Mother is gone. Ankhesenpaaten said Pawah killed her. Ankhesenpaaten abandoned me.*

"Princess!" The hushed whisper came. Aitye's hand touched her shoulder, breaking her from her nightmarish thoughts. She snapped her head to Atinuk. He had left the safety of the stone pillar and was beckoning her to come with a gentle wave of his hand. Aitye guided her toward him.

"It is time to leave this place of death, Princess Neferneferuaten Tasherit," Aitye whispered as they stood next to a royal cargo barge. It was small, yet it still boasted two small cabins, one at the stern and one at the bow.

General Paaten stood aboard; the two officers of Pharaoh's Fleet were nowhere to be seen. He reached out to Nefe, and, without much more thought, Nefe took his hand. He pulled her in and helped Aitye aboard next; Atinuk hopped over the edge and began to push away with the pole.

Paaten took to the stern and began to steer the barge downriver toward the sea. With a wary eye, Paaten watched Atinuk on the bow pushing the boat from the marshes with his pole.

The sun peeked over the two cliffs, and the Aten graced Aketaten, the great sun city Nefe's father had built in honor of the Aten, the sun-disc.

Nefe looked at General Paaten. One day she would summon the courage to ask him what had happened during her oblivious life of bliss. It seemed like life was good at the time.

But now . . .

The Nile breeze hit the side of her face as she sat on the edge of the boat opposite Aitye. It still seemed as if she should wake up at any point.

The sun city disappeared at the bend of the Nile downstream.

No, this is real. This is not a dream.

A slight panic arose in her chest, and her lungs

failed to expand. *I am leaving Egypt.* Air was trapped. *Mother is murdered.* She could not breathe. *Ankhesenpaaten left me.* Her vision blurred. *I am an orphan.* She grabbed at her chest, her throat, her mouth. *I am alone.* The world spun out of control.

She woke up on the deck of the barge with her head in Aitye's lap. Atinuk stood over her, looking down at her as she opened her eyes.

"Is the Daughter of the King well?" General Paaten called from the stern.

Atinuk looked up and nodded.

"What happened?" Nefe stuttered.

"You fell ill for a moment," Aitye answered with a soft voice. Her fingers smoothed Nefe's brow. Ankhesenpaaten had done that for her many times before. Nefe grabbed Aitye's hand. It only further reminded her Ankhesenpaaten was not with them. "Please stop doing that."

"As the Daughter of the King wishes." Aitye waited for Nefe to release her grip. It was her place as a servant to the royal family and steward to Pharaoh —to do as Nefe wished.

Atinuk knelt down as Nefe sat up. She leaned her head against the side of the barge. He wiped her face with a damp linen cloth, rather harshly, Nefe thought. She narrowed her eyes at him and jerked her head away as he wiped. "Stop that."

"I need to wipe your face," he said and lightly placed two fingers under her chin to hold her head still.

"Why?" Nefe asked. *Have I not been through enough? Why are you cleaning my face now? At this time?*

Atinuk thinned his lips in response and finished wiping her face. He returned the cloth to his belt, no longer white, but copper-colored.

Jabari's blood. A shudder came over her; she knew the shedding of her mother's blood had soon followed.

"King's Daughter." Atinuk's soft voice broke her from her thoughts. "I know you have always enjoyed a level of distance from others, and you have never been without your title. However, today, we must start anew."

He reached out to hold her hand, but Nefe slid her hands away from him as he spoke: "You will always be royalty to the three of us, but everyone else must not know your relation to Pharaoh Neferneferuaten; otherwise, all of our efforts would be in vain. Those who hunted your mother will hunt you as well."

Nefe looked to the two in front of her. Aitye was about her mother's age, and Atinuk seemed at least a few years older than Aitye. Surely, he was old enough to know when to speak to the King's Daughter.

Nefe put her hands over her ears and slid them to cover her eyes. "I have lost everything, even myself in the moment," she whimpered. "Must you tell me this now?"

"You are a woman of fourteen years, your majesty," Atinuk's voice came back rather firm, more harsh than it had been prior. "Other women have had to live through equally hard—"

"Do not compare," Aitye's soft chiding came.

Atinuk stood. He refrained from saying anything more and went to the bow of the boat. Nefe's hands slid down her face and fell into her lap. Aitye looked at her with pity or empathy in her eyes—Nefe was not sure which one.

Nefe averted her gaze. She was thankful Aitye protected her from whatever Atinuk was going to say, but she did not want to be stared at like that. She wished to be alone. Her gaze fell upon the small cabin at the rear. As if reading her mind, Aitye whispered, "May I help you to the cabin, Princess?"

She could not open her mouth, for if she did, she was not sure what would come out. Nefe nodded, and Aitye helped her to stand.

Nefe fell into the cabin's lounger after Aitye guided her to its edge. Aitye let the opaque drapes fall, blocking the morning sun from view. In the dimmed cabin, Nefe let out a whimper. Her gaze fixated on the feet of General Paaten up on the steering perch at the stern. They were the feet of the man who was taking her away from her home forever. She shivered as she replayed Atinuk's words in her mind.

It was all too real. It was all too fast. I am all too alone.

She curled up into a ball and wept.

No. No. This is only a dream, a nightmare, and soon I will wake.

But it did not stop her tears.

CHAPTER 3
ESCAPE FROM GUILT

GENERAL PAATEN EYED ATINUK IN THE CABIN AT the bow while he steered from the stern. Atinuk had his sling spread open over the lounger, with his bow and quiver of arrows at the lounger's head. A gleam of gold appeared when the morning sun shone into the cabin.

"How does he have gold?" Paaten muttered under his breath.

He replayed their introduction in the back of his mind.

This Atinuk knew who I was; he knew my name and my face. He knew we would come out of the tunnel; he knew what to say to me to get me to lower my guard. Who is this man? Is he one of Pawah's men? But he is a Canaanite. They do not care about our gods and would have no benefit in seeing Egypt fall.

He paused, reevaluating his last thought. A muscle in his forearm twitched.

"Unless . . ."

His weight fell heavy on his feet, and his stare upon Atinuk grew intense and cold.

Unless the Canaanites are mad at Akhenaten for leaving their tributary states to fail after they sent their tributes but never received protection in return.

He tensed at the thought.

Could this man be leading us all to our deaths? To make a public spectacle of Akhenaten's general and daughter and kill us all in the end? Perhaps that was his deal with Pawah; perhaps that is why I was merely kicked into the tunnel rather than stabbed.

"Who is this man?" he mumbled.

His free hand rested on his khopesh. A reprieve had come over him when Atinuk said he was a friend of Kiya and that he had land in Canaan. It had seemed the gods were answering his decades-long dream. He had left his wife in Canaan, in Damaski. The dream that had wrenched him from her arms had come to fruition. Nefertiti was the woman Pharaoh; she had yelled, "*Remember your promise, General.*" She had been shut out in darkness. All had occurred just as he had dreamed over the last twenty-nine years. He had suspected long ago he would fail this woman Pharaoh. He had accepted it, but he had hoped Nefertiti would not be her. But now that it had happened, he only had a primal urge to yell out and hit something. He had known it was coming, and yet he still failed her. He had tried everything to get rid of Pawah, even knowing that if he were successful, he might lose Niwa and their life together. If Nefertiti had lived, he would not be on a barge traveling to Canaan. The thought turned his cheeks pink and hollow.

How selfish am I? Surely the gods know I had hoped the woman Pharaoh from my dreams was not Pharaoh Neferneferuaten—not my friend, Nefertiti.

He heard her daughter crying in the cabin before him. He let out a shaky breath and shook his head.

If it was not Nefertiti, it would have been one of her daughters.

He thinned his lips as he thought.

Nefertiti would have wanted this to befall her, rather than her daughters. I wish it were none of them. I promise you, my friend, your daughter will be safe in Canaan.

"Bes—god of dreams," he looked to the sky, "it was easier when the woman Pharaoh was faceless." He lowered his chin in reverence.

The god-sent dream had been fulfilled and consequently his oath to the gods released. A pang coursed through his heart. He had been allowed to return to his wife for good, and yet Pharaoh's daughter would never be able to return home.

The sun rose over the Nile as Atinuk stepped from the cabin and drew Paaten's attention. Atinuk glanced at Aitye, who stood on the side of the barge. He fidgeted, as if he debated joining her.

Paaten narrowed his eyes at him.

So he is to kill Pharaoh's daughter and me, and keep Pharaoh's steward for himself?

Atinuk sensed the icy glare and snapped his head to Paaten. They locked eyes for a moment until he turned and went to the other side of the barge.

In my weakness, I had assumed Atinuk was part of the gods' plan for me to rejoin my wife and to help me carry out my oath to Pharaoh.

He reconsidered his initial assumption over and over again in his mind.

THE END OF THE DAY CAME, AND NEFE HAD YET TO emerge from her cabin. Aitye stepped up to General Paaten's perch and handed him some of the bread stored in the barge.

Her gaze fell to the stranger in the cabin at the front of the barge. "I do not trust him," she whispered, but then her gaze fell. "If I may speak freely with Paaten, General of Pharaoh's Armies."

General Paaten took a bite of bread. "I have deserted, at the command of our late Pharaoh. I am no longer General of Pharaoh's Armies. Speak freely."

She dipped her chin in gratitude. "Do you trust him?"

"No," he muttered and took another bite of bread. He noticed the woman was about the same age, weight and height of the late Pharaoh. *Forgive me, my friend.* "Your master has been killed." Guilt gnawed at his stomach for ultimately failing his friend whom he had come to respect, despite her many poor decisions. "You are free to seek another path."

She glanced at the cabin that concealed the princess. "I swore my life to Queen Nefertiti twenty-one years ago, and, at her passing, I swear my life to her daughter."

"You are a good woman. Our Pharaoh was lucky to have such a loyal steward in her presence."

"I had been by her side since she was thirteen years old and became Queen Coregent. I was offered freedom several times by Pawah, but I could not see my life without Nefertiti—my Queen, my Pharaoh, my master." Tears glistened in her eyes. "And yet, here I am without her. I failed her when she needed me the most."

Paaten reached out to brush Aitye's arm.

"You have not failed her. I have. Do not place that burden upon your heart. It is mine to bear." He lifted her chin and studied her face. A tear rolled down her cheek. He wiped it away, as he had done with the princess. She was young enough to be his daughter, and the princess, his granddaughter. These women had lost so much and still found the strength to continue and to forge ahead. It pulled a different thread of guilt that had wrapped around his heart for twenty-nine years. Now that his oath had been released, he could return home to his wife Niwa. He could fulfill the oath he made to his wife when he married her, and a peace settled within his heart again.

The gods knew it would be this way. This is the plan of the gods. I must trust it.

It had been nine years since he had seen his wife. He had not returned to her since the plague; there had been no more campaigns to the northern border. Pharaoh had wanted him by her side to protect her. Many times he had wanted to send a messenger to see if his family was alive or if they had succumbed to the plague. He longed to know if Niwa had finally thought him dead and pursued another. But the only two soldiers whom he could trust with such a task, Mai and Imhotep, were either gone to Re or not able to do it. Even if they had been able to go, ordering anyone to do such a thing would go against Pharaoh's order to remain in Egypt.

As he had done every time he returned home, he pushed away the thought that he would find her with another man, or passed and buried, or just gone. Yet, to resolve his fear, he reminded himself that she had said she wanted this life with him. He had told her he did not know when he could return. He had been able to see her every two, three, or five years, but never more than five, except most recently. He had always been able to send a message once a year, except most recently.

Nine years. With no message from me. She would think me dead, would she not?

All of his hopes were in his prayers to Bes to give Niwa dreams of his returning to her—dreams that were as urging and compelling as his had been that caused him to leave her in Canaan each time he had set in his heart to stay.

He focused on Aitye in front of him and realized his hand was still on her cheek. He pulled his hand away but kept her stare.

"It is my burden to bear," he repeated, pulling himself from his thoughts.

Her lips pressed into a thin line, and she gave a small nod of her head, clearly not accepting his full responsibility of what had happened to their leader.

He glanced to Atinuk. They were leaving Egypt forever, and they had a stranger aboard whom neither of them knew nor trusted. He could recall the past and muse on what he would find in Damaski later.

Paaten stood up from his perch.

"Sit here."

She obeyed, and once she settled into the steering seat, he took her place on the step. He guided her hand to the steering oar. "I do not trust our new friend to steer the barge to where it needs to go; I want you to learn. I cannot steer the barge every day and be alert every night until we reach Azzati."

"I will do my best," she whispered and rested her hand on the steering oar.

"We will dock once the sun is about to set in the west, but, for now, consider this your first lesson." His voice conveyed unwavering professionalism.

"General Paaten, why do we dock at night? Would it not be faster to sail by night and day?" Her shoulders had risen to her ears, and her voice remained timid, as if she were afraid she asked a silly question.

His jaw clenched at his title, and he rubbed his bottom lip. "I am no longer General, Aitye." His hand fell. "As much as we are ingrained to call each other by our titles, we need to call each other Citizeness or Citizen or by our names until we are out of Egypt. Even then, we do not wish to bring attention to ourselves."

She nodded.

"To answer your question," he began again.

She looked up with wide eyes, surprised that he was answering such a silly question.

"We dock every night because there are no lights along the Nile, and we cannot see where to steer." He did not want to tell her his eyesight blurred under the night sky; he did not want to admit age had diminished his night vision. "I have never been a member of Pharaoh's Fleet. Although I commanded them and took note of their actions when I was aboard a transport barge, I cannot steer at night, and I refuse to trust our stranger, should he volunteer."

"I understand, and I agree, Paaten." Her eyes lifted to his, and a warm smile came over her mouth. The way she said his name made him shift on his feet: it was soft, and there was a sparkle in her eye. He had seen it many times before when single or divorced women wanted to write him or even set up a house, but he had promised Niwa that no other woman would know his body or have his heart.

"Good," he returned, wondering what he had done to make Aitye look at him that way when she had not previously. "If you move your hand to the right, the barge will go left." He made sure not to touch her arm or hand in his instruction. "If you move it to the left, the barge will go right."

"Seems easy enough," she whispered, her eyes locked with his.

"Yes, it is easy enough. Try to keep to the middle of the river. In the unlikely event of a storm, I will take over. When we are about to dock, I will take over."

She nodded but kept her gaze on him.

"Look at the river," he ordered gently.

Her eyes shifted to the river. "Thank you, Paaten, for treating me as more than just a steward. Another would not have comforted me in my guilt or even answered my question."

Paaten took a deep breath as he realized the reason behind her sudden change toward him. "Any honorable man who lives by the principles of Ma'at would do the same, Aitye, royal steward or not." He took another bite of bread.

"You are honorable in your word as well. You leave everything to flee to Canaan to protect Pharaoh's daughter. Are you to take your wife or children?" Aitye asked, her eyes on the water.

"I have nothing here. My home was in Pharaoh's barracks in the palace, and I have no family in

Egypt." He took another bite. It was true. There was no lie in his mouth.

"You never married?" She eyed him with a knitted brow, glancing to his broad chest and arms.

"I never found an Egyptian woman to marry," he quickly spouted off and took another bite. "I must speak with the Daughter of the King now." He ended the conversation quickly. "I will return when the sun is almost set to dock the barge along the shore."

She nodded, and the sparkle in her eye dimmed.

———

PAATEN STEPPED THROUGH THE OPAQUE DRAPES AND the princess's quiet cries silenced. He sat down on the lounger by her feet and rubbed his neck.

What to say to her? She just lost her mother, her sister, and everything she has ever known.

"You think me a child?" the soft whisper came.

"No." He shook his head.

She lifted her head to look at him. "But Atinuk said—"

"Atinuk is a stranger. I know nothing of him. I do not trust him," Paaten whispered and peered over his shoulder at the man going through his travel sling once more. At this angle, it looked like he had plenty of gold. He wondered why he did not draw the drapes to conceal his trade goods.

She chewed her lip. "But he said he was a friend to Royal Wife Kiya."

"Yes, that is what he said, but there are too many unanswered questions I have about him." Paaten looked at Aitye's feet on the steering perch straight in front of him.

Nefe lowered her head again and sniffled.

"There were no riots, were there? There were no rebellions?" Her whisper barely floated over the soft lapping of the Nile waters against the barge.

His back slumped, and his hands fell into his lap.

How much of the truth should she know?

He peered over at her.

"That means Atinuk lied, and he is not who he said he is." Nefe wiped her nose with the back of her hand.

"There were no riots or rebellions last night, but I have seen them. They . . . " His voice trailed off. *What to say?*

He decided to be vague. "They plagued your father's and your mother's reigns."

"Why?"

"They made mistakes, but I want you to remember your mother and your father as you always have." He glanced at her and saw her purse her lips in thought. "I do not trust Atinuk. I do not know if he is who he said he is, but he speaks the truth in that regard."

He knelt down in front of her before she could ask any more questions. She hastily wiped away tears and sat up. He took her hand, unsure of what else to do. He never had to console his men. If they were losing, he simply made an empowering speech about Pharaoh, the gods, and ultimate victory in the face of traveling to Re. He doubted such an effort would pacify the young woman in front of him.

"He is also right in another regard," he whispered. "During our time with other people, we cannot refer to you as King's Daughter or treat you as royalty. You will be a Citizeness. We will need to call you by a name other than Neferneferuaten Tasherit. Those who want to hurt you will know your relation to your mother by your name alone."

She nodded. "I understand," she whimpered and wiped away another stream of tears.

He swallowed the lump in his throat that grew after he caused her to cry, and he second-guessed himself at bringing up the subject again so close to the morning's events. But she steadied her tears and her breathing, so he pressed on. "What name do you want to be called?"

She hesitated. "Would Nefe be a good name?"

He bowed his head before her and felt his heart burst open. There was something he had to do before they threw away the last of her royalty—something he was unsure if he could fully do himself.

"Daughter of the King, Neferneferuaten Tasherit, I cannot apologize to your mother, but I can apologize to you." He took a deep breath and leaned his forehead to her knee. "I am sorry I failed Pharaoh. I took an oath to protect her and her royal family. I do not deserve your forgiveness, but I will spend the rest of my life protecting you, Daughter of the King." He lifted his head and looked her in the eye.

She swallowed and attempted a formal dialogue. Her brow furrowed, and her words seemed to be pulled from another time and another place. Hatred and vacancy fought within her eyes as she spoke.

"Your loyalty knows no bounds, General," she stammered. "I know I am safe in your hands and"— she shrugged, trying not to cry—"if we truly do live a life that is away from all of this strife, perhaps you will not need to protect me."

He pressed his lips together and nodded. "Needed or not, that is my oath to you." He patted her hand. "I have had three years to prepare for this day; you have not had any time except for this morning. When you are ready to emerge as Nefe, we will be waiting for you."

CHAPTER 4
ESCAPE FROM GRIEF

A DECAN LATER, THE MEN-NEFER DOCKS GLEAMED in the distance under the midday sun. Atinuk stepped up to Paaten's perch and pointed to his General's golden collar and bronze armor. "You will need to dress like a citizen, Paaten."

Paaten ignored him. He already knew the time would soon arrive when he needed to shed his uniform of twenty-four years; he did not have to be reminded.

"I can take over the steering while you change. I have an extra collar in my sling, in case I needed to dress as an Egyptian. We can trade for your collar once we get to Azzati; it will give us plenty for food and wine, and perhaps even a donkey for Nefe and Aitye." Atinuk held out his hand to balance himself against the stern's steering perch.

Paaten ignored him again. He was not going to trade his General's collar unless the situation was dire. It seemed Atinuk had plenty of gold to trade for the items of which he spoke.

"Aitye, please come steer until we reach the Mennefer docks," Paaten called out. She jumped up from the bow's cabin lounger and came to take Paaten's place.

"You still do not trust me, I see?" Atinuk asked. He barely moved, forcing the tall former General to go around him.

Paaten leaned into Atinuk's space, almost knocking him into the Nile waters below. "No, I do not."

Atinuk followed Paaten to the middle of the barge. "Why not? Did I not offer you food, clothing, and land in Canaan?"

"You offer all of this without any request in return? You prey on us at a vulnerable time. You seek something other than what you say." Paaten's hand rested on the blade of his khopesh as he spun to stare at Atinuk.

"You know not of which you speak." Atinuk's eyes raged.

"How did you know my name? How do you know me?"

"You are . . . *were* the General, the highest in command of Pharaoh's Armies. Your collar and bronze armor give away your status." Atinuk averted his eyes at the end.

Paaten pursed his lips at that last action. "There is more." He squared his shoulders to Atinuk.

They locked eyes once more while Atinuk responded, "I have heard of your name in my travels and during my stay in the royal messenger apartments."

Paaten decided to question Atinuk until there was a lapse in his story—until he found a weakness or an inconsistency in what he had already said. "Are you a Canaanite messenger?"

Atinuk chewed his lip before he answered. "Of sorts."

Paaten readied his stance in case he had to kill the man. One hand rested on his khopesh, and the other clung to his chest strap, just a finger length away from his dagger's sheath.

"I do not like being toyed with, Atinuk." He unhooked his khopesh and popped the flat edge on the side of his leg.

Atinuk's eyes drifted to the shiny bronze weapon. "You will not kill me, Paaten."

"If you are a threat to the King's Daughter, I will surely dispatch you without hesitation." Paaten glanced around in his peripheral vision. The nearest barge would not be able to see a quick killing and a subsequent feeding to the crocodiles below.

"I am no threat." Atinuk raised his hands.

Paaten stared him down but kept his weapon gripped tightly in his hand. "Then answer the questions fully and without omission."

"Very well," Atinuk said and dropped his arms to his sides.

"Did you or did you not know we would be in that tunnel? How long did you lie in wait for us to emerge? Were you privy to the plan hatched by Pawah for Pharaoh? You knew my name; you knew my face. You told me you were friend to Royal Wife Kiya. How were you a friend?"

"Do not bring Tadukhipa into your suspicions." Atinuk's hands curled into fists.

"Who is Tadukhipa?"

Atinuk's jawline grew taut. "You Egyptians could not speak her name in the Mitanni tongue and thus called her Kiya."

"We *Egyptians*?" Paaten's knuckles grew white around his khopesh.

There is something motivating this man. He has a grudge against us.

"Tadukhipa"—Paaten butchered the pronunciation but pressed forward—"never mentioned a friend named Atinuk," Paaten growled. "What were you to her?"

"We loved each other once."

Paaten's hand tightened on his chest dagger as he deduced the stranger's motivation. "So you seek revenge for her death? You blame—"

"No."

Paaten eyed him, his mind racing. He had been too quick in his last accusation. His gaze fell to his Canaanite attire; he had admitted to being a Canaanite messenger of sorts, but Kiya was Mitanni.

There was an opening to a potential gap in his story, so Paaten decided to poke.

"You are Canaanite. She was Mitanni. How can you say you loved each other? She lived her life in her father's palace and arrived at Malkata when she became fifteen years of age. When would she ever have met you? Did you see her from afar and stalk her to Egypt? Had her caravan through Canaan given you a brief encounter with the princess? Did—"

"Stop!" Atinuk's muscles strained under his Canaanite leather tunic.

Paaten anticipated a swing, but although Atinuk appeared weaponless, the military veteran never underestimated his opponent.

The tension in Atinuk's neck released. "You know nothing, Paaten."

"I know what I know. I do not trust you, nor will I let you lead us into some trap in Canaan." He prodded his khopesh in Atinuk's direction.

Nefe's silhouette sat up in her lounger behind the semi-opaque drapes of her cabin, and Aitye's gaze darted between the men and the river.

"There is no trap. Only a shared land," Atinuk muttered.

"So you say. And now it is a shared land? You told us you had land."

He turned around and threw his hands up in the air before he faced him again. "Shared land . . . land; it is all the same." He paused and returned his hands to his sides upon seeing Paaten's look of distrust upon him.

"I loved the one you knew as Kiya. Her father dangled my life in front of her to manipulate her into doing what he wanted. She was stripped of everything she was, even her name, to become an Egyptian and live as Pharaoh's wife to save me. I knew one day I would bring her to Canaan. We had tried to escape there before, but we failed. That was why I set out from the Mitanni capital of Washukanni to find the Canaanite tribe of my great-grandfather."

Paaten shook his head at the unlikely story. "What were you to the Mitanni Princess? A Canaanite prince? The son of some vassal state lord? How did you survive stealing King Tustratta's youngest daughter away in a failed escape attempt?"

Atinuk shook his head, ignoring Paaten, and continued on with his story. "When I arrived at Aketaten, Tadukhipa was already ill with the plague. She succumbed to it not long after I left her room when your Nefertiti entered." His voice broke at the apparent memory. "The royal guards mistook me for a messenger, and so to fulfill Tadukhipa's last request, I remained under the guise of a Canaanite messenger. I learned the layout of the palace in order to protect the daughters of Nefertiti."

Paaten considered his response.

That may well be, but I still have unanswered questions.

"How did you know about the tunnel and that we would come out of it?"

Atinuk lifted his gaze to the skies. He let out a long sigh and closed his eyes for a moment. "Pawah and Beketaten drew me into their inner circle. I was given this gold"—he pointed to his sling hidden under the cabin's lounger—"to kill any who tried to exit the tunnel."

"So you are a conspirator against the throne?" He swirled his khopesh in his hand so that its bronze sickle blade hummed through the air.

"No," he shook his head violently as Paaten held his sword back ready to strike. He stood tall and unflinching, as if trying to show his innocence. It was enough to halt Paaten's blade.

I shall let him explain this one time.

"Tadukhipa told me there was turmoil in the palace. Not long after her death, I found out the leaders of the rebellious movement were The Fifth Prophet of the Aten, Pawah, and his wife, Beketaten, the daughter of Pharaoh Amenhotep III."

"How did you find that out?" Paaten's stomach roiled. He, the General of Pharaoh's Armies, had only found out that information two years ago, yet this man, a false messenger, had known for eight years?

"There were rumors among the royal messengers' apartments that if your King or vassal state or whoever sent you wanted to seek revenge against Egypt for not responding to the cries for help or aid, a secret movement was looking for recruits to overthrow Pharaoh Akhenaten. Many of us signed up to help. The foreign messengers held no loyalty to Egypt's King. They only wanted their King's request fulfilled. With a new King on the throne, they were more likely to be heard and their request granted."

"You willingly recruited into the movement's ranks?" He lifted his khopesh higher, almost slamming it over Atinuk's shoulder, but he halted at the steadfastness in Atinuk's eyes. There was no deceit there, but, still, something about him was not right. He decided to let the man answer, and he lowered his khopesh once again to his side.

"I knew if I were to protect Nefertiti's daughters as I had promised Tadukhipa, I needed to know who the source of the danger was and what they were doing. I pledged my loyalty to Pawah and Beketaten. I told them I was skilled with the bow. They told me to be where I was that morning I revealed myself to you."

Nefe came out of her cabin, her face pale and her jaw agape. She wielded a crooked pointer finger. A blast of rage propelled the words from her mouth: "You knew?"

"What did I know?" Atinuk looked at her with a knitted brow.

"You knew Pawah was going to kill my mother?" Nefe's hands jolted to her sides in heavy fists. Spittle formed in the corners of her mouth.

Atinuk rubbed his hand over his mouth. His eyes darted among Aitye, Nefe and Paaten, as if sensing the hatred. He raised his hands again. "All I knew was that they wanted me there at the end of the tunnel. They told me the location of the hidden door. One of the royal guard showed me its cleverly concealed design in the stone's carved motifs, only discernable from the slight change from stone to richly worked plaster to mirror the stone wall. He said it could only be opened from within the tunnel. My order was to sit there all day if I had to, until someone emerged and eliminate them."

Atinuk dropped his hands. "But, when I saw General Paaten and the two daughters of Nefertiti with blood splattered across their faces, I knew the time to fulfill my oath to Tadukhipa was upon me."

Paaten unsheathed his dagger, dropped his khopesh, and took two bounds toward Atinuk in one quick, fluid movement. He wrenched him by the collar of his leather tunic and pressed the blade against his throat. Their bodies leaned against the side of the barge, tilting it toward the water. Aitye yelled out and moved the steering oar to keep the barge from toppling.

"You knew, but said nothing." The growl in Paaten's throat rivaled the rage in his eyes. "You could have sent a messenger to me or to Commander Horemheb or to Pharaoh's own father, but you did nothing."

Atinuk did not blink, nor did he show any sign of weakness. "The last man who tried to warn you of a coming threat was slashed to pieces, and what was left of his living body was burned in front of us. Pawah is not a man to cross."

"You are a coward." Paaten knew then he only spoke as an Egyptian General. Atinuk held no loyalty to the throne. It also proved to him the depth of the corruption and how far the reach of the People's Restoration of Egypt had gone. The military had spent seasons trying to remove Pawah, and each assassination attempt had only strengthened the loyalty of his supporters. It seemed to Paaten that Pawah had secured his safety by pitting his supporters against each other, making them fear and distrust one another. One wrong word or deed and death would ensue. Pawah soured Paaten's thoughts. How had Pawah and Beketaten slipped under his nose all this time to build this network of sympathizers? Where were the Medjay? Where were the loyal members of Pharaoh's Armies? Where were the Nomarchs? Where were all of those who were supposedly loyal to Pharaoh?

Atinuk cut him off from his thoughts. "What good would I be to the daughters of Nefertiti if I were dead? I did not know whom I could trust. Imagine being alone in a foreign land amid the circle of those who want to see their ruler removed? Half of what I was told I assumed to be false. Even now, I do not know the full truth of anything."

He pointed at Nefe.

"The only thing I know for certain is that this is a

daughter of Nefertiti. I made a promise to the woman I loved to protect Nefertiti's daughters."

The thought of Pawah getting away with so much gnawed at Paaten's dedication to Pharaoh. He twisted his wrist, pulling Atinuk closer to the blade. There was still no deception in Atinuk's eyes, but then again, Paaten had sensed no deception among his men, Horemheb, Ay, and even Nefertiti during their roles in Pharaoh Akhenaten's demise. Had he been blind all that time? Had he lost his touch in identifying deception in a man's eyes? He stared at Atinuk, his gaze boring into his brave countenance. Should he trust him, like he trusted Jabari? Should he trust what he saw in front of him? *Can I trust myself?* Paaten needed to distance himself from this revelation or else risk overwhelming his heart. "You promised to protect the daughters of Pharaoh Neferneferuaten, yet you leave one behind?"

"I was already over the palace wall, General. *You* did not stay either."

Paaten pressed the blade further into Atinuk's neck but refrained from breaking the skin. He had not stayed, but his oath was different. It was to take them *if* they were willing . . . *if* he remembered correctly.

A slight hesitation passed over his memory. Had he just invented that condition so that he could go home to his wife? Was he to take both Ankhesenpaaten and Nefe? Maybe that was what he had promised to Nefertiti? But Ankhesenpaaten stayed. How could he have protected Nefe if he had gone back and dragged Ankhesenpaaten out? It was his fault she had fallen behind while they ran to the palace wall. He should have made sure both daughters were in front of him instead of leading them from the front.

"Royal Wife Ankhesenpaaten made her choice."

He lifted his blade from Atinuk's skin and released him. He took a step back. He still did not trust him, but what he had said so far seemed to be the truth—there appeared to be no deception in him. Why would he lie about being within Pawah's network? If anything, would not his lie be he had no association with Pawah? If Paaten killed him, he might be killing an innocent man, an unjustified kill in his mind. His heart would not be heavy in the afterlife because of an unfounded action made that day. He sheathed the dagger back into his chest belt. It did not mean there would be no basis to kill him in the future, but in the moment, he hesitantly decided to believe his story. Atinuk let out a slow breath through his nostrils as his shoulders relaxed once more. They were both in the same situation, it seemed, having made promises to royal women now gone.

"No!" Nefe's shrill scream pierced the air, breaking Paaten's thoughts. "No!" she yelled again and lurched toward Atinuk, her hands aimed for his neck. "You knew! You knew!"

Paaten grabbed her by the waist and lifted her up

before she could touch him. Her arms swung, barely missing Atinuk's face. Her legs kicked as Paaten lifted her off of her feet. A hard kick struck Atinuk in the thigh, sending him to a knee. Paaten backed up with Nefe in his arms.

The barge rocked side to side as Aitye screamed. She was holding onto the steering oar with both hands. "Stop!"

Nefe struggled in Paaten's large muscular arms. "You knew they were going to kill us, and you did nothing! Curse your heart to Ammit!"

Paaten whispered in her ear, "Daughter of the King . . . please, stop."

Atinuk raised his hands again in defense. "I could only assume. Pawah only told enough for the person to do what they needed to do. It could have been men who had betrayed him once again in your mother's assassination orders against him. It could have been any number of things."

Nefe stopped, and a pained grimace overcame her face at Atinuk's statement against her mother. "You lie! You are a liar! My mother did no such thing!"

Paaten grabbed her outstretched arms and pulled them back to her chest, holding her tight against him.

"You knew!" She struggled against Paaten's hold.

"I swear it. I did not know. I am sorry. After Akhenaten, after Smenkare, the whole group of men I was with thought Pawah had planned to marry your mother, not kill her."

Nefe went slack in Paaten's arms and buried her face in her hands. Sobs took over her small body as she only whimpered, "You liar."

Paaten lowered Nefe to her knees and sat beside her; Atinuk fell to his heels across from her, rubbing his thigh where she had kicked him.

Atinuk shook his head as he watched her cry. "If you need to blame someone, blame me. I am sorry. I wish I had known. I would have found a way to tell your mother herself if I had known that was Pawah's plan."

She said nothing but still wept into her hands. He reached out and rubbed her arm. "I am sorry."

Paaten snatched Atinuk's wrist and threw it back toward his chest.

There is still something amiss about him. Something he is not telling me, Paaten thought, *but, regardless, no one touches the Daughter of the King. I will not fail Pharaoh Neferneferuaten again. I trusted Jabari and . . .* He shut out his thoughts. His stare burned through Atinuk. *I will not fail again.*

Aitye called out from the stern. "Paaten, we are coming about the docks."

Atinuk's gaze fell upon Paaten, and then his eyes glanced down at his General's collar and bronze armor.

Paaten took a deep breath. It was time to remove the uniform. He hated that Atinuk had been correct on two occasions now, but still, it did not mean he had to trust or like him.

CHAPTER 5
ESCAPE FROM MEN-NEFER

Pᴀᴀᴛᴇɴ ᴅᴏᴄᴋᴇᴅ ᴛʜᴇ ʙᴀʀɢᴇ ɴᴇxᴛ ᴛᴏ ᴀ sᴛᴏɴᴇ ᴘɪᴇʀ on the outskirts of the Peru-nefer, the principal docks of Men-nefer, and stepped down from the steering perch. His gaze lifted towards the gleaming white-walled summer palace and the abandoned *Hut-ka-Ptah*, Great Temple of Ptah. Akhenaten's temple to the Aten stood in front of it, but the newer structure did not compare to the age-old Great Temple with its regal additions built over many generations.

Such legacy thrown away by a madman obsessed with the Aten-disc. Paaten shook his head at his former Pharaoh's temple to the Aten. His gaze fell to his barge mates; he had to go to the markets, but who should stay with the barge? He was not going to leave Atinuk with either of the women, so the option was to take Atinuk with him. A pinch of his mouth was the only indication of his frustration. *That will leave*

Nefe and Aitye vulnerable on the barge if anyone decides to make trouble . . . but it is the only way.

"Stay with the King's Daughter," he ordered Aitye.

"Yes, Paaten." His name slid off her tongue in that certain way again.

"You, come with me," he ordered Atinuk, ignoring the steward.

Atinuk nodded in reply and gathered his sling, leaving the vast majority of its contents under the lounger of the cabin at the bow.

"Let none board, Aitye."

She nodded, and a slight wave of fear came over her eyes.

"We will be back before the sun sets in the west." He gave her a warm smile to settle her fears. "We will trade for docking for the day; no one should bother you."

His gaze shifted to his khopesh that lay hidden beside her. He felt slightly off-kilter without the weight of his bronze weapon hanging by his side.

He youthfully hopped out of the barge, despite his age, and waited for the younger man to follow. In the brief moment while he waited for Atinuk to join him, he looked over the edge of the pier and saw his reflection looking back at him from the depths of the Nile. No gold collar graced his neck, and no bronze armor donned his torso. He wore his bead-lined shendyt and a noble's collar Atinuk had stolen during his stay at

Aketaten. He was almost whom he had wanted to be all those years ago when he married Niwa in Damaski: a simple man living a simple life with her. He only hoped his wife was still alive and still loved him.

"I am ready, Paaten." Atinuk tapped him on his shoulder.

"Good." Paaten brushed off Atinuk's tap. "Stay close." He eyed Atinuk as he walked off down the pier and paid the harbor fee to the harbor scribe.

Aitye stared at Paaten, who felt her stare on the side of his face.

"Be safe, Paaten."

He glanced at her and then to Nefe. *Aitye can be trusted, can she not? She was never a member of Pawah's followers, was she?* His mind raced through all the possible consequences of his decision to leave them with the barge, no matter how unlikely the scenarios seemed. *Aitye knows how to steer the barge. She could take the King's Daughter and leave us, or she could drown her.* He winced at the fleeting thought.

Even if she is trustworthy, I am still leaving her alone with the princess with no defense training. My khopesh is practically of no use. I could lose Atinuk in the Men-nefer crowds. He could come back before I do and take them away without me; I am his only threat upon the barge.

He clenched his jaw and looked back in the direction of Atinuk, who had realized he stood on the crowded docks without Paaten near him.

The lump in his throat itched. He had never

second-guessed his decisions before, especially one as seemingly small as this one.

Atinuk waved at him.

"Keep her safe, Aitye," he muttered, sealing his decision. He followed the foreign stranger into the Men-nefer markets.

I will not let him out of my sight, he reasoned.

He made Atinuk trade for honey, castor oil, linen wrappings, bread, wine, leeks, and cooked beans with the trade goods he had brought. He watched the people pass by him, and none seemed to know who he was.

However, as he trailed behind, he noticed the heads of those in the crowd turn toward Atinuk as he passed by. Paaten wished the man had stolen two Egyptian men's clothing.

"Are we to return now, Paaten?" Atinuk murmured, glancing over his shoulder to the crowds to make sure no one followed them.

"No," Paaten looked off toward the inner-city homes. "I have been preparing for this escape for three years at the command of Pharaoh." He eyed Atinuk, who would have to accompany him to the small estate he had set up here for the sole purpose of leaving Egypt. He did not trust the man alone with the King's Daughter.

"Come with me."

HE ENTERED THE MODEST COURTYARD AND WALKED into the single-story stone home. A man younger than Paaten hobbled to the door with his cane and a mangled leg. A woman came in from the outdoor kitchen in the back. She stopped in her gait upon seeing Paaten.

"Imhotep," Paaten dipped his head at the man. "Itet," he nodded to the woman.

Atinuk looked between the two men in confusion, but he remained mute as he stood by the door.

"It has happened, General?" he asked, wincing. Itet's hand went to her heart. The home fell silent.

The guilt he had tried to suppress constricted his heart. "Yes, by the hand of Pawah."

Imhotep's shoulders rolled forward, and his chin drooped to his chest. "May Pharaoh's ba and ka travel well to Re; may Pawah and his followers be cursed to Ammit."

Paaten placed two heavy hands on Imhotep's shoulders. "The corruption in the sun city was too great. Word shall travel soon. The power must remain with the position of Pharaoh, so I doubt her murder will be revealed to the people."

"I understand." Imhotep glanced toward the large travel sling leaning upon the table in the inner hall of the home. "Everything you have asked for is there."

"May you have peace in this life and the next, Imhotep. You have served Pharaoh's Army well, and this house will serve your family for generations to come. May your heart be light."

"May yours as well, General. Fare well in Canaan." His eyes darted to Atinuk before he turned his back to him and whispered so that Atinuk would not hear, "Enjoy your wife and your family. I shall not see you then in the afterlife?"

Paaten's lips pressed together. It was a risk he knew he took if he was not entombed like an Egyptian on Egypt's land. "I have made plans . . . so if you do, I shall be glad to see you."

A grin spread over Imhotep's face. "And I shall surely be glad to see you too." He wrapped a hand behind Paaten's neck and pressed his forehead to Paaten's. "It has been an honor to serve alongside you. Thank you for taking care of my family when I could no longer serve in Pharaoh's Army. I am indebted to you."

Paaten's chest swelled with gratitude. Imhotep, along with Mai, had been the foot soldiers he had taken with him in Damaski when he first saw Niwa again. They had found him out, but they remained loyal, knowing there was truly no threat there.

"You held my and my wife's lives in your hands that day so long ago, and you chose to keep my secret. You have prepared all I asked of you these last three years and did not spread rumors of the arrangement. It is I who is indebted to you."

Paaten lifted his head, glanced back at Atinuk to make sure he had not heard them, and walked to the travel sling. He pulled out the official piece of papyrus placed on the top of the sling, just as requested. He took the seal set and placed his seal against the deed.

"This home and half of all of my wealth is now yours, as agreed. The other half has already gone to the family of Mai, rest his ka." He picked up the heavy sling with one hand and placed it over his shoulder. He need not look at the sling's contents; he trusted everything was as he had requested.

"The story is this: I have perished in my sleep in Aketaten, or align to whatever message travels from there."

His gaze ran over his old friend's career-ending leg injury he had received in battle against the Nubians more than a decade ago. A prayer passed through Paaten's mind to the god of war Anhur: *Thank you for my physical prowess and capable body, even at my age. I would not have been able to keep my oath to Pharaoh and make this final journey to Niwa if I had been as Imhotep.*

"Thank you, General." Imhotep nodded his head.

Paaten shook his head. "Just Paaten. In peace, my friend."

A warm smile fell over Imhotep's face. "In peace, Paaten."

Paaten glanced at Itet and lowered his head to her as well. He had asked Imhotep many times to go to Damaski to deliver a message when he could not go himself. Imhotep had obliged every time until his injury forced him to stay home. Itet had been gracious of his requests, going months without her husband when he could have been home.

"In peace, Itet. I thank you for your grace."

She glanced between Paaten and Atinuk before she spoke. "In peace, Paaten," she whispered. Her eyes held joy for him. "Be well in Canaan."

He nodded his head, and his eyes warmed at the duo who had held his secret all these years.

Paaten and Atinuk left the home, and as they walked toward the city's principal docks, Atinuk peered up at him. "Now it is I who has unanswered questions."

Paaten snorted. "Then they shall remain unanswered."

Atinuk narrowed his eyes at him, but a smirk came over his lips. "Thus General Paaten says."

Paaten chuckled at the borderline blasphemous remark against Pharaoh from the foreigner. "You will do well to remember that in this band of runaways, my word is law."

Atinuk let a heavy sigh fall from his mouth. "At the end of all this, you will trust me, Paaten." Atinuk's eyes fell on Peru-nefer coming into view; their barge remained untouched. Aitye's figure sat on the middle of the barge awaiting their return as the bottom of the sun-disc touched the western horizon.

"I do not trust many people. If I do indeed trust you at the end of this journey, you will have earned back your life." He adjusted the heavy sling upon his shoulder as he strode. "At this present time, you have none of my trust, and you are lucky I did not dispatch you on the barge."

"Yes, I am quite fortunate," he said, adjusting his own sling. "But I am half your age, old man, and I let you have the opportunity to dispatch me on the barge."

I am not even sixty yet, but he is clearly in his mid-to-late thirties. Is he implying I am seventy or more? Paaten scoffed at Atinuk's implied insult.

"You are not *half* my age; and you did not *let* me do anything. Though, say what you need to for your pride. Heavy hearts of pride do not travel to the afterlife."

"Neither do hearts buried in foreign lands, or so I have learned about your people's beliefs," Atinuk murmured as he nodded his head in acknowledgement to a man passing by. "So, I assume none of our little band of runaways will have an afterlife."

"I have made preparations for us, not you. I will have to trust someone in Canaan to carry them out once we have passed from this life," Paaten mumbled.

Atinuk hummed and lifted his chin. "That will be hard to do since you trust few people."

There are those in Damaski I trust, you fool. Paaten wanted to punch the smug smirk off of his face, but instead he changed the subject and asked, "Where is this *shared* land of which you speak, Atinuk?"

Atinuk adjusted his sling again. "In Canaan."

Paaten flicked his gaze to the sky. "Yes, you said that already. *Where* in Canaan?"

Atinuk stared at the barge for a moment before

he finally cleared his throat and answered, "Damaski."

Paaten peered at him; he had not heard of a landowner named Atinuk the last time he was in Damaski. *If Atinuk said he spoke with Kiya before the plague took her, he is not new to Damaski since I left there. He is hiding something; he lies.*

"Where in Damaski?"

Atinuk scratched his head full of hair before answering again. "In the outer city by the river."

Paaten narrowed his eyes at him. *What is he hiding? Last time I was in Damaski, Niwa did not have many neighbors, and I certainly do not remember this man.*

Paaten stopped walking. After taking a few more steps, Atinuk noticed his pause and also stopped, turning to face him. "Is all well?"

Paaten inclined his head. "I sense deceit from you."

Atinuk pursed his lips and then turned them into a smirk. He shrugged. "I cannot help you with your distrust. I have spoken the truth." He nodded his head toward the barge. "Sun is almost down."

Paaten lifted his hand to his chest strap and ran his thumb along the dagger's hidden handle. "It is."

They locked eyes.

Atinuk spoke. "We should not leave the King's Daughter and her mother's steward alone in the dark."

Paaten tapped his finger on the hidden dagger's blade. "No, we should not."

Atinuk chuckled and sized him up. "One day you will trust me, Paaten." He turned his back to him and continued on to the barge.

Paaten watched him walk away. "If that day comes, it will not come quickly." He took a few large bounds to catch up with the foreigner.

CHAPTER 6
ESCAPE FROM BLAME

NEFE ATE LITTLE. SHE SLEPT EVEN LESS. SHE HAD stayed within her cabin ever since she nearly strangled Atinuk. She could not bear to be around the others on the barge, much less to converse with them. She kept her vacant gaze on her limp hands in her lap. The hollowness in her chest contradicted the heaviness that dwelt there. Her back rounded in defeat, and her shoulders pulled her head down.

Her sister had chosen their half-brother over her. Her mother was dead. She was running for her life from a man who would probably never endure his rightful punishment. Her fingers twitched as Ankhesenpaaten's screams from the tunnel resounded in her memory.

She had sat in the tunnel, frozen and unable to move, watching the last moments of her mother's life play out in front of her. Perhaps if she had helped

Ankhesenpaaten grab her mother's hand, they could all be together. Perhaps she could have saved her mother . . .

Her hands. They did nothing. She did nothing.

I did nothing.

Her eyes burned, but no tears fell. Her thinned lips curled down as she sniffed away the imagined tears. *Now I am running to save my own life, like a coward. I let these people*—she glanced at her barge mates—*make me believe it was what my mother wanted, but if I were my mother, I would want to be alive with my daughters beside me.*

She glanced to Paaten. *He did nothing.*

Her gaze shifted to Atinuk. *He said nothing.*

And finally, her stare fell upon Aitye. *She did nothing. She should have taken my mother's place. She was her steward. Her oath meant nothing.*

Her eyes once again fell to her own hands. *I am alone by my own doing, and now I am fleeing Egypt with three cowards toward an unknown future in an unknown place.* She eyed the barge. *This is clearly a military barge, one of the ships of Pharaoh's Armies. How will we not be caught with this barge? We will surely be noticed. And if the threats are true, we will all be killed as the cowards we are.*

Aitye entered her cabin with a pottery bowl of beans and bread atop it. Nefe did not bother to look up.

"Princ—Nefe," Aitye stuttered. Her head drooped. "Forgive me, your majesty. I will never be at ease calling you only Nefe." She handed Nefe the bowl, but Nefe did not reach for it.

"I will leave this here." Aitye placed the bowl beside her. "It is the last of the beans that we traded for in Men-nefer. We will need to dock at Per-Amun before we continue to Canaan."

Nefe blinked with a stony face. *They can do whatever they want. It changes nothing. These cowards.*

Aitye shuffled in place, and Nefe wished she would leave. Her once-limp hands balled into fists on her lap.

Aitye rubbed her hands together and licked her lip. "You need to eat. I know you are hurting, but we are going to be on foot soon. You will need your stren—"

"You command the King's Daughter to eat?" Nefe growled and peered up at her mother's steward. Anger fueled her will to speak and snuffed out her sobs for the moment. "Who are you to do such a thing?"

Aitye took a step backward, shaking her head. "I am only requesting you eat, your majesty. Walking to Canaan is no easy feat. You—"

"We would not have to be running to Canaan if you, along with those two"—she pointed to Paaten, on the steering perch, and Atinuk, who had stopped to see why she yelled—"had fulfilled your oath to Pharaoh." Nefe trembled. She dropped her pointer finger to her side.

She swept her glance at all three of them, standing like silent sentinels.

"None of you did anything!"

Nefe brought her fists under her chin; her gaze once again fell to her hands. "And neither did I," she whispered under her breath. Her shoulders began to slump as her jaw twitched. Her tears begged for release, but she held them prisoner. Her will was dissolving. She could not cry any more than she already had in front of these people. Soon, she would wake up. Soon, she would be back in her bed at the palace. None of this would be real. She would gladly give up the last nine years of her life if she could have her family with her again. All of her sisters, her father, her mother, her grandmother—all of them would return. She could feel complete again. She would not be alone.

Alone. I am alone.

No.

Wake up!

Aitye took a step forward and pulled Nefe into an embrace. Nefe recoiled at the interruption to her thoughts, and she thrust her hands into Aitye's chest, knocking her away. Anger once again inflamed her will. "Do not touch me, as is your place, *Steward*."

Aitye regained her balance and narrowed her stance. Her chin lifted. "If you think you are the only one hurting, *Princess,* you are wrong." Her eyebrows furrowed, and the once-sympathetic gleam in her eye vanished.

"I helped raise you, Princess Neferneferuaten Tasherit, as well as all your sisters." Her bold voice caused Nefe's heart to skip a beat.

But you are not my mother, Nefe thought as Aitye continued.

"I grew up alongside your mother. I became a steward for her when I was fifteen years old. I fought to save her life when the rebels broke into Malkata. I saw her in pain. I saw her suffer. I saw her when she had nothing else to lose. I helped her to endure." Aitye's voice remained calm and gentle, yet bold and firm.

Nefe gritted her teeth as a red hue flushed her face. She had never even seen her mother for an extended period of time, and she could not recall an instance when her mother had ever consoled her. *Aitye has consoled me, but she is not my mother.*

"*I* was with her when she was exiled from Aketaten. *I* helped her learn to cook for you and the rest of her daughters. *I* felt her joy when she became with child for the last time and gained reentry into your father's sun city. *I* was by her side through all six pregnancies and deliveries, and *I* was there through the entombment of each of her four daughters. *I* had to keep her from her babies when they became ill with the plague, so she would not travel to Re and leave the country in even more turmoil. . . . "

Nefe remained mute, unable to form a coherent reply during Aitye's reproof. She was right, though.

She had probably done all of those things for her mother; she had no reason to lie.

Yet, Nefe wanted her mother with her. All of her life, she had wanted her mother, but Kiya and Aitye were there instead. Hearing Aitye's list of services to her mother made her shoulders shrink back at the life her mother had lived. Nefe had been happy in the royal harem, living a normal royal life alongside Ankhesenpaaten and her sisters. She was only five years old when four of her sisters traveled to the Aten or Re, whichever it was, but she wished for them nonetheless.

". . . *I* shielded the palace from her anguish when Kiya traveled to Re. *I* dabbed her brow with cool water when she lay sick from her life of pain."

Aitye took a step forward until she came toe-to-toe with Nefe. Her eyes glistened with unshed tears.

"She may have birthed you, but she was *my* friend. *I* was her confidant." Aitye leaned toward Nefe, who stood her ground. "You are *not* the only one hurting."

Nefe chewed on her lip. *Then why did you not save her?* The yell could not get through her constricted throat. She kept her mouth shut for fear her rebuke would turn into a wail and cause her to fall on her knees into a sobbing heap upon the deck.

Aitye leaned back and smoothed a hand down her linen dress. "I gave an oath to live for your mother, and I know she would want me to take care of you, as I have always done."

You cared so much for Mother, yet you still let her die. I do not want you to take care of me. Her jaw clamped shut, and her thoughts hit the barricade behind her lips. She held her breath and focused on remaining upright.

"In this new life, we can be whatever we want to be. I *choose* to be your steward. Do not ever forget it." Aitye wiped a tear that finally escaped, and she steadied an angry breath. "Your majesty," she whispered to end her tirade.

Aitye turned to go, but then she peered over her shoulder. "Eat your beans, Daughter of the King. You will need your strength."

She let the drape down on her way out of the cabin.

Nefe watched her walk to the center of the barge with Atinuk, who looked back at her through the semi-opaque drapes.

"I hate you," Nefe whispered under her breath and sniffled. She crossed her arms. *The hypocrite; she says Mother was her friend, and yet she lets her die.* Aitye stood at the edge of the barge. Atinuk's gaze left Nefe and shifted to Aitye. Nefe turned to face Paaten's feet on the steering perch.

In that moment, Nefe only wished for Ankhesenpaaten by her side. Ankhesenpaaten would be there to hold her while she cried. Ankhesenpaaten would stroke her head and tell her that, together, they would find peace in this new life. But without anyone to comfort her, fear took root in her heart; her body quivered in the warm Nile breeze. There was no one there to tell her the future would be fine, or that she would be fine. No one would be there to catch her when she fell; there would be no soft place to land. Her family was gone.

Her head slightly shook as she collapsed into the lounger, her focus to remain standing now gone. She lay down and closed her eyes.

"Wake up," she whispered to herself.

CHAPTER 7
ESCAPE FROM ANOTHER LIFE

ATINUK WATCHED AITYE EXIT THE CABIN AND SAW Nefe glowering at her. Aitye's cheeks were flushed. His throat itched as a lump grew there. His gaze darted back and forth between Aitye and Nefe until it finally landed on Aitye.

Her arm had ripped open again—fresh blood seeped into the linen wrapping. He grabbed the honey and castor oil from the barge's storage in the deck and walked over to her. He had seen her over the years as she tended to the daughters of Nefertiti; a certain admiration for her had developed in his mind. The way she spoke with her hands, the way she held her chin even though she was a steward, and her fierce loyalty to Pharaoh all drew his attention.

She even remains graceful as she chides Nefe, just as she chided me. Gentle. Firm. Loyal.

Never did he think she would be on the barge running away with him, but now that she was . . . he pushed the thought away. *I love Tadukhipa.* His shoulders slumped. *Loved. I was too late to take her back to Canaan.*

He looked out over the Nile before squaring his shoulders to her. *We have barely spoken to each other these last two decans.* He glanced to Paaten, who was eyeing him. *Mostly because of the autocrat.*

His gaze fell back to Aitye. *I could never harm Nefertiti's daughter.* The small beads in Aitye's wig gleamed in the sunlight. *I could never harm Aitye.*

He traced the profile of her face for a moment, until she snapped her head to him.

"Do you wish to speak to me?" Her voice was venom, and angry tears burned her eyes.

He shook his head and shrugged.

"No."

He pointed to her arm and held up the small amphoras of honey and castor oil with his other hand. "You are bleeding again, though."

She peered down to her arm and shuddered. Her jaw clamped, and she stared at the wound as if reliving the memory of how she got it.

"I deserve it," she muttered, and the Nile once again took her gaze.

His brow furrowed. "You deserve to be injured?"

She nodded.

"Why?"

"If I had been able to light the torch, General Paaten would have been able to see. My Pharaoh may not have been with Re right now." She squeezed her hands together. "I just could not stop shaking. My fingers . . . my hands." She shook her head as her hands began to tremble. "She gave me the torch; I had time to light it. I should have lit it."

Atinuk surprised himself and placed a hand over hers as she continued. She appeared unfazed by his touch, too lost in her own thoughts.

"The King's Daughter is correct. I did nothing to save my master. My oath to Pharaoh means nothing now." Her chin drooped, and she took a shaky breath.

He squeezed her hand so that she lifted her gaze to him.

"Your oath means you choose to serve her daughter over seeking a life for yourself despite this new freedom." He let his hand fall away, afraid to keep it there. "There is no greater living sacrifice than to live for someone else."

Tears welled in her eyes, and she pressed her lips together. "Thank you, Atinuk."

He locked eyes with her. He had promised Tadukhipa to take Nefertiti's daughters with him to Canaan, but, after that, could he live for himself? Could he find it within himself to take a wife, have children? Even though King Tustratta had granted him freedom at Tadukhipa's promise to wed Pharaoh Amenhotep III, he still felt his life as a palace servant tied him to the Mitanni Princess. He had loved her. He still loved her. But he found it hard to live with only the ghost of her. Something held him loyal to the Mitanni Princess's memory, but his heart urged him to feel again after all this time. Aitye was gentle and kind, like Tadukhipa. He had seen the way she tried to console Nefe. He peered at the princess over Aitye's shoulder. Nefe reminded him of Tadukhipa when they had tried to escape from the palace together. Nefe and Tadukhipa were around the same age when they had made the attempt.

He pushed the memory away as his gaze once again fell to Aitye.

She had drawn his eye over the years as he snuck about the palace reluctantly doing Pawah's bidding, but he had chided himself every time he thought about her, still declaring loyalty to the deceased princess. However, as Aitye stood before him, telling him about her innermost fears, she was as he had imagined her to be. She captured him entirely. The possibility of a life in Canaan, but with Aitye instead of Tadukhipa, caused him to pause.

Aitye's blood drew his attention. "Let me tend your wound," he whispered.

She peered again at the blood-soiled linen and nodded.

He took off the bandage and saw she had ripped the scab open. "It will take time, Aitye, to live with the guilt." His eyes darted in memory as he applied more honey and castor oil. "I have spent half of my life trying to make up for my own mistakes; I had spent thirteen years building a life for Tadukhipa in Canaan, planning how I would take her away from here. Tadukhipa gave up everything she knew for my life and my freedom. I could not live knowing she was here alone. I have spent the remainder of my life thus far for her. I will honor her wish to provide for Nefertiti's daughters . . ."—his gaze drifted to Nefe— "daughter."

Silence followed. He had left himself vulnerable as he finished wrapping her arm.

"But?" she asked.

He locked eyes with her.

But I do not know if I can keep my heart reserved for Tadukhipa anymore.

He traced the outline of her face. "Tadukhipa passed from this life eight years ago from the illness that swept through the lands. I was too late in coming for her. My entire life has been for Tadukhipa." He shook his head. "Eight years is a long time to live with something you cannot change."

Even this woman's eyes listened to him; there was such gentleness in them. "I realize that now. You should too."

Her chin quivered. "It still does not take away the pain."

He turned to look out over the barge's bow at the calm waters of the Nile and the coming fork in the river. "It does not, but life somehow goes on. You learn to tolerate it."

He pointed to the fork in the river and moved his finger toward the western river path. "You can live in the past, or"—he pointed to the eastern river path toward the land of Goshen—"you can live for the future."

His hand again fell to the side of the barge as he swept his gaze back to the woman he wanted to comfort. "Tadukhipa is gone. Nefertiti, your Pharaoh, is gone."

He took a deep breath of the river air. "Do not be like me." His lips formed a despondent grin. "Starting today, I choose not to live in the past. I will uphold my promise to her, but I cannot live for her anymore."

Aitye did not return his grin. "Then maybe you did not truly love her as I love Pharaoh."

Atinuk's grin faded. *In time, she will see.*

There was no benefit in arguing whose love for whom was greater, so he just murmured, "Perhaps."

He returned his gaze to the Nile waters as Paaten began to steer the barge toward the land of Goshen.

CHAPTER 8
ESCAPE FROM TRUTH

Paaten steered the boat toward Per-Amun, the easternmost port of Egypt's empire in Goshen. The port city skyline held a pillar of smoke billowing into the sky.

Nefe stood next to one of the front two poles of her cabin's frame and drew back the drapes to look out at the city in the distance. Aitye awoke and emerged from the other cabin to come to the middle of the barge to look at the same spectacle with Atinuk.

Atinuk looked back to Paaten, who only stared at the smoke as he steered. They were dangerously low on supplies; the next-nearest port after Per-Amun was Azzati. He let out a low, slow breath; they had to dock. They could not make it to Azzati on the supplies they had onboard.

He slid the barge next to the stone pier, and Atinuk dropped the triangular limestone anchor.

Paaten shielded his eyes from the sun as he peered into the distance. His eyesight was not as good as it had been when he was younger. He squinted and tilted his head back to see against the glare of the sun reflecting from the gentle Mediterranean waves. Blurry images of people and the market came into view.

A large Cypriote boat nearly blocked the sun as it docked against the stone pier next to the barge.

Paaten looked around at all the sea ships in the area. "At least, there are many people here," he muttered to himself. His eyes drifted back to the smoke billowing up into the sky. "But what could have caused that?"

Paaten's gaze fell back to Atinuk. "And what to do with him? Do I keep him with me, leaving the King's Daughter and Aitye alone and vulnerable? Ours is a small royal barge that would be easily seized in a trade center full of foreigners. Or do I trust him enough to stay with them and be here when I get back? Or do I take the King's Daughter with me and leave Aitye and Atinuk?" He rubbed his neck. "I can always get another barge. Pharaoh's Army has become so lax; it is disgusting." He spat into the water.

Perhaps if I had not been so focused on carrying out Pharaoh's ridiculous orders for the Aten, I could have seen the corruption in the ranks. I could have seen where Akhenaten drove a wedge between the men's duty and their loyalty.

He ran a hand over the handle of the steering oar. *I just walked up to the Fleetsman and told him I needed a barge. They gave it to me with no further questions asked, telling me to have it back within the month.*

He sneered at the misadministration of Pharaoh's vessels. "That would never have occurred under the reign of Pharaoh Amenhotep III." His chin dipped in memory of the great King. "Egypt, what have you become?" he whispered. His gaze fell to Nefe. "An Egypt that we must flee."

As he stepped down from the steering perch, he ran his eyes down Nefe's small frame, and an image of Pharaoh Neferneferuaten filled his mind.

I will not fail you again, my Pharaoh.

"Princess, you will come with me into the market. You are to stay close and say nothing."

Nefe turned her head as if she heard him but chose to ignore him.

Paaten stepped behind her. "You will come with me to the—"

"I heard you, Paaten." She dropped the drape and retreated into the cabin.

"We need to not waste time. The longer we are here, the greater our chances of being known." He spoke to the drape but saw her faint outline through the somewhat-opaque linen.

"I am coming," she huffed and swished the drape open.

Atinuk stood in front of her. "I should go, Paaten."

"You will stay here with Aitye and guard the barge. You have your bow and quiver. My khopesh is right there," Paaten said, pointing to the stern's cabin lounger as he grabbed Atinuk's travel sling. "We will be back before the sun sets." He hopped out of the barge and held out his hand to Nefe, who reluctantly took it.

Paaten placed his hands on her shoulders once she stepped onto the stone pier. "You are going to be my granddaughter should anyone ask—"

She swiped his hands from her shoulders.

"—and I will need to call you Nefe."

The Cypriote crew began unloading next to them, and Paaten knew they needed to move quickly or risk being pushed into the water by the traffic on the pier.

"Call me what you wish. Tell whatever lies you need to tell," Nefe muttered. She spun on her heels and walked away.

Paaten stared at Atinuk before he followed her. "Cause no trouble," he ordered Atinuk. He pointed to the strong warriors with red-and-white sashes across their chests and waists who stood sentinel on the docks to ensure order. "The Medjay are not ones to be trifled with."

He hoped he had not made a mistake in trusting him with the barge. Perhaps he and Nefe should have stayed on the barge and let Atinuk and Aitye go to the market, but Atinuk was clearly a foreigner. They had a limited amount of trade goods, and he knew the merchants in the marketplace were apt to take advantage of foreign traders, especially when the principles of Ma'at seemingly had been all but forgotten by the jaded and persecuted people.

He let out a deep breath as he caught up to the princess. *I cannot keep questioning my decisions. I made a few bad ones, but I will only make more if I keep doing this to myself.*

CHAPTER 9
ESCAPE FROM IGNORANCE

NEFE MARCHED STRAIGHT AHEAD TOWARD THE markets. At any other time in her life, she would have been overjoyed to see the markets of the common people. She would have loved to leave the sanctuary of the royal harem, but this was not any other time. It reminded her of her failure, her cowardliness, and her spineless barge mates. The smell of the fish, the dialects being spoken, and the distinct odor of the foreigners created a wall of sensory overstimulation as she stepped from the stone pier, almost knocking her backward upon coming into contact with it. The fresh smell of the sea was lost in the myriad of new smells and sounds.

Paaten's hand grasped her shoulder. "This way," he said as the shouts of people behind them started.

"...Move..."

"...Keep walking..."

I do not want the man responsible for my mother's

murder to touch me. Nefe rolled her shoulder to remove his hand.

Paaten's hand came back, but this time with a heavy grip, guiding her through the congestion at the entrance of the stone pier. She tried to swipe his hand away, but he kept his hold on her. The harsh whisper in her ear came afterward, "You will stay by my side; I will not lose you too."

Nefe crossed her arms and let Paaten keep a grip on her shoulder as he moved her through the crowd. They stopped at a table to trade for bread, beer, and dates. The two women who owned the market stall ignored them, along with the other three people perusing their array of food items.

Nefe strained to hear the women's conversation as Paaten smelt the beer and bread for freshness.

"Hittite Prince slain . . . "

Her brow furrowed. *But I thought the Hittite Prince was part of the ruse for mother's murder.*

" . . . Army burned that horrid caravan . . . "

Her gaze drifted to the smoke.

A man tried to get the merchant women's attention. "How much for this amphora?" he yelled at her in Akkadian.

" . . . dirty, filthy Hittites . . . "

"Woman, how much for this amphora?" he snapped at one of the women while pointing to a large amphora of beer.

She glared at him. "Its equivalent in olive oil, Mycenaean," she snapped back.

"Oil for beer? You fool," he rebuffed. "I will give you a hin of olive oil for this hekat of beer."

She waved him off, and he left in a huff.

Nefe stayed mute but caught the eye of one of the women.

"You look quite innocent, young woman. Never seen a Mycenaean before?" She laughed, but the other woman pointed at her.

"You are quite beautiful. You resemble Pharaoh Neferneferuaten. I hope you are not as foolish as she."

Paaten put down an amphora of beer and cleared his throat. "She is my granddaughter."

"Well, you should be proud to have such a beautiful granddaughter. I have a son who wants to set up a house with a horrid woman. She is lazy and overcooks the beans." She eyed Nefe. "Are you interested? My son is as handsome as you are beautiful."

Nefe bit her tongue as a tear welled in one of her eyes. *Is this to be my life now: bartered away to some boy of some merchant woman?*

"She is not interested," Paaten spoke for her.

The woman turned her eye to him, seemingly to rebuke him, but her mouth closed as she sized up his muscular body. "Well, my husband has traveled to Re. Are you interested? I am a wonderful cook."

"I have a wife," Paaten mumbled and held up the hekat of beer that the other man had wanted. "How much do you want for this beer?"

She eyed him up and down. "I do not think you have a wife. So, for you, I will take a shat copper for it."

"You are most kind," Paaten placed a shat copper into her palm. "But I do have a wife."

"I hope she enjoys you." The woman looked at his strong arms and body. "I would."

"She enjoys me plenty," he muttered.

The woman's lip pouted, and the lustful gleam in her eye faded. "Well then, is that all you want, Citizen?"

Paaten looked at the smoke and pointed. The woman's eyes kept looking at Paaten's strong, defined arm, rather than following the line of his finger. "What has happened here? I overheard you saying something about the Hittite Prince?"

"Yes, Pharaoh's Army slew the prince and his caravan," the woman snorted. "I am glad too. Our *Pharaoh* should have known better than to hand Egypt to the Hittites!"

Nefe gritted her teeth and clamped her jaw as her stare intensified upon the woman. *Do not speak of my mother in such a disrespectful manner!*

Paaten ignored her and dropped his hand. "Who ordered that action?"

The woman scoffed. "How should I know? I am only relieved to know the throne will not be tainted by Hittite filth. It has already been stained by Akhenaten and then Smenkare." She curled her lip and shook her head in disgust. "I hope Ammit devours both of their hearts . . . "

Even though Nefe only faintly knew who Ammit was and the demoness's place in the afterlife, her hands curled into fists. Her breathing quickened. *You dare speak of my father and uncle in such a way? You dare refer to them without the royal titles they deserve?* She snapped her gaze to Paaten. *Strike them down for speaking in such a way against the previous Pharaohs.*

" . . . and I hope Neferneferuaten-Nefertiti gets what she deserves for trying to give Egypt into the hands of the Hittites . . . "

Nefe opened her mouth to chastise them, but Paaten's heavy hand fell on her shoulder to stop her.

". . . such a vile people they are. Our enemies! She wants to marry their prince? She is a—"

"She did restore Egypt to our gods," Paaten interjected. The Egyptian marketgoers nodded their heads and pursed their lips, alerting Nefe to their eavesdropping on the conversation.

Yet no one chastises this woman for speaking about my mother in this way? Not a single person here. Nefe looked at the four Egyptians in the huddle around the stall.

"Just in time, too. I was starting—" the other woman began.

"Indeed," Paaten said, turning Nefe and himself to leave. "Thank you for the trade."

"You come back here if your wife is ever done with you," the woman called after him and then pointed to Nefe, shaking her finger. "If you want a good man for a husband, you come see me too."

"Indeed," Paaten said again with a polite smile as they disappeared into the crowds.

There were so many people, Nefe did not try to move Paaten's hand off of her. Instead, she grabbed on to it. In that moment, she realized how alone she was: how far she had traveled from the palace at Aketaten and how different her world was from this world outside the royal harem's walls. Fear twisted in her stomach as the endless blur of faces pushed past her. Each bump or accidental poke caused her heart to race.

Do all of the people want my father and uncle to be given over to Ammit? Do they all believe my mother deserves a death such as murder? Her fingertips sank underneath Paaten's hand, and she clung to it. *This life is nothing like what I envisioned. I cannot do this. I am afraid. I am scared.* Her lip trembled as she pressed against Paaten in the crowd, not wanting to be pushed or prodded anymore. She wanted to be home. She wanted her sister. A dread built in her stomach as her truth settled in once again: *I am alone.*

"In peace, Citizen," an old man nodded to Paaten. "Mistress of the House," he acknowledged her.

Nefe looked around. Paaten had guided her to the front of a new stall.

"Are you well, Mistress of the House?" The old man leaned in to study her face.

She nodded with a pressed smile.

He nodded and patted her hand that she had rested on a stand in his stall. "Good. Good."

Paaten traded for cooked beans, bread, turnips, radishes, and dates. They left with his travel sling full, one arm draped around the hekat of beer, and one hand on Nefe's shoulder. The crowds began to thin out some, but Paaten still kept a hand on her shoulder. She slowed her step to walk beside him. Peering up at him, she pursed her lips. She had so many questions, but she did not want to talk to him. He had failed her mother. He was a coward.

As if sensing her concerns, he mumbled, "Not everyone respected your parents." Paaten gently squeezed her shoulder. "Thank you for staying your tongue." His eyes' alert gaze continued to scan the passersby. "We do not know who is loyal to the throne and who is loyal to the People's Restoration of Egypt."

"The what?" Nefe tilted her head. "What is that?"

He nodded as a man passed by them. He guided her to the stone pier. "There are those who want to see the entire royal bloodline from Akhenaten gone." His voice was low, and he looked straight ahead as if to not draw attention to the grandfather and his granddaughter.

"Why?" Her voice shook as she began to eye each man and woman who passed by. She stepped up to the stone pier and spun around. "Why, Paaten?" she whispered.

He visibly swallowed. "Remember your family

how you want to remember them; it is not important anymore."

"Move!" a yell came from behind them. At the command, Paaten prodded Nefe to walk along the pier toward their barge.

"It is important to me," Nefe muttered.

"The only important thing is to protect you and fulfill my oath to your mother." The gruffness of his voice had returned.

She bit back, hard. "Because you could not keep her safe?"

"I have asked your forgiveness in that matter, and now, I ask that you think of your mother and your father in the way you want to remember them." His voice remained calm and without angst, as if her comment had not fazed him in the slightest. He let go of her shoulder as she walked in front of him. His voice traveled to her from behind. "There is much you do not know and much you will never want to know. I do not wish to be the one to taint your memory of them."

"There is nothing to taint." Nefe bit her lip. *Nothing to taint. These people are only envious of the throne. They wish their lives to be in the palace, so they spread lies.*

But that woman's words pounded in her ears: " . . . *I hope Neferneferuaten-Nefertiti gets what she deserves. . . .*"

What had her mother done to incur the wrath of such people? What had her father and uncle done to have their hearts cursed by the people they were appointed by the Aten to protect? Had she been blind all of her life? Maybe Paaten was right in that she did not want to know.

No! I have to know. It is the reason why I am fleeing Egypt, is it not? Paaten is wrong. One day, I will find out the truth. She stared off at the many ships, boats and barges docked at the Mediterranean seaport. The pier ended somewhere in the vast sea in front of her, just as her future ended in a sea of unknowns. In that moment, she wished to curl up on the lounger and weep for her fragile memory of her life in the palace, now shattered and broken.

Her feet hurt, and she dropped her head. As she walked, the sun glimmered on her gold and precious-gem-encrusted sandals peeking out from under her long linen dress: an obvious sign of royalty.

I suppose no one looks at feet while walking in the market.

CHAPTER 10
ESCAPE FROM TRADE

Atinuk pulled his quiver across his shoulder as two sea-hardened Cypriotes approached and eyed Aitye. They slowed their walk down the pier as they came upon the barge. Their eyes went to him just as their stench reached his nostrils. "Canaanite," they huffed in Akkadian. "You have a nice woman for your barge. How much?"

"She is not for trade," he returned, holding his bow by his side.

One leaned on the side of the barge. "Women on the sea are always for trade," he muttered. "I have—"

"Nothing I want. Go to the Per-Amun markets to trade."

The Cypriote stood up and ran his hand down the strong Egyptian cargo barge. "Egyptians." He shook his head. "They also trade for what they cannot build. Take this boat, for example. I know our King Alashiya builds almost all of the wooden boats for

Egypt in exchange for Egypt's bountiful gold, grain and leather." His tone mocked the fallen state of the empire. "I probably helped build this one." He ran a finger along the wooden side, flicking it off at the end of its run.

"You trade for this boat?" The other Cypriote eyed Atinuk, who lifted his chin in response. Taking his silence for an answer, the Cypriote continued, "You obviously have desires that you trade for, Canaanite." He threw a hand toward Aitye. "So do I."

Aitye curled her lip, clearly repulsed by the seaman. She backed into the cabin and knelt by the lounger. Atinuk shook his head at her when she reached for Paaten's khopesh hidden underneath the lounger's linen skirt.

"She is an odd thing," the Cypriote said, taking note of her actions. "How much to trade for her?"

Atinuk ignored him. "Go to the Per-Amun markets to trade."

"I do not trade with the Egyptians. They do not marry off their women, much less trade them."

Atinuk's gaze shifted to Aitye. Did the Cypriote think she was not Egyptian? She certainly looked Egyptian to him. "She is an Egyptian woman."

The Cypriote laughed. "That is a Libyan dressed as an Egyptian."

Atinuk shook his head; it made no difference to him. "Begone, Cypriote."

"She fools you, Canaanite. Why not let me take

her off of your hands? One less mouth to feed. Besides, there are no other women for trade here."

"Begone, Cypriote. I will not say it again." He drew an arrow from his quiver and rested it against his bow, hoping to scare the man into submission.

The Cypriote's eyes glanced to Atinuk's weapon. "You think you are intimidating with that hunter's tool?" He pulled out a bronze dagger from underneath his tunic. "Shall we see who is quicker? You to draw and release your arrow, or me to throw my dagger? If you win, I shall leave or die, depending on your aim. If I win, I shall leave you for dead and take your woman."

Atinuk had fought off men like him before when he wandered about the city-states of Canaan trying to find his great-grandfather's tribe, but he had never killed anyone. Additionally, he did not want the attention it would cause, nor did he want Egypt's Medjay to take him to the main city courtyard for killing a man.

"Do you fear death, Canaanite?" the man hissed. His companion watched the exchange, but Atinuk saw him draw his dagger in attempted secrecy.

"I fear an unfair death, Cypriote. Your compeer draws his weapon as well."

"Then maybe your crew should not leave you alone with such a beautiful woman and such excellence in seacraft." His hand smoothed over the side of the barge once again.

"Remove your hand, or I will affix it to the barge

with my hunter's tool. I will shoot the hand of your compeer as well if he does not sheathe his dagger."

They laughed again. "You nomads; you always think you are superior to the sea- and city-dwellers."

Atinuk remembered his last few years of training by traitorous Egyptian bowmen. Pawah had seen it as a sort of insurance, should the bowmen return their loyalty to Pharaoh. Knowing what he did now, Atinuk assumed that is why Pawah had stationed him, the foreigner, at the end of the tunnel with orders to kill anyone who exited. Pawah could not risk the turn of an Egyptian's heart, should a royal step through the tunnel. As a foreigner, Pawah probably thought he was indifferent toward killing a royal.

He readjusted his grip on the bow and lightly grasped the bowstring with his drawing hand. *Pawah was wrong, and so is this Cypriote who underestimates me.*

The man leaning on the barge gave a slight nod to his companion, and Atinuk anticipated an attack. He let his arrow fly at the compeer's dagger hand just as he raised it to throw his weapon at Atinuk. The other Cypriote gaped at his crewmate before turning and raising his arm to throw his dagger, but Atinuk had already nocked another arrow.

Zip.

His arrow hit the Cypriote's hand that still rested on the barge.

"Ah!" His dagger dropped to the stone pier by his feet while his compeer behind him held his wrist, screaming in pain. His dagger also lay on the stone pier by his feet. Two of the dock's Medjay approached, one with his khopesh ready to strike.

Atinuk clenched his jaw and breathed through his teeth. He had only heard stories of Egypt's Medjay. He wanted no part of them. *Yet here I am doing the opposite of what Paaten told me to do.*

One Cypriote began to speak in Egyptian at the Medjay. The white-and-red sashes of their uniforms danced in the sunlight and the sea breeze.

Again, they underestimate me, he thought as he overheard their lies. Atinuk cleared his throat and spoke in Egyptian as well. "These men are liars. They wanted to trade for the wife of the barge's owner, and, when I refused, they decided to take both his barge and his wife by force." He pointed to their daggers on the stone pier. "They drew them and were going to kill me; they did not think I was quick enough with the bow."

The Medjay considered the evidence and the statements from the three of them. Aitye peered out from the lounger, clearly afraid. Upon seeing Aitye, one of the Medjay broke the arrow that affixed the Cypriote's hand to the barge. He slid his hand off of it, while the man groaned in pain. He gathered up their daggers and thrust them, handles first, into the Cypriote's chest. "Leave. You are no longer welcome at the port of Per-Amun." He waved them off toward their barge.

They grumbled, but since each sported a wounded hand, they did not dare fight the Medjay, whom they probably feared due to their reputation alone: The Medjay were fierce and ruthless enforcers of Pharaoh's law.

As the Cypriotes slunk back to their ship, one of the Medjay turned to Atinuk, while the other hooked his khopesh back onto his belt. "When the barge owner returns, leave. You are no longer welcome to the port of Per-Amun either." They looked to Aitye and nodded their heads to her. They examined the barge a little more closely. "This is an expensive barge, Canaanite. It looks to be that of Pharaoh's Fleet. Who did you say was the barge owner?"

Atinuk had been thinking of what to say to someone at each port if any asked, so he was quick to answer with his preimagined story: "He is a rich Egyptian nobleman from Hut-Waret, I believe. I am not sure. As I was returning to Makedo, he hired me to keep watch over his wife and barge while he took his daughter to the markets. She wanted to see Per-Amun."

They each tilted their heads and considered his response. One asked, "What are you doing in Egypt, Makedan?"

Atinuk cleared his throat. "I am a messenger from the city elders. They sent tribute and a request of aid to Pharaoh Akhenaten, but I was not received until Pharaoh Neferneferuaten heard my message." Atinuk observed the Medjay as they continued inspecting the barge while they listened to his story and made their silent judgements.

"Thank the gods for Pharaoh Neferneferuaten," one of them muttered.

The apparent leader of the duo snapped his head to his subordinate and glared.

Silence followed.

The leader puffed his chest at his subordinate's obedience to his unspoken command of silence before returning his gaze to Atinuk.

"Very well, messenger. Give Egypt's regards to our vassal state of Makedo in the land of Canaan," he said and nodded in acceptance of his story. He and his partner continued their patrol down the pier to make sure order was kept. But Atinuk noticed the assumed leader kept peering back at him.

They will return.

Atinuk looked toward the shore. "Make haste, Paaten," he mumbled. The salt-scented air of the sea breeze carried soft cries from the other end of the barge to his ears. He looked back to see Aitye wiping her eyes.

The onlookers had dispersed, and everyone seemed to be going about their business. He assumed it was safe for him to journey to the stern cabin to comfort the woman he admired. His valor in protecting her and the barge strengthened his stride. He placed his bow on the lounger as he knelt beside her.

"I did not know what those Cypriotes said, but I heard what you told the Medjay." She stared at the passersby on the pier in a near-trance. "Thank you for protecting me," she whispered.

Her hands rested on the lounger, and he covered one of them, breaking her trance. He perused her face before locking eyes with her. "You never have to thank me for that."

He reached for the linen on her arm and checked the wound; it looked like it would heal nicely. There would be a light scar upon her smooth skin but nothing to mar her.

"They said you were a Libyan dressed as an Egyptian?"

She chuckled amid her tears and nodded. "I believe it was my great-grandparents who were taken from Libya as chattel servants."

"Chattel servants?" Atinuk asked as he reached for the honey and castor oil. *Captives of war?*

"Yes," Aitye said lifting her chin. The corners of her lip fell.

I hope she does not believe I think less of her because of that. Perhaps I asked with too much surprise.

"Their children were free and grew up as Egyptians, but, with nothing to their name, they stayed in Pharaoh's palace. Each generation, we have advanced in the servants' stations. I am proud to have been the head steward of Pharaoh Neferneferuaten."

"I do not doubt it. You are loyal and"—he searched for the right word—"dedicated." He rubbed honey into the scab on her arm.

She paused, a scowl brewing on her face. She

yanked her arm away from his touch. "Just because I am Libyan—"

"I take no concern with your origins." He smiled and gingerly took her arm back into his possession. "I am Canaanite, as you know. My great-grandmother was taken as a servant in the Mitanni house of King Shuttarna, King Tustratta's father. My grandmother and mother each advanced in their stations as well. My mother was the wet nurse for Tadukhipa."

"You were a servant?" Aitye's brow furrowed. "Is that what you meant by Tadukhipa gave you your freedom? I thought you were speaking about your freedom after trying to escape with Tadukhipa from her father's palace." She slightly chuckled at herself for seemingly not understanding he was also a servant in a prior time.

"No, my freedom from bondage." Atinuk paused at the sad memory but returned to the present, to Aitye in front of him. He had hurt her feelings. "I was only curious about your heritage; I meant no harm in my words. If I was not clear in my intention and tone, I apologize."

She pressed her lips together and nodded. "So you do not think poorly of me for my status and Libyan origins?"

"No." Atinuk shook his head, watching her brown eyes settle. "A servant may be a King"—he gestured to her—"or Queen, in another world."

"Well, I assure you, my family does not descend from royalty of any kind."

He smiled at her slight chuckle and massaged the castor oil into her wound as well.

"Neither does mine, but"—he shrugged—"the royals could not be what they are without their servants."

She snorted and repressed a laugh. "This is true."

He looked at her scab as he massaged. His treatment of it was finished, but he did not want to let go of her arm. He poured a little more castor oil on it and massaged again.

"When you were granted freedom," Aitye asked, a little timidly, "did you have to leave your family?"

The question ripped open a part of his heart he had closed long ago. He shifted as he sat back on his heels. "I never knew my brother. He was traded to the Assyrian King before I was born." He spoke directly and without any emotion about this part of his past he did not want to remember. "My mother told me to leave her; she was a woman advanced in years. She said the gods had granted me this privilege, because servants are not freed in the Mitanni lands. She told me to leave before the King changed his mind." His eyes burned as he stared at Aitye's scab. "So I left my mother as a servant in his palace. I am not proud."

Aitye's hand smoothed over his arm. "I am sorry, Atinuk."

He lifted his gaze to her. Gentleness. Understanding. Her eyes spoke many things.

"I have never forgiven myself," he said. "Just as I

have never forgiven myself for arriving too late for Tadukhipa."

She grasped his bicep. "'Servant' is just a status. I am sure your mother still fares well."

His lips grinned at the sad irony, knowing Aitye was treated well as a servant, but it was not the same for his mother. "In Egypt, yes, servants are well-treated because each Egyptian lives by the principles of Ma'at. They cannot treat another person with ill contempt or else they risk their hearts being eaten by Ammit on the scales of the afterlife. With the Mitanni and the other foreign empires, servants are not people—merely disposable possessions." Tears again burned his eyes. "And I left my mother as one of them."

She paused, but her hand never withdrew from his arm. "Your mother wanted you to be happy. She knew if you were to stay or to try to free her as well, the King may have enslaved you again."

"I know, and I knew it then too." He shook his head. "But I did not even try."

"If I have learned anything from my time in the palace as a steward and learning about mothers and their children, it is this: They would rather their child be free without pain and strife than to live their own life of luxury. My Pharaoh, for example, distanced her children from the throne to save them. Even now, she has traveled to Re, and her daughters live. I believe she would be sad in knowing her daughter Ankhesenpaaten turned back to that life."

He hung his head, but Aitye lifted his chin. "Forgive yourself. It is what your mother would have wanted."

"It is so simple to say, Aitye."

She paused, and with a slight chuckle and grin, she whispered, "I believe we have had this conversation already, but our roles were reversed."

He grasped the wrist of her hand that held his chin and coaxed her hand into his. "Yes." He remembered that day staring at the fork in the river.

"Did you not say something about living for the future?" she reminded him with her grin growing larger.

A slight hue came upon his cheeks. "Yes, I did."

Her grin faded. "I know it is hard. It seems like we live with the guilt our entire lives, hmm?" She searched his eyes.

"Like I said, you learn to tolerate it." He shrugged. "But it does bite your heart every now and then."

She nodded and drew her hand out of his. Before she could withdraw her arm too, he applied more castor oil and massaged. He decided to move past that subject, and hopefully, if he was lucky, he could experience holding her hand once more.

"Do you have siblings?" During his time at the palace, he had never seen her go anywhere but the servants' chambers at night with the other women. She had no husband, no child; she never seemed to have any familial relationship with any of the other stewards or servants.

"No. I am the only child of my mother, who traveled to Re when I was young. I am alone." He finished his massage and reapplied the linen bandage.

He shook his head. "You are not alone."

Instead of a smile, he received an expressionless stare in return. "You act as if you know me already," she told him.

He stood up, watching her eyes as they followed him. He fidgeted with his fingers before he grabbed his bow. "Eight years is a long time to spend in Pharaoh's palace with the ghost of a woman you once loved." The sea breeze tingled his cheeks as he looked out over the vast sea. "As I told you, I have now decided to live for the future and its endless possibilities."

He dropped his gaze to hers. *Perhaps, one with you.*

Her face remained expressionless while their gazes locked. He had not quite answered her implied question, but he was not ready to admit to her that he had been watching her.

He bounced the upper limb of his bow in his hand and hoped he would never have to admit it. He slowly exited the cabin, but before he let the drape drop, he peered back over his shoulder.

"Perhaps you should stay in the cabin until Paaten and Nefe return. We would not want another man to lose a hand after desiring your beauty."

"You mean my body?"

He traced her full lips and large brown eyes with his gaze. *No, your beauty.*

He nodded in a false agreement with her. The drape fell behind him. He heard her lie down behind the lounger, so no one would know she was there.

CHAPTER 11
ESCAPE FROM THE MEDJAY

Nefe looked up; the red-and-white-sashed men stood in front of her. Each man's hand rested on a khopesh securely tied to his waist. They looked official and frightening; a pit opened in her stomach as their eyes fell upon her. Paaten's hand strongly guided her to step onto the barge. Atinuk extended his hand to help her onto its frame. She followed the implied commands as the two officials stopped in front of the barge.

"Nobleman, it is good of you to return with your daughter," Atinuk said with a slight bow of his head, keeping his eyes darting between Nefe and Paaten behind her.

Daughter? Nefe thought. *I thought I was his granddaughter.*

Paaten narrowed his eyes at Atinuk before acknowledging the Medjay standing before the barge.

His deep voice carried in the sea breeze. "In peace, Medjay."

"In peace, Nobleman."

Nefe clenched her teeth. *Something must have happened while we were at the market.* She glanced around. The blood stain on the side of the barge abruptly halted her scan. *Blood. Is that blood?* A scream raced to the top of her throat, but Atinuk locked eyes with her, slowly lowering his chin, as if coaxing the scream back down.

"I hope you enjoyed the markets at Per-Amun, Citizeness. Your mother is lying down." Atinuk gestured toward the cabin on the barge's stern. "She requested your presence when you returned."

Nefe ducked her head and hurried away, out of the potential inquiry from the men known as the Medjay.

Aitye had lifted her head at the sound of voices. "Mother," Nefe said, stealing a peer over her shoulder to see if the Medjay still stood there. They remained.

"Daughter." Aitye spoke with a warmth Nefe remembered—it was how Aitye spoke to her when she was young.

"Are you well?" Nefe asked. She did not think the men at the front of the barge could still hear them, but she did not want to find out. Nefe played along, although she could not find it within herself to call Aitye her "mother" again, since Aitye had so cowardly forsaken her oath to her mother.

Aitye shook her head. "Two men tried to take me

by force, but our hired help from Canaan protected me and the barge."

Nefe knelt down beside her. "That must have been frightening."

Aitye nodded, but her attention was already elsewhere. Her eyes and ears focused on the men's conversation at the front of the boat.

" . . . I was on my way to Makedo—" Atinuk was saying, but one of the Medjay held up his hand to silence him.

Nefe wondered who these *Medjay* were; she had never heard of them, but Paaten seemed to hold his distance, and Atinuk obeyed them. She squinted to make them out in the blazing sun. Visually, the two Medjay rivaled Paaten in strength and build, although they were not as tall as he. *Almost as tall as he,* she reconsidered. Their muscles rippled in sweat under the sun. They each had a khopesh, a whip and a dagger on their belts.

Are these the enforcers of Pharaoh's law?

She shuddered, remembering the gossip of the royal harem describing the beatings the people received when they did not worship the Aten in truth. *Silly people,* she chided the subjects of past gossip. *Who would ever go against one of the Medjay?*

"We would like to hear it from Citizen Paaten." The Medjay lowered his hand to rest on the handle of his khopesh fastened to his belt; both of the Medjays' gazes turned to Paaten.

Paaten nodded toward the Medjay, still standing on the stone pier. "As you wish—"

Nefe swallowed the lump in her throat; her eyes grew wide. *How was he to know what Atinuk had said in his absence? What if their stories did not align? What then? Were the Medjay to take them to town and hold them for questioning by the Nomarch? Were they to take and beat them for lying to the officials of Egypt, like those who had refused to worship the Aten in truth?*

"—my wife and I decided to grant our daughter's request, as she wanted to see the markets at Per-Amun before she set up a house. I asked my wife to stay behind with the barge, as I have heard there are many places in Per-Amun where nonlocal women may end up disappearing—"

"Yes, that is true. You were wise to go with your daughter." The Medjay eyed him. "Why did you not bring your house servants or guards with you? If you truly are a nobleman, you should have known guards are practically a requirement in the large port cities."

Nefe's jaw strained. *How is Paaten going to answer these questions?*

She realized her hands gripped the lounger when Aitye placed a hand over hers. Any other time she would have slid her hand out from underneath Aitye's cowardly hand, but her thoughts consumed her as she leaned forward to hear what Paaten said in response.

"I do not live in the bigger cities"—Paaten glanced at Atinuk, who gave a slight nod of the head—"such as Waset, Aketaten, or Men-nefer. I have no need of guards. I gave my stewards leave until we returned and left the servants behind to tend to the estate."

Nefe's fingers spread out as the tension in her shoulders crept away down her back.

Paaten handed the travel sling to Atinuk, who took it and stored it in the cargo hold beneath the deck.

"But the next time we decide to come to Per-Amun, I will be sure to hire a few guards," Paaten added.

"Yes, hire more than a few guards: some to remain on your barge and some to go with you to the market. Foreign messengers are usually not as good with the bow as the one you found, Citizen Paaten." The Medjay narrowed his stance, and his hand fell from his khopesh. "And most noblemen do not look as fierce as you."

Paaten gave an appreciative nod of his head. "I was born into a family full of healthy men such as yourself."

They chuckled for a half a moment and looked over the barge once more. "Well, it seems all is in order," one Medjay said as he rested a large hand on the side of the barge. He pointed a finger toward Atinuk. "Make sure the Makedan repairs your barge."

Paaten leaned over the side of the barge to peer in and saw the broken arrow and the stain of blood on the deck.

"What happened?" Paaten looked at Atinuk.

"Two Cypriotes tried to take the barge and your wife, Citizen Paaten," the Medjay said with a pat of his hand against the barge. "Your Makedan hired hand defended them."

"I am indebted to your bravery." Paaten inclined his head. "Where are these two Cypriotes?" He turned his attention to the Medjay.

"They were sent back to their vessel and are currently nursing their wounded hands." The Medjay popped a curt grin. "The Makedan could be lethal with that bow of his."

Paaten cast a sidelong glance at Atinuk and nodded. "I see."

The presumed leader of the two Medjay beckoned Paaten closer. Nefe and Aitye leaned in to better hear what the Medjay was going to say to him. "We know this is a barge from Pharaoh's Fleet. What is your rank, soldier?"

Nefe's stomach gurgled. *I knew it! We are going to be taken ashore and killed. Everything was for naught. Mother, I am sorry.*

She cut Paaten with her eyes. *Why did you not obtain a noble's barge? You could have taken anything but a royal barge! You failure! You cursed—*

"I am a Troop Commander. It was loaned to me by Pharaoh's Fleetsman at Aketaten to use for travel with my family, as I have stated." Paaten's answer was firm and concise.

Nefe held her breath. *What? How can a member of Pharaoh's Army use Pharaoh's barges and ships as their own?*

The Medjay leaned back. "Be more careful with Pharaoh's barge, Troop Commander Paaten. Leave Per-Amun and return the barge to Aketaten."

Nefe's jaw fell agape, and she felt Aitye's stare upon her. She forced her jaw closed. *These enforcers of Pharaoh's law do not enforce the law of Pharaoh? This is Pharaoh's barge!*

"I will return it at the end of the month, as I have already told the Fleetsmen at Aketaten." Paaten stood firm, unafraid, but still respectful of the Medjay.

They stared at Paaten, until the leader of the pair narrowed his eyes at him. "Do you have any relation to the General Paaten?"

He pursed his lips and shook his head. "No."

"I have never seen him, but he is described as a tall and daunting man." The Medjay dropped his gaze to Paaten's toes before snapping it back to his face. "Curious."

Paaten nodded. "I have received such comments on many occasions. This is not new to me."

The leader stared at Paaten for a moment longer, as if waiting for Paaten to flinch or to give some other tell of deceit.

"As you were," the leader finally said. The two Medjay stepped back toward the row of seamen walking along the pier. "May you have peace on your return journey to Hut-Waret and Aketaten, Nobleman," the head Medjay said.

Hut-Waret? Nefe thought, now confused. *Did he*

not just say Aketaten? What is happening in front of me? She glanced toward Atinuk, and a new thought entered her mind. *If he does not disembark, they will wonder why he remains aboard if he is supposedly from Makedo.*

Paaten seemed to know her concerns and did not hesitate to respond. "My daughter wants to see Azzati now," Paaten chuckled and waved in Nefe's direction. "For her, I will do anything. Thank you for your blessings. In peace."

The Medjay eyed Atinuk, as if waiting for him to get off the nobleman's barge, but Atinuk spoke. "Nobleman, I have protected the barge and your wife, as instructed. Since you are continuing on to Azzati, may I obtain passage to there? In return, I will protect your barge once more before I return to Makedo?"

"Yes, that is an acceptable trade, Atinuk. I would be honored to have you aboard after you so bravely defended my barge and my wife," Paaten said and smiled, patting him on the shoulder.

The Medjay seemed to accept the exchange, and they walked away, stiff and firm, muscles drawn tight, as they peered this way and that to keep the order.

Nefe's mind numbed. *First, I hear disparagement about my mother, then about my father, and now we are harassed by the Medjay?* Her stare upon Paaten turned into a glower. *You were the General of Pharaoh's Armies! How could you let this happen?*

Once they were out of sight, Paaten's hand on

Atinuk's shoulder gripped his leather tunic, curling the fabric into his fist. Paaten pulled Atinuk's face close. "What really happened? Why were the Medjay here? I told you not to cause trouble."

Atinuk yanked back and out of Paaten's grip. "I defended Aitye and our barge from two Cypriotes."

"If that is the truth, then why were the Medjay here observing *us* and questioning *us*?" Paaten towered over Atinuk.

"Probably to see if I, the foreigner, told the truth to them about whose barge this was when the Cypriotes almost attacked." Atinuk scoffed and put some distance between Paaten and himself. "You are welcome, by the way." He turned and waved at him over his shoulder.

He began to pull up the anchor while Paaten eyed him.

"Are you not going to put away the hekat and return to your steering post?" Atinuk asked. "I would like to leave Per-Amun now if you are ready."

Nefe stood up. "I am ready as well," she announced to no one in particular. Her mind was tired of sorting out what she had learned in the past half-day about her parents and this scare with the Medjay.

Paaten narrowed his eyes at him, still in distrust, while Nefe did the same to Paaten.

"Yes, pull up the anchor," Paaten ordered. He packed away the hekat of beer and took his position while Atinuk pulled up the triangular stone anchor.

Nefe sat on her lounger and watched Atinuk heave its weight up from the waters below.

"We should help them. We are short of crew." Aitye lifted her head to Nefe.

"I am the King's Daughter," Nefe said and narrowed her eyes at Aitye. *How dare she want me to help ready this vessel, like a servant of Pharaoh.*

"With all respect due to your mother and father, you are no longer royalty."

Nefe sneered. "I will always have my birthright; you speak blasphemy against the throne."

"I am only stating the obvious, *your majesty.*" Aitye was about to turn, but then she opened her mouth to speak again. "The sooner you come to accept that, the more we can all heal from what has happened."

"Heal yourself. I want no part of the failings of those on this barge." Nefe shook her head as she watched Paaten take his place on the steering perch. "Such failures. How could my mother and father even command Egypt with such failures around them?" *Perhaps these incompetents are the reason why the people felt that way about my mother and father.*

Aitye's eyes averted upward, and her lips pressed into a thin line. "There is much you do not know," she whispered before returning her gaze to Nefe. "If you knew all of what we did, you would feel foolish."

"Then tell me." She crossed her arms.

"In time. You are still hurting and trying to come to terms with what has been lost to you. When you are more stable in mind, then I will reveal all to you."

"You patronize me." Nefe sneered her lip. "Steward."

Aitye licked her lip and gave a slight shake of her head. "The King's Daughter Neferneferuaten Tasherit perished along with her mother. You must rebuild your identity, and it is not starting off well—"

"Silence your tongue," Nefe yelled at her.

"I obey you in this instance because of your mother." Aitye set a hard glare upon Nefe.

Nefe's stomach roiled and burned all the way up to her throat. *So this is the same disrespect and disobedience that my mother and father must have endured. Such a mockery of the crown and of the Aten!*

"But you will continue to obey me," Nefe said with much more composure. "I am the Daughter of the King."

"You need to accept your new life." Aitye spun around without being dismissed and left the cabin.

"I am the Daughter of the King," Nefe repeated in a whisper. "I am the Daughter of the King." Her eyes burned with unshed tears. "I am the Daughter . . . " Her whisper got lost behind pressed lips as she struggled to keep her tears at bay.

CHAPTER 12
ESCAPE FROM TRUST

Aᴛʏᴇ ᴇᴍᴇʀɢᴇᴅ ꜰʀᴏᴍ ᴛʜᴇ ᴄᴀʙɪɴ ᴀɴᴅ ᴜɴʜᴏᴏᴋᴇᴅ the long pole from the side of the barge. She began pushing the barge away from the pier with the pole, but she struggled.

Atinuk noticed her glance at him, so he quickly finished wrapping the anchor and rushed to help her. He stood opposite of her. His hands were near hers, and their chests faced each other.

A small corner of her lip upturned as he gripped the pole.

"Push," he whispered, turning his attention to the pole, unsure what to think of her. Was she happy he came to help her? Had he come too quickly when she glanced at him? Had she thought about what he had said; could she see a possible future with him as well?

"When you do," she said and waited for him to lean forward to press the pole against the stone pier. She expelled her breath on his neck as she pushed alongside him. He froze for a moment, remembering Tadukhipa's breath on him some twenty years earlier.

"Once more, Aitye," he said, again letting his grip slide up the pole a little so that he brushed her hand as he extended the pole over the water.

"When you do," she repeated, and once again her effort's exhalation was upon his neck. They pushed until they came to the end of the pole and it could no longer be used. Atinuk slid his fingers over hers as he brought the pole in from the water. "I can do this, Aitye."

"So can I," she whispered.

He grinned at her teasing. "I know, but I want you to rest after today."

She had not moved her hand out from under his as she worked on removing the pole from the water with him. "You rest. You are the one who had to use your bow."

He stepped forward, making her step backward until she was at the edge of the barge with her back against the side. He ached to do that dance without the pole between them, without anyone else on the barge. But eyes were on them, most certainly now, and he did not know what Paaten would do to him. He lifted the pole up and out of her grip.

She gave him a smirk as he sidestepped her and lowered the pole over her head to the side of the barge. Leaning over, he hooked the pole into place while the side of the barge pressed into his belly. *If she had done this, the lapping waves below would have surely toppled her into the water, considering her lack of height alone.*

He lifted himself up as the next wave hit, giving the barge a small rock. "If someone is at risk to fall into the water, I would rather it be me," he told her before he straightened up.

She said nothing, but her eyes evaluated him.

"Are you angry?" he asked.

She shook her head but still evaluated him. After a moment, she said, "Thank you for bandaging my arm." She pushed away from the side of the barge and walked to her cabin at the bow. His eyes followed her, and as the drape fell once she entered the cabin, the hot stare of Paaten fell upon him. Atinuk turned to meet his stare and then looked out to the sea. "I can steer, Paaten. You need more sleep than you are currently getting."

As usual, Paaten ignored him.

"Still do not trust me, I see." He thought he had said it low enough that Paaten would not hear him, but his words must have carried on the breeze.

"No, I do not," Paaten agreed.

Atinuk let his head fall back as he looked to the sky. "I have saved Aitye and the barge from theft and robbery. What do you not trust about me?"

"You have withheld information from me, and you will not tell me what it is. Therefore, I must assume you wish us alive either to betray us to our enemies or to trade Egypt's Princess and General for gold and grain." Paaten kept his gaze to the water as he steered the barge to catch the sea winds in the sail.

Atinuk snorted. "That is simply not true."

"How am I to believe you? I believed the Chief Royal Guard; I trusted him, and you saw what happened."

Atinuk chewed his lip as watched the great man's jaw grow taut at his mistake. He leaned against the side of the barge and crossed his ankles. He understood why the General did not trust him, but there was nothing for him to fear.

How to make him see?

"You have withheld information from me. The same can be asked of you, great General. How can I trust you?" Atinuk tilted his head at him.

Paaten narrowed his eyes. "I have told you everything you need to know."

Atinuk shrugged his shoulders and crossed his arms. "Well, I say the same to you."

"It is unacceptable for you to do so."

"Why?"

"This is my barge."

Atinuk chuckled with a shake of his head. "This is Pharaoh's barge," he corrected.

"I commandeered it. It is my barge."

Atinuk watched the single sail catch the wind and lurch the barge forward. He balanced himself against the side while Paaten caught the momentum just in time to head up the coastline.

Surely, after our time together, he must trust me to some

extent? He needed to know Paaten at least trusted he would not harm them; he had to at least make Paaten believe that.

"Do you believe me when I say I do not want any harm to befall you or the women on this barge?"

Silence, and then, "No."

How can he say that? I protected Aitye and the barge, just now, just then at Per-Amun. Atinuk looked over his shoulder. *We can still see the dock. How can he say this?*

"Even after . . . ?" His voice trailed off.

"An attempt to prove a false loyalty? A scavenger who protects his windfall for trade in Canaan?" Paaten shrugged. "There are many reasons why you would choose to protect the barge and Pharaoh's steward and not leave the King's Daughter and General at the docks."

Atinuk lifted a hand in the air in surrender for the day. "Do you at least believe me when I say I have land in Damaski?"

"A *shared* land, I believe is more accurate." Paaten still had not looked at him; his gaze was utterly fixated on his task.

Atinuk flicked his gaze to the heavens. "Yes, a shared land."

"I do not believe you."

No surprise there.

Atinuk let a heavy breath fall from his lips, but then he saw Paaten glance at him.

"I know some of the residents in Damaski. When

we get there and they recognize you, then I will believe you."

Atinuk smirked. *I know something you do not know, Paaten.* He inclined his head and hummed with a slight nod of his head, "Then be ready to believe."

CHAPTER 13
ESCAPE FROM DREAMS

THE SUN NEARED THE WESTERN HORIZON, AND Paaten decided to drop anchor off a barren shoreline. Aitye readied the cold beans and bread while Atinuk dropped the anchor in the calm sea. Nefe remained within her cabin as Paaten descended from his steering perch.

He looked at her silhouette in the setting sun and then searched the surrounding waters. No ships were there, and he hoped none came. He had only been on the sea the few times he and his regiments had traveled by way of ship to the north, but he knew ships sailed throughout the day and night. Any ships passing by could hit them, or their crews could rob them. Even though Egypt controlled the land, the seafaring peoples could be vicious.

His eyelids drooped, but he snapped them open. He had to stay awake to see the ships' lights if any came. He looked at Aitye preparing their meal. *Eat and stay awake*, he thought as he entered the cabin of the King's Daughter.

"My Princess," Paaten knelt to one knee before her.

She sat up on the lounger and crossed her arms. "What do you want?" She looked away from him, and her lip curled in disgust.

"You will always be royalty, but this is a new life— one where you cannot be known as royalty. Join us and eat a meal. Do not isolate yourself. You have lost much, and isolation only feeds your sorrow."

"You speak as if you know this to be true?" She peered at him. "When have you ever lost as much as I have?"

Nine years of separation sank into Paaten's stomach. Almost thirty years of isolation in Egypt gnawed at his heart. "Daughter of the King, your mother wanted you to live a happy and carefree life away from all the turmoil in Egypt. Do not bring that turmoil with you. That is not what your mother would have wanted."

"You do not speak for my mother," Nefe growled.

He folded his hands upon his knee. "In this way, I do. I was a close friend to your mother, a trusted ally, a confidant; I know this is what she wanted for you and Royal Wife Ankhesenpaaten."

"And yet," Nefe spread her hands about the cabin, "Ankhesenpaaten is not here."

"No. She chose to reject your mother's wish. You chose to accept it. We cannot go back now. It—"

"I know," Nefe yelled and curled her hands into fists. "I know we cannot go back, but I want to. I want everything to be as it was before." She shot up and started pacing in the small area, made even smaller by Paaten's presence. "I just want everything to be as it was before."

Paaten stood up as well and folded his hands over his belly. "It will never be—"

"I know!" She spun around to face him; tears welled in her eyes. "I know," she yelled again.

His voice fell to a whisper, as he could only internalize her pain. He could not help her. "I am sorry, Daughter of the King." He had no other words.

"Yes, you should be sorry. You should hate yourself. You did nothing to help my mother. My mother would be alive if it were not for you. You failed her in every sense. You"—she blubbered through her words—"I hate you!" She bounced a fist on his chest, but then she squeaked out a small "ow" and rubbed the wrist of her attacking hand.

Paaten knew this young woman would not accept any consolation from him in the moment, so he only took a deep breath. "I have apologized for all of those truths. I do not reject them. I accept every blame and every burden." He traced her face with his eyes. He hoped she never found out the truth about her parents; her idolization of their memories was now all she had left of her sham of a life. "Please, Daughter of the King, join us for our meal."

"Get out," she growled, her shaky breath coming out through her nostrils.

Paaten dipped his chin at her wish and left the cabin.

Aitye and Atinuk kept their gazes averted as he sat down on the middle of the barge near the communal platter of food. Aitye poured water for them to dip their fingers in before they ate. Atinuk used the bread to scoop some beans to eat, but Aitye slapped his hand. "We must first serve Nefe."

"Nefe?" Atinuk asked and raised an eyebrow. "I thought her name was King's Daughter."

Aitye's shoulders rose to hide her neck. "We must first serve the King's Daughter." Her eyes darted between Paaten and Atinuk, and a pink hue graced her cheeks at her blunder.

"No, I am glad you called her Nefe. That is who she is now." Atinuk ran a finger along her hand on the deck of the barge, but at Paaten's stare, Aitye slid her hand away.

While Aitye prepared the princess's dinner, Paaten sized up Atinuk. *What is he hiding? Why is he trying to seduce Aitye?*

Atinuk's eyes followed Aitye as she rose and took the royal her dinner; a warmth befell his eyes, and a small grin appeared on his lips.

Paaten narrowed his eyes at him. *To keep a woman for himself when he sells us to the highest bidder in Canaan? To turn her against us?*

He let slip a light shake of his head when Atinuk returned his gaze to him.

Why is he here?

"What? Why are you shaking your head?" Atinuk asked, raising a radish to his mouth. "You do not like that I eat before you? Or do you not like that I am the only one on the barge who calls her Nefe?" He pointed the vegetable toward the stern's cabin.

Paaten selected a turnip and took a bite, refusing to answer the man, but he still held his gaze in what remained of the sunlight.

Weight set into his legs and his arms; his eyes wanted to close as he ate. Aitye had returned, and they shared their meal mostly in silence. Paaten quietly observed Aitye and Atinuk's unspoken banter between their eyes.

If I can no longer trust Aitye, I can trust no one on this barge to help protect the King's Daughter. He drank his beer until his cup was empty. *With the princess's treatment of Aitye, it would not be any surprise if Aitye rescinds her word and leaves her for whatever Atinuk has planned.*

Aitye rose, took the platter and cups, wiped them down and stored them while Paaten sat staring at Atinuk just as the last of the sunlight left the sky.

"I can see you are tired, great General," Atinuk teased. "Sleep. I will watch for ships in the night."

"If I sleep, you will stab me."

He heard Atinuk's sigh come in the twilight while

his eyes adjusted to the light of the moon and the stars, a feat that had become harder with his age.

"Then sleep and have Aitye take first watch."

"After you seduce her?" Paaten shook his head.

"I seduce no one."

Paaten scoffed, but already the lure of the night made him close his eyes.

He popped them open.

I will stay awake.

"You need to sleep, Paaten, and sleep well. You will need your strength when we trek from Azzati to Damaski," Atinuk reasoned.

Paaten hated to think the man was right yet again.

A presence appeared next to them. "I agree, Paaten. If you do not trust Atinuk, I will take first watch for ships and will wake you when I tire."

"If *I* do not trust Atinuk?" He peered in her direction, making out the faint moonlit highlights of her face. *I thought you did not trust him either.*

She shifted her weight. "If *we* do not trust Atinuk."

He paused, watching her increasingly fidgety movements in the moonlight. "Are you with me, Aitye?"

"Yes, Paaten."

He kept his back straight. *I must sleep. I will need my strength. Especially if Atinuk decides to betray us. I will need to be able to fight.* Paaten looked at the sea—no lights. *This may be the night to do it. We are not along the*

Nile; there are no potential robbers. Nothing but dark sea and calm; no winds. Not even a whistle. The sail is collapsed. He realized his eyes had closed. "Take first watch, Aitye." He slumped over to his side, putting his arm underneath his head.

"Yes, Paaten." She returned to her cabin and pulled the drapes up so she could see. He heard Atinuk plop down too.

"All will be well when you wake, Paaten," Atinuk murmured. "If I were going to kill you, I would have done it by now."

"Unless I mean more to you alive than dead," Paaten mumbled.

He heard Atinuk chuckle. "Get some sleep, old man."

Paaten wanted to respond, but a deep sleep's enchantment had already taken his tongue. The rest of his body soon followed. After two months of travel and light dozing to make sure nothing and no one attacked in the night, he dreamed back to a time he was with his wife:

He chased Niwa through the small field. Her eyes peeked at him through her long brown locks flowing behind her as she turned to peer at him; a grin of laughter spread wide on her face. Her scent of oil, honey and wine whipped about him as he ran. Scooping her up in his arms, their laughter pounded in his ears. His lips were on hers, and she kissed him back with the passion he had fallen in love with.

But as soon as it had begun, a slap's sting seared across his face. Niwa stood before him. She was older than when he had chased her: a few small lines in the corners of her eyes, a more sullen smile.

"Because he is my son!" Niwa yelled at him, her cheeks red with a passion of a different kind. "I bore him and raised him. You may be his father, but he is my son."

His eyes burned. A tear seeped from the corner. He realized he was crying, but he did not match her anger.

"I want to be here," Paaten whispered and reached to touch her cheek, but she pulled away. "I wish to be here, Niwa," he urged. His desire had no words or tone to describe the depth and truth to that utterance.

"But you are not," she yelled again and slapped his hand away.

He was losing her. *Bes! Amun-Re! Hathor! Pakhet! Answer me. Help me.*

"What do you want me to do?" he asked, both of Niwa and the gods and goddesses.

She crossed her arms; her hitched breath burst through flared nostrils. "Pigat tells me that if I were to remarry another, my son's inheritance would be dependent on whether my new husband claims him."

An image of her and the Hittite man, Washuba, entered his mind. A wave of nausea passed over him as he prayed. *Marriage is sacred and honored; you let me lose my wife by serving the oath I made so long ago?* He felt silly praying such a question. Who was he to the gods to ask such a question? He swallowed his pride before them.

"So you wish to marry another?" He lifted his gaze to his wife. "Washuba?"

"I love our son so much, Paaten. I would never trust another man to claim him, and thus, I will never remarry." Her words choked in her throat. "I suppose, then, I will wait for you, whenever that may be." She shook her head; tears streamed down her face.

"Washuba is honorable," he said, not wanting her to cry. He loved her and was willing to let her go if it meant she cried no more. He selfishly wanted to see if she liked the idea. "He would claim my son, as he has claimed the children of the widows that you have helped him save from the land of Hatti." Paaten's heart as well as his voice broke as he spoke.

He feared the worst in her response, but at least with Washuba, he knew she would be safe. He had only met him the few times he had been at the estate while Paaten was there. He seemed honorable for a Hittite, and he remembered the way Niwa spoke of him. It had turned his stomach in the beginning. He had wanted to kill him, but he was a part of Niwa's life. Washuba had saved many women from the same life Niwa had endured while she lived in the land of Hatti.

"Washuba," she pressed her lips together and shook her head again. "Paaten, I do not love Washuba. He is a good man, but I can never love him, as I have told you."

His breath hitched in his chest, and relief loosened some of the tension in his shoulders.

Her arms fell from her chest. She bit her lip and looked up in obvious turmoil before she found his gaze. "I do not want to marry another even if I could. I . . . " She wrung her hands. "I . . . I only fear you will never return."

Although his heart was settled by her statement of truth, it still broke as he watched his wife hurt and ache enough to lash out at him in her own way.

"Half of our lives are gone," she cried in a whisper; her anger diminished and was seemingly replaced with sorrow. "When and if you do return for good, how many years shall we have left together? One?"

He hoped not one. *Many years together*, he begged of the gods. "You agreed that no matter how little time together our life would have—"

"I know what I agreed to." She thrust her hands to her sides and let her tears fall down her grimaced face. "I did not think it would be like this."

He tried to calm her and pull her into an embrace, but her anger burst into flame once more, reborn with a vengeance. She thrashed from his arms. She wanted to spew many words from her mouth, but only a simple command escaped:

"Stay here, Paaten. Stay with me."

His gaze never left her jade eyes. The command was so simple. Had he been a weaker man, he would have done as she wished, as he desired. *Curse my strength, my duty to my oaths.* He had given his word to the gods that he would fulfill his oath to Pharaoh, and they still held him to his promise. "The god of dreams, Bes, sends me—"

"Your gods," she mocked, throwing her hands in the air. "You told me my gods were not real." She thrust her hands toward him. "What if your gods are not real either?"

He shook his head, praying and hoping her questions did not anger them. "Then why do you have the dreams, Niwa? Why do I have the dreams? I have prayed for these visions—"

"Because that is what our hearts want, Paaten. I want you. And I want you here with me and your son. Yet you want to serve Pharaoh and only secondarily want to be here with me. Egypt prevails once more, just as it did when you first left. You told me yourself your heart is torn in two."

He took a step toward her, shaking his head. "I once told you that before we were wed. When I left you the first time and every time since, I told you and I tell you I leave my whole heart with you; it has not changed—"

"Has it not?" she spat, taking one step backward. Her brow furrowed, and anguish crossed her eyes.

The urgency of their precious, fleeting time together pressed upon him in their bedroom.

"I thought with a child, you would most surely stay. I thought perhaps I was not enough for you, but with your child, your *son*, I thought you would consider me, *us*, worth staying for."

His chin dropped to his chest. Hatred of himself seeped into his heart. Was that why she had asked him that question every time he returned, only to leave again? Did she not know his heart?

"You have always been enough, Niwa." He lifted his gaze to her. "Even with no child, you have always been enough. I . . . *hate* leaving you. I worry that you will not be here when I return. That you have passed from illness or that your love for me will have vanished. I fear that you will want another and have no more room in your heart for me."

"Then do not leave. You will have nothing to fear then."

His heart sank; her response confirmed the

possibility of his fear being realized. "I have tried that, Niwa. For months after we were wed, I rejected the gods while I was here with you. They only punished me in return and compelled me to go. They have told me plainly when they will relieve me of my oath, and that is the day I am free to return to you: when I remember my promise to Pharaoh, a woman Pharaoh. When she is shut out—"

"The King of Egypt is a man! A young man! Who has a long reign ahead of him and—"

He rushed to her, silencing her. He ran his hands over her neck and cheek. "One day, there will be a woman Pharaoh, and that day is when I can leave Egypt and return to you forever."

Her lips trembled, and her body pressed against him. "Stay with me now, please." Her breath warmed his nose as he lowered his forehead to hers.

"I want to stay," he whispered. He could not bear to see the tears well in her eyes again. "I want to be here with you every day. I want to see our son learn to walk and hold a sword. I want to grow old with you."

Tears burned both of their eyes.

"I want you," he whispered again, nuzzling her nose with his. "I only want a life with you, and one day, I will have that life. The gods made it plain, but I must keep my oath to them. I have kept my oath to you, and I will always keep my oath to you, my love. One day, I will return forever."

Her mouth turned into a grimace as tears rolled from her cheeks. He kissed her, and she opened her soul to him. He feared it might be the last time.

Please, Bes, Hathor, Amun-Re, do not let me lose my wife in my service to Pharaoh.

He wished that night would last forever, for the next day, he had to leave. He pushed her hair behind her ear and caressed her face as he kissed her, holding on to every gasp, every breath, every taste, every scent, every image of his beautiful wife. Cherishing it. Imprinting it. He wiped an escaped tear from her cheek, and her hands slid to his back in a full embrace.

"Stay," she whispered on her breath. A tear rolled down his face and onto her lips. It was the only response he could give as he kissed her. As if urging him to stay, her fingers dug into his back, harder, harder . . .

———

SOMETHING PRODDED HIM. PAATEN'S EYES POPPED open, and his body sprang upright. His eyes adjusted in the moonlight, and he saw Atinuk, who was kneeling down and pressing the nock end of an arrow against his arm.

He tried to snatch it, but Atinuk's words stopped

him in his reach. "You were thrashing in your sleep."

His hand fell, and he noticed Aitye and Nefe huddled in their cabins, staring at him.

"They became frightened," Atinuk whispered.

Paaten palmed his face, letting his fingers drag across the skin. His spine slumped; his chin dropped to his chest. The dream had been so real, so vivid, as if it had only just happened. But that day, that day in his dreams . . . it had been fourteen years ago.

"Bes," he whispered. "Why that dream?"

The tension in his shoulders dwindled as he hoped the dream came to him because he would see his wife and son soon. He faced Aitye's cabin. She was lying down. "Why are you not on watch?"

"Atinuk saw I was tired, and we could not wake you, Paaten." She sat up. "Please do not be angry. No harm has come to us."

"He holds an arrow." Paaten pointed at the weapon in Atinuk's hand.

"To wake you from your nightmare," she urged.

"It was not a—" Paaten curled his hands into fists and took a deep breath.

Atinuk sighed. "You need your sleep, Paaten. That looked like a very taxing dream. Just sleep. I give you my word I will keep watch until morning."

"What good is your word, Canaanite?" Paaten mumbled under his breath.

"As good as yours, Egyptian."

Paaten peered at the man, who stared back at him with a cunning gleam in his eye. Even in the moonlight, Paaten could tell there was something important Atinuk kept from him. "Doubtful."

Atinuk bounced the arrow in his palm. "As good as yours," he repeated in a whisper.

Paaten lay back down and nestled his head in the crook of his arm. "Ammit waits for you should you—"

"I know all about the curses." He hopped up to his feet and went to the opposite side of the barge to look out. "Just sleep."

Paaten's gaze shifted to the King's Daughter. *I cannot bear to fail again.* But the midnight's dark draw once again forced his eyes closed. *This one night, I will trust Atinuk. If he were going to kill me, he would have done so already.*

CHAPTER 14
ESCAPE FROM DETECTION

EGYPTIAN SOLDIERS FLOODED THE AZZATI DOCKS and markets. In fear of being recognized by his men, Paaten sent Aitye and Atinuk to trade in the markets. He asked them to trade for Canaanite clothes and sandals, among other essentials.

When Atinuk and Aitye returned with their trades, they found Paaten sitting on the lounger of the bow's cabin with his khopesh lying across his lap.

"Is all well, Paaten?" Atinuk asked, looking up and down the pier. Nothing seemed to be out of place. Nefe's silhouette rested on the lounger in her cabin at the stern with the drapes drawn.

He said nothing but took a deep breath.

Atinuk helped Aitye aboard. "They have a donkey for trade. Our plan was to disembark at Azzati and travel by land to Canaan." He opened the drape and placed his sling of trade goods next to what remained of his original trade goods from Aketaten. "Their donkey is a good trade. I hope it is still available when I return with more gold—"

"I am changing the plan." Paaten stood, towering over Atinuk, khopesh in his hand.

Atinuk stood as well. He eyed Paaten with a quick glance to the weapon in his hand.

"Why?"

"Pharaoh's Army is here. Even if we were to leave at night, the patrols would find us." Paaten shook his head. "A soldier would recognize me, and it would put us all in danger."

Atinuk's brow furrowed. "Why would that put us in danger? We may even have an escort."

"The punishment for desertion is execution," Paaten whispered, narrowing his eyes at him.

"That would only affect you." Atinuk stopped after the words had come out.

"No. It would affect us all. Even if it did not, do you think I trust you to protect and take care of the King's Daughter in my absence?"

Atinuk crossed his arms. *Still not going to trust me? I know why he does not want to go through Azzati, but now I just want to goad this on.*

"I have protected Aitye from the Cypriotes in your absence; I can protect the King's Daughter without you."

Paaten switched to the Akkadian tongue. "I see how you stare at her, Atinuk." He leaned in. "Your loyalty is not to the King's Daughter; your infatuation with Aitye may be the only reason why you have not tried to rid the barge of the rest of us."

Atinuk's jaw fell slightly agape at the fact Paaten could speak Akkadian so fluently. He was surprised Paaten still distrusted him so. He had protected the ship each night while Paaten slept. He had done exactly as Paaten told him to do at Azzati. He came back with Aitye, safe and unharmed. *What more can I do?*

"You think too much, Paaten."

"Says the man willing to sacrifice me, so you can travel on land." He choked up his grip on the khopesh. "What do you wish to do with the King's Daughter? Have her killed in a public execution for her father's failure to come to the aid of a Canaanite vassal state?" He slid his hand over the flat side of his khopesh as he spoke.

Atinuk swallowed the lump in his throat. He would be a liar to say this tall, well-built, muscular man, even in his late fifties, did not strike some fear into his heart, especially as he toyed with the weapon that had probably killed thousands. He stood tall as well, but he was still a head shorter than Paaten. Atinuk's strong build was also different from Paaten's —more lean than bulk muscle.

Paaten spun the khopesh in his hand. "What is it that you plan to do with her? I will not ask again."

Atinuk glanced to his bow near Paaten's feet. He

had only killed his dinner with the bow; he had never had to take another man's life.

"I plan to take her to my shared land and provide for her, as I promised Tadukhipa."

"You pause before speaking." He lifted the sickle blade's tip so that the little sun that fell into the draped cabin glinted from its bronze body.

Atinuk stood his ground, knowing any flinch might send this paranoid Egyptian into a full-on slaying.

"I am only in awe that you still do not trust me." He pointed to the sickle-shaped weapon. "And still threaten me."

"You still withhold something from me. I will not fail in my oath to Pharaoh; I will protect the King's Daughter with my life."

"I believe you." Atinuk nodded his head. He crossed his arms, knowing if the man decided to strike, he did not have much hope in surviving the attack—especially in this small space. With the drapes drawn and their speaking in the Akkadian tongue, the Medjay would do nothing, thinking they were foreigners in a foreigner's brawl.

But we are aboard an Egyptian vessel . . .

"Then what do you plan to do with the King's Daughter?"

"I already told you. Whether you believe me or not is your decision. I have not withheld anything in that regard." Atinuk bit his tongue. *Why can I not learn to control my words better?*

"In that regard?" Paaten lifted his chin and spun his khopesh again.

Atinuk glanced at a passerby on the pier, who stared at their silhouettes through the semi-opaque drapes, as he walked on toward the docks. "You are drawing attention, Egyptian. We are speaking Akkadian and look like we have stolen this Egyptian barge, and our shadows through the drapes show your weapon."

"Then answer me. What have you withheld from me?" Paaten took a step toward him.

Atinuk knew what he withheld, but he was not ready to let Paaten know yet. He still had not made up his mind about the former General. "You will learn in time."

"When I lie fatally wounded and you have taken the King's Daughter?"

"No," Atinuk swung his head. "I wish no harm on any of you. That is all you need know right now," he told Paaten. "Please put your khopesh away. I take an oath I will provide for Nefe in Canaan. I swear upon Tadukhipa's memory I wish no one on this barge any harm."

Paaten narrowed his eyes. "Our Chief Royal Guard swore his life to protect Pharaoh, and yet he lured her to her murder."

"I am not the Chief Royal Guard. I have nothing to hold against Nefe or her mother or her father."

"You blame Pharaoh Neferneferuaten for bringing

to Egypt the plague which took your beloved," Paaten pointed the khopesh to Atinuk.

Atinuk raised his hands in a show of innocence. He dipped his chin and let out a heavy sigh while he shook his head. "I blame myself for not reaching Tadukhipa in time. How can I blame the Pharaoh of Egypt, who was friend to the woman I loved? Pharaoh was only trying to protect her homeland from such an illness."

Paaten's lip twitched. After a few moments, he lowered his khopesh to his side. "I still do not trust you."

"Well, know if you kill me, you kill an innocent man." Atinuk shrugged and stooped to return the remainder of his trade goods to his sling. "Apparently we are not making the land trek to Damaski from Azzati. How do you propose we get there?"

Paaten sat down on the lounger. "We need to get to Berytus."

"Why?" Atinuk's brow knitted as he stopped mid-action and peered up to him. *That is the most ridiculous plan.* He shrugged in defiance. "The Hittites control its sister city, Kubna, after Akhenaten failed to protect his vassal state. Now, they come for Berytus. I am sure, with the Hittite Prince's slaughter, they will only fortify their forces at the border." Atinuk shoved a hand toward the northern sister cities of Kubna and Berytus. "Or did you forget that is why your army has such a large presence at Berytus? And why there is such a large presence here? They are moving north to intercept."

Paaten's hand curled into a fist, and his jaw tightened. "There is much land to cover if we disembark here, with lots of patrols looking for wayward travelers like us. They will assume us to be thieves seeking to rob the royal caravans that pass through this part of Canaan. If we go to Berytus, we can slip behind the fighting at the border, and it is a shorter land distance to Damaski. Neither army will follow us through the mountain pass at this time of the year."

Atinuk shook his head at the stupidity of that plan. "I say we disembark here, hide as much as we can, and if we are caught, we can pretend to be a family in search of new land."

"I am not the easiest person to hide, and if we are caught, I will be recognized," Paaten grumbled. He appeared to think on it, if only for a moment. "No. It will be less risky if we dock at Berytus, go behind the northern border, and slip into the Canaan lands undetected. Pharaoh's Armies will be too distracted with the Hittites to care about us."

Atinuk's lips pressed into a thin line, and he tilted his head up at the man seated in front of him.

"Thus General Paaten says." Atinuk gritted his teeth.

"Do not patronize me," Paaten muttered before finally switching back to Egyptian. He pointed to the steering oar. "Aitye. Take the steering oar." His gaze dropped to Atinuk. "Atinuk, raise the anchor. We are leaving this place."

Atinuk rolled back on his heels and carried out the order with a grimace on his face. *Stupid plan. Foolish decision.*

CHAPTER 15
ESCAPE FROM THE STORM

THE CLOUDS TURNED DARK, AND THE BARGE rocked from side to side in the growing waves. Atinuk staggered toward Paaten, trying to keep his balance. Aitye and Nefe each clung to one of the poles of the cabin's frame on the stern.

Atinuk lifted a pointed finger to Paaten. "You said we should sail north! We could be on land if you had listened to me."

"With Pharaoh's Armies; do you think they would take kindly to a traitor, a foreigner, a steward and a princess appearing to desert their homeland?" Paaten tried to refute as his eyes searched the coastline for any sign of the Berytus docks.

"You said we would be safe in the barge," Atinuk yelled at Paaten.

"I am not a Pharaoh's Fleetsman," he growled. "The coming storm has sprung upon us." He pointed at Atinuk. "Tie down everything. We must get the barge to shore."

"The cliffs have no docks," Aitye yelled back.

"This is Berytus; there has to be a dock somewhere." Paaten scanned the shoreline amid the creeping fog.

"Well, it is not here!" Atinuk yelled back. Paaten's gaze fell to Nefe. She remained mute; her face was fallen, as if she did not care. No anger, fear, nor panic lived in her eyes.

I cannot fail her.

The winds picked up. Paaten shielded his eyes from the wind and again looked up and down the jagged coastline, squinting to try and see in the conditions. Time was not on their side. Pharaoh's Army patrolled the area near Berytus. He studied the cliffs. They were tall and steep. There was little chance the two women would be able to climb. He glanced at Atinuk. *He might. I could.*

He shook his head as the wind whipped at his back on the steering perch. *Is this where it all ends? Have I failed Pharaoh yet again?* His gaze fell to Nefe, who stared at him with a vacant gaze.

No. I will not fail.

The waters were deep all along the cliffs of Berytus. He knew that from his dealings with the Fleetsmen during his career in Pharaoh's Army. The barge could go to the cliffs and not run aground.

The storm was almost upon them. The barge

KING'S DAUGHTER

rocked viciously from the growing waves. They were not going to be able to find the docks in time.

I will not fail. I will not fail again. Nefe will live. I will protect her.

He spotted a cleft in the cliffs that might accommodate the barge, and he pointed to it. "We will sail there and stay for the night." He used the heavy winds in the single rectangular sail to propel the barge, but the fog overcame his sight. The winds whipped back and forth, jolting the barge away from how Paaten steered it to go. Rain fell. First, only a few drops, and then it poured.

The fog only grew thicker. Paaten dug his heels into the steering perch and used all of his strength to hold the steering oar and prayed to the father god Nun to withhold his water's chaos.

Let us make it to the cleft.

Atinuk slid from side to side of the barge, tying down their slings and their cargo holds. A heavy wave crashed over the side, further drenching the passengers. Paaten turned into the wave to keep it from capsizing the barge.

The winds ripped the bottom of the sail from the mast; the sail flipped around aimlessly as it held to the top of the pole.

It will not end in this watery grave!

He had no choice but to obey the will of the waves. He let out an "Ah!" and pushed the oar to the side to move the barge along the waves and currents to keep them afloat in the storm.

"Hold on!" he bellowed. The drapery of the cabins caught in the winds; both cabins were yanked from the deck of the barge and whipped up and away into the air. Aitye and Nefe fell from the shock. Nefe bled from the cheek because a wayward cabin pole had kicked her in the face on its voyage. Atinuk staggered over to them and pulled them to the edge of the barge.

"Hold on!" he repeated Paaten's message.

Their combined weight at the stern lifted the bow in the air at the next high wave. "Atinuk! Get to the bow!" Paaten called and gestured with his head; his hands were securely fastened to the oar.

Atinuk heard him during a miraculous lull in the winds and sprinted to the bow. He lunged and took hold of the bow's side, plummeting his weight into the deck. The bow dropped back into the water.

"Aitye!" Paaten called and she looked up. "You and Nefe, each take to the sides!"

She nodded and dragged Nefe to the starboard side before she crawled over to the port side. Another wave crashed into the boat.

What was I thinking? Hatred of himself burned his cold body. *This is a river barge, and I took it out on the sea.*

The cliffs loomed ahead, and through the dim light, he saw nothing that reminded him of where he was before. The cleft was gone.

It was right there.

The winds whipped through his soaked shendyt and loincloth.

172

"If the storm takes the barge," Paaten muttered as the splash of a wave sent chills down his back, "we will have no hope of fleeing to Canaan. We may not even have our lives."

CHAPTER 16
ESCAPE FROM DEATH

THE WIND AND RAIN BLEW ALMOST SIDEWAYS AS
the barge bumped against a rock.

"Tie down the barge!" Paaten ordered, throwing a
thick rope to Atinuk amid a thunder clash; his voice
was lost in the storm.

Aitye held Nefe as they clung to the sides of the
barge while the waves crashed over the threshold.
The waters pinned them against the barge's sides,
threatening to strip away life-giving air. The cold
waters pulled at their fingers, begging them to let go
and embrace the icy tide. They were quickly being
pulled to the middle of the barge where the waves
were greater.

A coursing wave bumped the barge against the
rock again. Atinuk glanced at the two women as he
muddled through the sinking ship to grab the rope
that did not make it to him in the howling winds.

"We are going to sink!" he yelled at Paaten; his

voice was lost in the winds too. He snatched the rope from the water and hopped over the raging waves to the bow. He looked up at the cliffs. Their only way to survive this night was to scale up the cliffs, but even if they could accomplish such a feat, the Egyptian army might be camped there.

If we are even still in Berytus anymore . . .

He hurled the heavy rope around the pointed bow and looped it around a nearby rock. Once secured, he heaved, pulling the raised bow of the boat to the rocks. He glanced over his shoulder; Paaten did the same to the stern. The cabins were long gone, but the travel slings were tied securely to the deck of the barge. Any remaining food they had was no doubt ruined. The bumping against the rock ceased, but the waters persisted in even angrier waves.

Atinuk succumbed to one such wave, and out of the corner of his eye, he saw Aitye and Nefe slip from the side. They were dragged toward the sea. He braced his legs against the port side of the barge as he reached out and grabbed one of their arms. His feet hit the side, and he pulled on the arm to keep it near the barge. He prayed to whatever gods there were—Egyptian, Canaanite, Mitanni, or even Fate herself—that the wood planks of the barge would hold strong. The wave subsided for a moment and Atinuk took the brief reprieve, hoisting Aitye back onto the barge. Another wave surged at the bow, bringing Nefe, who clung to Aitye, with it. They crashed into the starboard side, and Atinuk knew it would drag them back out to the sea in an instant. He heard a growling yell in the moment his head was above water, but it was muffled. A rope plopped in front of his head. Without thinking, he grabbed it with his free hand, and it pulled taut.

Ah, Paaten! he thought just as water closed over his head again. Using as much strength as he could muster, he pulled Aitye's arm so she could grab the rope just as the waters pulled them toward the sea. Atinuk let go of Aitye and grabbed Nefe.

A break came in the wave. He wrapped one end of the rope around Nefe's waist and locked the other end of the rope around his arm, tucking it fast against his side. "Press onward," he yelled to Aitye, and the three of them used the rope to walk to the stern of the boat, where Paaten pulled them up out of the waves.

"We have to get off the boat," Paaten cried and pointed up.

The cliffs seemed to hang over them due to their immense height. Paaten held on tight to Nefe, wrapping her up in the rope and fastening her to him.

Atinuk looked to Aitye. He had nowhere near the strength or height of Paaten, and Aitye was a full-grown woman; Nefe, a small, young woman. Nevertheless, he tied the rope around Aitye's waist and chest, fastening her to him. He leaned to her ear and yelled so she could hear him. "You will have to help me climb. I cannot carry you. But if you fall, I will catch you."

Fear surged through her eyes, but she nodded and turned to the rock, balancing herself against the raised stern of the barge.

In his mind, Atinuk continued speaking to Aitye. *Be brave. Be strong. Be like Paaten. Just not as stupid. He got us into this mess.*

Paaten placed a foot on the edge of the stern and, with the next wave, leapt toward the rock. Nefe clung to his back as he took hold of the cliffside. The water crashed just below his feet. He looked up. Atinuk saw him breathe deeply before he began to ascend.

Atinuk stared at Aitye as they both held on to the raised stern. He shimmied over to her side and found her gaze. He took her hand and turned her to face the dark, wet rock. He breathed with her; his heart raced.

Do not look up.

Paaten had cleared the space, and, with the next wave, Atinuk yelled, "Jump!"

He leapt and landed on the rock. One of his hands slipped, but the other hand and one foot caught. He looked to his side; Aitye was not there. His gaze dropped; she was flailing in the water right below him. The wave was pulling away, and an intense tingling washed over his racing heart.

No!

He braced against the rock, tightly hugging whatever he could grip. His toes dug into the crevices. The waves pulled her out under the high side of the stern. She gripped the wooden oar. Her weight made it creak against the thick, tightly woven reed rope that held it firmly to the steering perch. The pull of the rope against his waist choked the breath from him. He tightened his stomach to hold her against the pull of the waves.

Again, the wave rushed shoreward, releasing the tension of the rope around his waist. Aitye came crashing into the rock. He ascended in the slight reprieve of the wave. She grabbed on and climbed as best she could, but he felt the tight strain of the rope as she lagged behind.

She just has to clear the crest of the wave, and then I have to make sure we make it to the top of the cliff.

The water beat against her back and thrust her into the rock. A lighting strike lit up the sky, and he saw blood on the side of her head.

"Aitye!" he called out. "Climb!"

She struggled as the wave pulled at her once again, but she held onto the rock.

"Keep holding!" he urged. He lowered the position of his foot and shifted his hold. He reached down to grab her wrist, almost letting his fingers slip. He snapped back to the cliff and readjusted his grip. The wave returned, thrusting her body toward the rock again. She yelled out in pain. He grabbed her upper arm and yanked her from the water.

Her hands clawed at the rock until she finally found something to grip. Her chest heaved in a frenzied panic. Her body shivered as if an evil spirit had taken it over amid the howling winds. They both pressed their bodies against the cliff as they found each other's eyes. Her face turned pallid.

Another lightning strike lit up the sky as white as Aitye's knuckles while she gripped the rock. Blood fell from her head. Atinuk's eyes quickly ran over her body in the brief light and found no more blood. He placed his hand over hers. "We will make it," he yelled at her.

Her body only shook in response as it dripped from the rain and the icy waters of the sea.

"I need you to climb," he yelled again, hoping she heard him.

Do not look up. Do not look up.

He looked up and saw Paaten's leg disappear into the cliff face, or was he already at the top and climbing over the edge?

Curse you, Paaten.

The sheer height of the cliff caused a wave of nausea to roll through his stomach. He gulped his breaths to keep his dinner down. His chin slowly fell parallel to the waves. He calmed himself. He let go of her hand and readjusted his hold on the cliffside.

"We have to climb, Aitye," he yelled again. He reached up to find a good grip, a difficult task on the wet rock. He again looked up and again regretted it. *How did he reach the top so fast? Do not compare. Just go. Live. Do not look up.*

His gaze fell to the rock in front of him. *Focus. Do not look down either.*

He climbed until the rope pulled taut. Closing his

eyes, he whispered, "Please, Aitye. Please climb." He breathed through his mouth as pangs of numbness attacked his cold fingers. He looked down.

She had not moved.

"Aitye!" he yelled, knowing it was in vain. He tried to climb once more to tug her upwards, but the pull on his waist nearly caused his hand to slip off the rock. "Climb!"

He clung as best as he could to the rock and reached down to tug on the rope. He looked down again. "Climb!" he yelled in a small break in the wind and tugged on the rope again.

It seemed to break her from her trance, and she shifted her hand out above her and found something to grab. He waited for her, knowing if she slipped as she climbed, he would go down too. His fingers and feet would not be able to hold the both of them. He could barely hold up himself.

His body ached in the numbing winds as he waited for her. He quickly patted her hand once she was next to him before grabbing the rock again. "Good, Aitye. We only have a little more to go, but we have to keep climbing!"

She nodded, and they both ascended, one after the other.

Streaks of agony coursed through his calves and forearms. His muscles seized up, halting him. He let out a moan and pressed his forehead to the rock. Aitye could only watch him, knowing the pain. Atinuk had seen it happen to her every time it was her turn to climb. Her eyes were bleary, as if her body were acting alone on its instinct to survive.

He breathed through the pain and then glanced up. They were about halfway to the top, or at least he hoped they were. *How did Paaten ascend so quickly?*

A snake jutted out from the cliff and fell toward them.

"No, no, no," he muttered.

The cursed thing will just have to hit us.

But at the next lighting strike, a rope hit him in his face. He cried out at the sting against his frozen flesh. It dangled just in front of his eyes begging him to take it, but the pain in his body still raged. He wanted to take that rope, but his fingers did not want to let go of the rock. His calf seized him at every twitch or stretch of his leg.

He moaned again.

Aitye stayed mute as the rain blasted against her face and head. *Paaten, so help me. If I live through this, I will make the commands from now on.*

He nodded to her and released one of his hands to take the rope. His grip on the rock slipped, but he took the rope with both hands, leaving his face to swing and hit against the cliffside. He licked blood from his lip. Once the pain in his legs subsided, he tried again to climb using the rope. He found enough of a foothold to gird his waist with the rope and lock it under his elbow. He sat back into the rope and shook his free hand against his thigh to summon the feeling in his fingers. He looked up in the pouring rain and then back to Aitye, before reaching for her.

"Climb!" he yelled again and hoped her footing was sure.

She did, slowly, until he could get to her, stopping at each grip to pace her body.

"Paaten," he whispered. "You better have this rope tied around a rock or something to help you pull us up."

She reached an arm around his neck. He swung her so that her legs wrapped around his waist and her head buried into his neck. The extra weight caused the rope to dig into his elbow, which was still locking it. He tightened his grip on the rope. Her ear was close to his lips. "You are going to have to hold on to me. I cannot hold you."

She nodded, teeth chattering, and tightened her arms, one under his arm and the other around his neck. Her hands interlocked behind his back and weakly pressed against him. With Aitye securely holding on, he took the end of the rope on one side of his body and pulled up. His other arm choked up the rope. His feet walked up the cliff wall as they ascended. The rope burned, and his fingers ached. The rope seemed to disappear into the cliff face—not at the top. Paaten was pulling, but it was not enough to raise them much higher before his grip started to give out.

I am not sure how much longer I can hold on.

He looked at Aitye's body clinging to his own. In

a flash of memory, he remembered fording the river with Tadukhipa when they attempted to escape her father. He had failed her. He had made it past the river, but his body gave up, letting them fall back into the hands of her father's empire. He had been the reason she was sent to Egypt. He had been the reason she died in the plague. A deep breath filled his lungs. His eyes lifted to the point where the rope disappeared into the cliff face.

Not like this.

He released the memory, giving his body new strength; he pulled up on the rope and choked up on his grip. Paaten pulled.

Almost there.

Again, he rose.

His fingers bled as he tightened his grip and again choked up on the rope. Paaten pulled.

Again, he rose.

His wrists throbbed, and yet he climbed.

Again, he rose until Paaten pulled Aitye off of his chest and helped him into the small seaside cliff cave. The sideways rain still beat against them, but at least there was a semi-flat surface big enough to fit the four of them. Paaten crawled back into the cave about a cubit and lay down on his back next to Nefe. The rope was threaded through the rocks in the back of the cave, but Paaten's muscles twitched nonetheless after he had climbed with Nefe on his back and had pulled Atinuk and Aitye to safety. Aitye lay down next to Nefe. She shivered, and, at the next lightning strike, Atinuk saw a blue tinge to her lips.

She is cold. She is going to die.

He looked at his hands; they were raw, swollen and bloodied.

No. She will not die like this. He lay down on top of her, shielding her head from the rain. He rubbed her arms and patted her cheeks. Her eyelids fluttered at his warmth.

"Aitye, you need to stay awake," he said in her ear, not realizing the winds' howl was not as great in the cave. His statement echoed, so he whispered it again, realizing the tremble in his lips and the shiver in his body.

"Make sure you keep your feet dry. Without them, you will not make it," Paaten mumbled as he positioned himself in the small cliffside cave.

Atinuk looked down at his feet drenched in their leather shoes and Aitye's in her sandal: one was missing. He sat up and took off his shoes and Aitye's sandal and rubbed her feet dry and then his. The water pooled further inside the cave, but at least with their heads shielding most of the rain, their feet would stay dry. He lay down on his side next to Aitye and gathered her into his arms, pressing his body to hers.

"The leather keeps you warm but does nothing for her," Paaten mumbled again as he motioned for Nefe to move closer to Aitye.

I hate when that man is right.

Atinuk rose to his knees once more and shimmied out of his wet leather tunic. The wind and rain pierced his skin like tiny dagger cuts, but he bit his tongue. Clad only in his loincloth, he lay down and pulled Aitye's body to his. He threw his leather tunic over the four of their heads to keep the rain off of them.

Paaten grabbed the other end to keep it down against the wind. He wrapped an arm around all three of them and leaned into the huddle.

The warmth from the two additional bodies helped. Atinuk watched Aitye's eyes close as his vision blurred. His own eyelids felt heavy, and his heartbeat slowed down. He laid Aitye's head on his neck and pressed himself against her. At least his leather tunic kept the wind and rain out of their cave, he reasoned. Warmth had already begun to fill his core once again, and he hoped Aitye would benefit. He intertwined her legs with his, hoping to keep them warm. He slid his arm under her neck and wrapped his other arm down her back. Her head rested on his twitching bicep.

"Aitye," he whispered in her ear, but her head rolled back; she was unconscious.

No. Not like this. Please, not like this.

CHAPTER 17
ESCAPE FROM THE CLIFFS

NEFE HELD ONTO AITYE'S BACK WHILE ATINUK clung to her front. Paaten had wrapped his arms around to Atinuk's side and warmed the group. Atinuk's eyes drooped. The blood from his hands had soiled Aitye's dress and smeared on her perfect face. His swollen lip thumped, along with his heartbeat. There was a shallow gash on Aitye's head and shoulder. Most of her nails had been broken off, some severely. He smoothed the back of his hand over her forehead to keep any more blood away from her face. She was warm—perhaps, a little too warm—but her cheeks were cold as stone. He pressed his forehead to hers, studying her face.

The memory of fording the river with Tadukhipa came back to him.

She is not Tadukhipa. He pushed the thought aside. Tadukhipa was gone, but Aitye and Nefe were not, he reminded himself. He owed it to Tadukhipa to keep Nefe safe, but during his time on the barge, he felt his loyalty in love to the deceased Mitanni princess slipping much more than it had already.

I miss you, Tadukhipa. I had spent half of my life working toward our shared future. I still believed in us.

He had spent the first eighteen years of his life with Tadukhipa. She had been his friend; she gave up everything she knew in exchange for his freedom from servitude in the Mitanni palace. He had set in his heart to track down his great-grandfather's tribe in Canaan based on the stories passed down from his mother and grandmother. He would set up land there and then go to Egypt and take back Tadukhipa. But he had been too late.

He smiled with a bittersweet hum, remembering his lips against her ashen face, only a few hours before she died. Now, his lips brushed Aitye's face, pallid from exhaustion.

Aitye; please live, Aitye. I can only lose so many people I love in my lifetime.

He placed a soft kiss on her forehead.

"Stay with me," he whispered. Her eyes rolled under her eyelids.

His legs twitched even after their respite. He looked to the sea from the cliffside cave's opening. His leather tunic lay soaked on the cave floor. They would either have to go back down the cliffs to the barge or continue up. At the thought, his legs twitched more. They begged for more rest. He moaned as one leg seized up on him again.

Aitye's fingers pressed on his chest as she stirred in her sleep. Her hot breath warmed his neck.

The morning sun lit up the cave as it reflected off of the sea's waves. Paaten's hand squeezed on Atinuk's arm and sharply withdrew. He heard the old man grunt and stretch.

The beast awakens. This is his fault. We could have been on land this entire time, and we would have been safe. No one would have recognized him. We would have been fine. I wonder if he will want to go down to retrieve any surviving supplies before ascending to the top of the cliff, or if he will want to find a dock and abandon ship there?

Later in the morning, Paaten gathered their wet items and laid them out to dry. He peered out of the cave, looking both up and down. Then he too, still spent, lay down. He mumbled to Atinuk, "The barge is still tied to the rock, but half of it has been overcome with waves. We will need to go down and bring up our supplies and trade goods. I saw my travel sling still tied to the plank. I did not see yours."

"All it had left was grain and copper; bribes from a murderer." Atinuk studied Aitye's face once more. The color was returning to her cheeks.

Nefe lifted her head and glared at him. Her cheek was already beginning to heal.

"I am sorry, Nefe. I meant no harm by my words."

She narrowed her eyes. "The General is right not to trust you, you double-dealing foreigner."

Atinuk sighed. "I did as much as I could, Nefe. I promise you I had no intention of killing anyone, and I knew nothing of his plan to murder your mother."

"So you say." Nefe lowered her head, clearly tired and no longer wishing to discuss the subject.

"We need water and food and bandaging supplies," Paaten muttered, seemingly ignoring everything else. He raised his hands to look at the broken flesh.

"We ate well yesterday morning. Can we fast, rest, sleep, and go down tomorrow?" Atinuk's eyes never left Aitye's face. His body was exhausted.

"The barge may be washed up tomorrow and may draw attention from Pharaoh's Army camped above." Paaten's hands fell to his sides, and he let out a deep breath, causing a slight echo in their small cliffside cave.

"We will need to hope our Canaanite clothes and shoes are still with the barge; otherwise, we will not get past Pharaoh's Army easily, if at all."

He sat up and stared at Nefe. "My apologies, King's Daughter. I must rip your dress for temporary bandages."

Nefe lay there and dug her head into Aitye's back. She said nothing.

He placed a hand on her ankle and patted before he grabbed the hem of her soft linen dress and tore a strip. Nefe whimpered, and her lip trembled.

Atinuk could only imagine what was going through Nefe's mind as Paaten tore her last indication of royalty. He pulled himself from Aitye and tore a strip from Aitye's dress. They wrapped their hands and squeezed their fists. Atinuk winced and noticed Paaten did as well.

"I will go down," Paaten announced, but Atinuk shook his head.

"I should go," Atinuk said. "I cannot pull you up, and I weigh less than you, should you need to pull me up."

Paaten pointed at Atinuk's shredded hands and twitching calf muscle. "You will slip and fall and drown." He shook his head. "I will go. I can climb back up unaided, if need be."

Atinuk stared at Paaten's hands; although not as bloody as his own, they were still raw and red. The linen bandages did not do much for either of them. An involuntary smirk overcame his mouth, though, as he thought about what Paaten said.

"Why are you smiling?" His curt question caused Atinuk to drop the smile and meet his gaze.

"You care if I drown?" He saw a glimmer of concern pass over Paaten's eyes, but then Paaten opened his mouth.

"If you drown, I will be relying on the King's Daughter and Pharaoh's steward to help me." The concern was gone, and he stared at Atinuk, rigid and unmoving.

"Yes," Atinuk nodded his head and pursed his lips. "Glad we cleared that up."

Paaten looked at Nefe. "You will need to help

Atinuk pull up whatever I attach to the rope. Can you do that?"

Nefe nodded, her face sullen.

"I do not need help," Atinuk scoffed, a little insulted.

"Look at your hands," Paaten pointed. "They need to heal. I cannot carry Nefe up and then leave her alone while I come back down for Aitye. Even if I did, I might be able to carry Aitye up, but I cannot carry you."

"I do not want you to carry me." Atinuk shook his head with an exaggerated swing. *How dare this man think that he would carry me up the side of the cliff?*

"I already pulled you up once." Paaten shrugged and waved a hand in dismissal of Atinuk's concern.

"No, I climbed up. You only helped a little bit," Atinuk corrected.

Paaten lifted his eyebrows with a thin press of his lips. He cocked his head. "I made sure you did not fall and drown."

"We would have made it." Atinuk lifted his chin.

"You might have, but"—he pointed to Aitye— "she would not have, and since you were tied together, you would not have either."

Atinuk gritted his teeth.

Curse him. I hate when he is right. At least, he is not calling me weak . . . well, he is calling me weaker than he.

Atinuk's gaze fell to the sleeping Aitye, and he ran a finger over her temple. "Thank you for *helping* us."

Paaten gave a sad smirk in gratitude. "She will come through." His voice wavered.

"She will." Atinuk nodded, but at the slight tremble of Aitye's body, he changed his tone. "Yet we would not have had to endure this at all had we disembarked at Azzati like I had wanted to do."

Paaten's face fell expressionless.

"This was still the best way. We would have been caught; I would have been executed. Those not loyal to Pharaoh would have killed the King's Daughter. You would have been exiled or taken as a bond servant, and Aitye, executed as well for deserting Pharaoh in her palace."

"You do not know that." Atinuk pulled Aitye into his arms. He rubbed her arms and back to keep her warm.

"The risk was too great." Paaten rubbed his neck and winced as he did. "Berytus is a much bigger port with more trading partners and posts. We can hopefully salvage our Canaanite clothes, slip into the market, get what we need, and be on our way to Damaski behind the line held by Pharaoh's Army. If the gods grant us their blessing, Pharaoh's Army will only be concerned with the Hittite threat at the north of Berytus."

"If you say—"

"I do say, and I did say. We are at Berytus, and we will get to Damaski." Paaten stared at Nefe for a long moment during Atinuk's silence. "You will be safe in Canaan, Daughter of the King."

She narrowed her eyes at him. "Because you could not keep us safe in my father's palace."

Atinuk's eyes darted between the two Egyptians. He half expected Paaten to growl something back at her or at least see his hand curl into a fist, but his gaze fell. His shoulders slumped.

He nodded. "I failed your mother, but I will keep my promise to her. You will be safe."

"Except Ankhesenpaaten did not come. You cannot protect her." Her voice stabbed the otherwise-serene morning air.

"She chose to stay," his calm voice countered.

"She chose Tut over me." Her breath hitched.

"I chose you over the Coregent Tutankhaten."

Silence.

"You let them kill my mother," Nefe said sullenly, her voice cracking. The accusation hung in the cave for a moment.

"I have asked your forgiveness in my failure." Paaten hung his head. "I know it may never come, but I will keep my promise to your mother. You will be safe. I will protect you."

Atinuk stared at the man.

He makes a lot of promises. I wonder if he keeps them all.

"It seems we are all failures." Nefe eyed Atinuk and the unconscious Aitye before returning her gaze to Paaten. "I hope we all travel to the Aten so we do not have to endure such failure."

Paaten cleared his throat. "Never wish for the

afterlife while in this life, Daughter of the King. We have this life so we can grow into ourselves."

"I care not. My desire is to go to the afterlife, so I can be with my family again. Then, my life can be as it was before."

"It will not be as before," Paaten muttered.

She rose to her elbows. "What do you mean? Yes, it will."

"The Aten is not the premier god of Egypt. We travel to the fields of *Re* when this life continues in the afterlife. We become an Osiris. Your father"—he bit his lip and shook his head as if debating what to say—"your father, he . . . believed not as we should."

"No, Mother was the one who—"

"Saved Egypt." He closed his eyes. "She saved Egypt from your father." He sighed and opened his eyes.

"I do not understand."

Paaten's eyes questioned Atinuk, pleading for him to intervene.

Atinuk shrugged. The Egyptian religion and rituals were too complex for him to learn secondhand from a group of rebels in the eight years he snuck around the palace. It was not his place to tell Nefe what had happened.

Paaten returned his gaze to Nefe. "You do not need to understand. Just know this life can be good, and I promise you will be safe in Canaan. Do not wish to make the journey to the afterlife just yet."

She lay back down and crossed her arms over her chest. She rolled her head and looked at Atinuk. "Will life be good in Damaski without your Tadukhipa?"

The question stung; it restrained his breath within his chest. It had been unexpected, but somehow, he found himself nodding and pulling Aitye closer to his bare chest.

Nefe shivered by herself as she lay back down on the rock. Even though the wind and rain were gone, warmth would not come until later in the afternoon when the sun's rays penetrated their small cliffside cave.

"Atinuk, lay Aitye next to the King's Daughter, and help me down to the barge before anyone sees it." Paaten placed a hand on Nefe's arm. "Keep each other warm. I will be back."

She rolled into Aitye and ignored Paaten as he crawled to the edge of the cave. He took the rope and tied it around his waist and chest; Atinuk did the same with the other end of the rope.

"I will be back. I will tug on the rope twice when the travel slings are ready for you to pull up."

Atinuk traced the length of the rope as it weaved in and out of the rock at the backmost part of the cave. "Will the rope be long enough to reach the barge tied through the rocks in the back like that? It was barely long enough to make it to me, and we were almost to the cave."

"You were not *almost* to the cave, but you are right." Paaten sighed behind him and crawled back. "Without the help of the rocks, you will not be strong enough to pull me up if I fall. We need the full length of the rope to reach the barge."

Atinuk quelled his desire to punch the man for that statement, even though it was the truth.

And so it will be as I said in the first place. I will go down.

"You should go down, and I will catch you should you fall."

Atinuk said nothing but untied himself to unweave the rope. After he had retied himself, he crawled out of the cave. "I will try not to slip and fall and drown."

Paaten braced himself with his long, strong legs at the mouth of the cave, holding the rope around his waist and using one arm as a lock. "Good; I do not want to have to save you if you slip and fall."

"I would rather die," Atinuk smirked.

"Duly noted." Paaten sat back, expressionless once again.

"I know that means you care about me." Atinuk patted Paaten's ankle as he slid out, ensuring his feet had a good hold of the rock. The agony seared up into his legs, but he kept the smirk on his face and held back the moan in his throat.

"I do not care about men I do not trust," Paaten responded coolly.

"Of course." Atinuk shook his head at the old man before he disappeared from view.

THE BARGE WAS IN RUINS. THE ROPE WAS TOO short. The waves still crashed against the rock. Atinuk stood on what was left of the stern. He tottered his way toward Paaten's travel sling that floated on a barely attached wooden plank of the barge that moved with the ebb and flow of the waves.

The cold water shocked his feet and needles pricked his toes, even while they sat nestled in his leather shoes. He let out a long, slow breath to steady himself. His hands throbbed and dripped blood. The wood plank bowed as his weight closed in on the sling, stopping Atinuk in his approach.

His eyes surveyed the wreckage. The bow was still tied to the rock, but the middle of the barge was all but gone. "Food is gone. Beer is gone. Honey and castor oil are gone. My sling is gone, as well. " He heard a soft clang with each wave, and he turned to see Paaten's khopesh wedged between two of the stern's planks. "Paaten will be happy to have that," he muttered, remembering how the man threatened him with it. He scanned the bow section again, searching for his bow and arrow, his sling, or anything useful.

"Nothing."

His gaze again fell to Paaten's travel sling. Paaten

had never opened it in front of him, and he only hoped the man was smarter in his packing planning than in deciding at which port to disembark. He was going to have to swim toward the sling and hope the waves did not take him out to sea. He looked at the rope holding the stern together. "Too risky," he muttered, envisioning the stern crumpling without the rope in place to hold it to the rock. With no other options, he lowered himself into the water and gritted his chattering teeth. He held onto the wooden plank and hoped it did not break with his added weight. He winced and grunted at the salty sea's sting upon the open sores in his hands.

As soon as he untied the sling from the plank, it started to sink.

"No, no!" Atinuk yelled. He grabbed it and hoisted it up over his shoulder, which plummeted his head underneath the waves. He quickly tied it to his back and reached up to the plank, but the sling acted as a weight and pulled him down. He kicked as hard as he could, clawing upwards with both arms. He only continued to sink. His chest began to burn with aged air as the surface drifted farther away.

I am not going to make it; I have to untie the sling. His hand went to the knot on his chest. But before he pulled, his foot landed on something hard. He reached down.

Wood.

His foot slid along it. *And it goes upward.*

He stepped along the inclined wooden mast that

had caught in the rock as it sank beneath the waves. Air bubbles escaped his lips, and his chest hitched as he desperately tried not to breathe. Darkness encroached on his vision as he climbed with the dead weight on his back.

He looked up and saw a plank floating on the surface of the water. *I have no choice. Jump.*

He bore down and jumped from the mast with the last of his energy. His calves cramped, and he let out his air in one underwater scream.

His fingers gripped the edge of the plank as he took in water. He choked as his other hand rose into the air, only to be covered by a wave. With the ebb, he raised his head from beneath the wave, spurting water from his lungs and clinging to the plank; he hoped it would not break. The strain of the sling on his back nearly suffocated his strength. He took another breath just as a wave hit him in the face once more, almost knocking one arm from the plank. But with the next ebb, he secured his hold. He crept along the plank with each ebb and flow of the waves, kicking the entire time to help with the load on his back. He crawled out of the water and finally sprawled out on the remainder of the stern. His feet stilled in the water, spent and tired. His vision blurred as he looked up the sheer cliff. The rope hung overhead. How was he supposed to get that heavy, wet sling up four cubits of rock, tie it to the rope, and then tug twice?

Remembering Paaten's advice from the night

prior, he slid his feet out of the water by bending his knees. His shoes were gone. He had kicked them right off of his feet.

His loincloth was soaked, and his hands were again bloody. The seawater burned the gashes with an eye-wincing sting. He blinked as the sun peeked over the edge of the cliff, signaling it was midday.

The warmth of the sun's rays felt good, but they drained him of what little energy he had left. They enchanted his body, making it still.

He lay there until the sun was fully overhead. The rope still hung there. "Maybe Paaten can pull me up with his sling and khopesh tied to my back?" He grinned. "I will let him be the hero he thinks he is."

A chesty chuckle burst forth. He shook his head as he rolled to his stomach and pushed up. The sun was sweltering, and his loincloth was almost dry. The sling was still wet on the bottom, but drier on top. It at least was not as heavy as it had been. He secured it to his back by using the rope that had tied it to the plank, wrapping it around his waist and chest.

He unwedged Paaten's khopesh from the stern and carefully slid it between the skin of his leg and his loincloth, making sure the handle was secured by the rope that held the sling to his back.

Then, he looked up and sighed. He could barely curl his hands into fists. A low growl in the back of his throat accompanied the pain as he tried. He wiggled his toes as he stepped up on the side of the stern. His calves seized and twitched. He let a long breath escape as he stretched them, lowering his heels.

This is going to hurt. He winced as he looked up at the bloody trail coming down the side of the cliff. "Berytus, you take much of my blood."

He let out another slow, long exhale, and, when the next wave arrived, he jumped. The weight of the sling seemed to punch him in the back as he landed, thrusting his body into the rock. Blood oozed from the makeshift linen bandages on his hands. *At least, this time I did not almost fall.*

The water lapped at the rock below his feet. Every muscle drew tight as he reached up to find another hold.

Climb.

He reached the rope as sweat poured from his back with the sun beating on his head and shoulders.

He glanced up and hoped the man was waiting for him. He reached a shaky hand out to the rope, taking hold of it and wrapping it around his wrist a few times before grabbing it again for extra grip. He tugged twice.

Nothing is happening.

He tugged twice again.

Nothing.

He tugged twice again, and finally, his arm jolted up from an apparent pull of the rope at the other end. He swung out to grab the rope with his other hand. His feet landed on the rock, and he used every bit of strength to keep himself attached to the rope. He walked up the side of the cliff, letting Paaten pull him up like he had bragged about doing the night prior.

"Besides, my hands need to heal," he muttered.

CHAPTER 18

ESCAPE FROM EXHAUSTION

Paaten pulled with one last heave when the rope went limp. He collapsed backward as Atinuk crawled into the opening. Paaten's knees buckled, and his feet shot out of the cave.

Aitye had grabbed Atinuk's shoulder and helped pull him into their sanctuary.

The blood-stained rope lay in a heap behind Paaten. Nefe was sitting up and trying to push the rope to the back of the small cavern with her feet. The bronze of the khopesh clanged against the rock as Atinuk collapsed into the opening. Paaten's heavy travel sling blocked the light of the sun into the cave, casting its shadow over the faces of Nefe and Aitye.

Atinuk pulled the rope tied on his chest, and the travel sling rolled off his back and onto the cavern floor in between the two men. The small clanks reverberated in the small space.

"Be . . . careful . . . with that," Paaten ordered in

between breaths. His chest heaved; his vacant stare rested on the rock overhead. *I am too old for this.*

"Next time, we do as I say." Atinuk lay still on his belly, his cheek flat against the cavern floor. His calves cramped. His fingers and toes bled. The accursed khopesh had nicked him in the leg a few times during the scaling of the cliff. "We should have begun the trek at Azzati."

"No." Paaten's fingers twitched as his arms lay out on either side of him.

Both men's feet dangled out of the cliffside cave.

Aitye tore a strip from her linen dress and dabbed the brow of Atinuk, gently moving his hair from his eyes as his head lay near her. She leaned over and also dabbed the brow of Paaten. "What shall we do with the travel sling, Paaten?"

"Open it." Paaten's chest rose with a heavy breath. "There should be honey, castor oil, and bandages . . . " He groaned as he moved his fingers, swollen and red.

Why did the storm have to hit us? We would have been fine if we had just made it to the docks. We could have been that much closer to Niwa.

"You had honey and castor oil?" Atinuk murmured. "Why did you let me trade for that in Men-nefer?"

"Pull out the bronze cups too, Aitye." Paaten's vision blurred as he tried to remember the full contents of his sling. He had left specific instructions for Imhotep. "Gather us water from the back of the cave."

"Water?" Atinuk gasped, his lips parched and peeling.

"Fresh water," Nefe mumbled. "Pooled in the back."

Clank. Clank. Clank.

Aitye did as she was told. "King's Daughter, I know it is beneath you to serve, but in this instance, would you take these cups and fill them with water while I tend to Paaten's and Atinuk's wounds?"

Paaten's gaze shifted to Aitye's outstretched hands holding the bronze cups. Dried blood lined her nail beds, and the weight of the cups caused her exhausted arms to dip and sway.

Nefe blew a hot breath from her nostrils, but she snatched the cups and did as requested. As Nefe crawled back, Aitye rummaged through the sling and pulled out two hins stuffed into a roll of linen. Aitye first tended to Paaten's hands, then Atinuk's hands, and then her feet while Nefe held the cup for each man to drink.

Paaten rolled to his side and onto his knees and crawled further into the cave. He pressed his back against the side opposite of Aitye. His feet had some shallow cuts, but his leather sandals had held up the prior night. He looked at Aitye's feet, now bandaged. *Not good.* He looked at Atinuk's feet still hanging out of the cliff. Blood dripped from his toes. *Not good.*

"Where are your shoes?" Paaten muttered to Atinuk.

"Lost, getting your sling of goods that we could

have been using all this time." Atinuk raised his elbows to slide his hands to the rock by his chest, and he pushed his body up. He crawled inside and sat next to Aitye.

"Your feet need to be bandaged."

Atinuk blinked slowly at the obvious statement but did nothing. Aitye bent over to pull his feet into her lap. He grasped her wrist. "I can do it, Aitye. Let me bandage your hands first."

Paaten gestured to Nefe. "Can you help find the almonds and dates?" He had no strength to state her title.

"You had food too?" Atinuk snapped his head to Paaten.

"My sling was for the trek and for use in urgent situations. Since we had yours as well, I decided to use your trade goods for the day-to-day needs on the barge." Paaten rested the back of his head against the rock.

Atinuk glared at him before he began to tend to Aitye's hands.

Nefe lugged the sling farther into the cave and opened it in the space between their feet. She began to sort through the items, whispering their names as she searched for the almonds and dates. "Amphora, more bandages, natron, susinum, flax and needle, amulets of . . . " She stopped and looked at Paaten, dangling the faience amulets in the air by their cords. "Who are on these?"

"That is Hathor. That is Anhur. That is Isis. That

is Bastet. This is the Eye of Horus." Paaten pointed to each one; the last one he touched with his finger. "For protection."

Her brow knitted. "Is that not the Aten?"

"The Aten is the sun-disc, a small aspect of the god Amun-Re, the premier god of Egypt." He looked upon the daughter of Akhenaten, and part of his ka fell into despair.

You did your daughters such a disservice by not teaching them about the true gods of Egypt, Akhenaten. I honored your commands as Pharaoh, but I cannot see how your heart will not weigh heavy on the scales of Ma'at.

She placed the amulets down gently and glanced at Paaten. "If you say so, but Father said—"

"He said many things, your majesty." Paaten pointed to the sling. "Now, please find the almonds and dates." His hand fell to the cup beside him, and he drank.

She narrowed her eyes at him. "Father said the Aten is the one true god of Egypt."

"Your father—" Paaten clamped down on his teeth as he wiped his mouth with his forearm. He took a small breath and began again. "Remember your father the way you want to remember him, but it is his declarations that have made us flee Egypt to keep you safe."

Her jaw fell agape, but with the emergence of a red hue on her cheeks, she said nothing more.

"There should be a decan's worth of minimal food and drink in there for four people." Paaten again motioned to the sling to guide Nefe to return to her task rather than dwell on the past.

"Four? How did you plan on there being four of us?" Atinuk snapped his head to him again just as he finished with Aitye's hands.

Paaten's eyes darted between Atinuk and Nefe. *I wish he would just think and use his head. Such an impulsive man. No thought behind his words.*

"What?" Atinuk asked, looking to Nefe as well, not realizing his blunder.

"I had planned for two daughters of the King, Aitye, and myself. Pharaoh had specifically commanded me to take Aitye with me since she had been more of a mother to them than she."

Nefe stopped her search and sat back on her heels.

Another reminder that her sister did not come with us. Another reminder that she is the last of Pharaoh Neferneferuaten's line. Paaten gave Atinuk a slight shake of his head.

Atinuk pursed his lips and ducked his chin. He began to work on bandaging his feet and toes.

Foolish. At least he is not an utter fool and can see the error of his ways.

"My mother said that?" Nefe's eyes widened and glistened with coming tears.

Paaten nodded. A weight fell on his body as the moment progressed. He had not the strength to defend himself against the foreigner, nor did he want to endure Nefe's impending questioning.

"Food, please," he urged and again gestured to the sling.

Nefe pulled out three women's Canaanite tunics and one man's tunic wrapped tightly. She unfurled one of them, and a pair of leather shoes and a leather belt tumbled out. She looked at him with thinned lips.

"Your majesty, please, put those away. Do not let them get soiled with our blood. We need to be as inconspicuous as possible when we make the trek to Damaski." Paaten sighed and shook his head.

Her eyes only questioned him.

His stomach gurgled. He reached over and snatched the clothes from her, hoping the linen bandages would keep the blood off of the tunic. "Put these away." He carefully refolded and rerolled the tunics around the shoes. He leaned forward and on to his knees. He packed the bundles neatly away in his sling. Aitye had done a fairly good job on bandaging his hands. He could barely touch his fingertips together, but at least the blood was still contained within the linens. He searched through his sling instead of letting Nefe do it, fighting off the exhaustion in his muscles and eyes.

Flax thread and needle, two daggers, one knife for food, five pairs of reed sandals, amphoras of wine and beer, four blankets, a small bow and some arrows for hunting, nine years' worth of letters to Niwa—his heart broke as he saw the ink had smeared and the papyrus was near unusable—*bronze plates and cups, a cooking pot, my*

General's collar, bronze armor, chest strap dagger, bow drill . . . that would be good for a fire if we had anything to use as tinder . . . where are the almonds and dates?

He pulled out the bow drill and a pair of reed sandals in anticipation of building a fire, hoping he was not stupidly wasting a pair of shoes. He again searched.

"Ah," he said as he pulled out the sacks of beans, almonds, and dates, albeit saturated with water. *Right next to the gold, copper, silver, and . . . grain.*

He grimaced as he also pulled out the grain.

Most likely ruined. It has been wet for almost a day.

He opened the sack. Nothing looked like it had germinated.

"We may be able to save the grain," he muttered and set it aside. He grabbed the cooking pot as well before closing up the sling. He looked at Nefe's dress. "Can you tear off some strips of linen so we can start a fire? It will also help keep us warm."

Nefe scrunched her nose. "Why do you not use the linen you brought?"

"That is for urgent situations, your majesty. We still have a land trek. I would hate to be out there and be bloodied with no linen bandages to wrap an injury."

He arranged some stones in a circle before he took Nefe's dress and ripped it, despite the glower she gave him. He took the linen strips and ripped them over and over to increase their flammability, then put them in the middle of the circle of stones.

Looking at the tinder material, he sighed. *Damp, but mostly dry. We will have to try and see.* Off to the side, he wrapped the bow drill's cord around its spindle and began to rhythmically saw the bow drill back and forth to spin the spindle on its accompanying fireboard. After a while, an ember appeared. He got down low and lightly blew on it, then carefully added the small, glowing bit of hot charcoal to the tinder pile. Thankfully, the fire took hold of the bits of frayed linen. He tore apart one of the sandals and frayed them as well, so he could add the pieces as necessary to keep the fire fueled. He set the cooking pot on the circle of stones and began to dry out the grain around the makeshift fire pit. He put a few handfuls of beans into the cooking pot and poured Atinuk's cup of water into it as well.

"Can you bring us some more water, your majesty?" Paaten asked, handing Nefe the two cups.

Nefe snorted but did as she was asked.

Paaten sat back and again rested his head against the rock, even more tired after the short burst of energy. Atinuk ripped the linen bandage with his teeth as he applied the last bandage to his foot.

Aitye grabbed the sack of almonds and gave Paaten and Atinuk a handful before taking a handful herself. Nefe came back with the water cups, and Aitye poured one into the cooking pot to make sure the beans had enough water. Nefe sat next to Paaten, and they all watched the small fire, entranced by its light flickering within the cave walls.

Paaten bit into an almond, thinking it would have its usual crunch, but it seemed after having been soaked overnight, it was much chewier and softer than usual. *A respite for my teeth.* He chuckled to himself.

"What makes you laugh, Paaten?" Atinuk stared at Paaten with an unamused glare.

Paaten rested into the rock wall. "Nothing that concerns you, Canaanite," he spoke in Akkadian.

"Why do you speak in a different tongue when you know they cannot understand it?"

"I am practicing, since the primary tongue in Canaan is Akkadian," Paaten responded in Egyptian and shrugged. He wished the day over. The sun was setting; the light was dim inside the cave. "They have been learning Akkadian these last two months; I am sure they can understand some of it."

He ate the rest of his almonds by shoving them all in his mouth.

"I do not think they do; I think you speak Akkadian so they do not see how you talk to me." Atinuk pointed a bandaged hand in Paaten's direction while Paaten chewed the almonds he had thrown into his mouth. "You have done nothing but intimidate me and isolate me from our small group. You did not even let me steer the accursed barge. Aitye could have woken you if I ended up being a person you could not trust. You let me go to the market and trade my goods when you already had food and even bronze plates and cups—"

Paaten swallowed and cut him off. "What is it to you? Is it not just the briber's gold and grain from a murderer, as you said?" Paaten lifted his head as the simmering flame reflected in his dark eyes.

"It would seem you do not share well." Atinuk leaned back and popped another almond in his mouth.

"I share well when I am with those I trust." Paaten grabbed the other reed sandal he had pulled from his sling and began to disassemble it.

"So you trust me now?" Atinuk grinned and popped another almond.

"No, but we have no other options since you failed to retrieve your sling from the barge." Paaten chuckled inside beneath his hard exterior. He found goading Atinuk mildly entertaining.

"I failed . . . !?" Atinuk lightly bounced the back of his head against the rock. "How can you not trust me? I went down to the barge, risked my life in your place—"

"You did what you had to do—"

Aitye interjected, speaking in heavily broken Akkadian. "I think you are speaking of trust; I trust Atinuk, Paaten. He could have let me die in the water, but he pulled me to safety."

The chuckle in Paaten's heart ceased. "Had it been the King's Daughter or I who had fallen into the waves, I am not so sure he would have saved us," he muttered. Then he saw Aitye knit her brow and purse her lips.

She does not understand.

Atinuk leaned forward, his face fully illuminated by the firelight, and responded in Akkadian. "Just because I can see a life with Aitye does not mean I wish harm upon you or Nefe."

Paaten gave up disassembling the reed sandal and instead ripped it apart with ease. "Yet this great love for Tadukhipa, the one that compelled you for all of your life in your decisions—it is now just thrown away to the wind once you have met Pharaoh's steward?"

"You will not speak of Tadukhipa in that way." The attack in Atinuk's voice caused Aitye to place her hand on his forearm, even though she did not fully understand the language in which he and Paaten spoke.

"Why? You seem to have forgotten her." Paaten ripped the reed strips apart into smaller strips as he eyed Atinuk and Aitye's hand upon his arm.

"I will never forget her. I planned a future for us. This future. She was supposed to come back to my shared land, and now it is Aitye whom I bring back." Atinuk struggled to keep calm.

Paaten paused a moment, believing what Atinuk said. He knew Atinuk had not the strength for such a passionate defense, so it surely must have been the truth. Paaten felt the chuckle return to his heart and felt the need to goad again.

"And the King's Daughter," he said with a flat face.

Atinuk sighed, and his back bowed. "Yes, and the King's Daughter."

Paaten narrowed his eyes, but Atinuk only shook his head and closed his eyes, leaning his head back against the wall, his energy clearly expended.

Maybe this Atinuk is trustworthy after all.

Paaten returned to the Egyptian tongue to tell the group: "The beans will be ready to eat in the morning. I suggest we rest a few days here to heal before we go up." He fed a damp reed strip to the fire to keep it going. The warmth of the fire calmed the slight shiver in his legs, and its warm glow fell on their four faces. Aitye said nothing while Nefe nibbled on her almonds with a vacant stare.

"I am tired, and I will sleep." He spoke aloud. He handed the reed strips to Nefe. He grabbed one of the blankets and waved his hand to the rest of them, hoping they understood they each had a blanket to use. He was too tired to speak at that point, so he crawled farther back into the cave where they had slept before and lay down. His head rested on the cold rock. The warmth of the fire slowly made its way through the air. His eyelids fell heavy over his eyes. His body ached, needing the restoration of sleep. Soon, he dreamed.

"Remember your promise, General!" Nefertiti called to him through the dark tunnel. The yell resounded again and again, vibrating his very core.

"Remember your promise, General!" the yell came again. He stood alone in the tunnel again, knowing this woman Pharaoh would not live. He had accepted the truth long ago. He had interpreted Bes's dream: when Nefertiti was shut out from him in his dream, she would travel to Re. His promise was to her, not to the gods, not even to Pharaoh. To her.

The darkness in the tunnel gave way to the light of a nearby flame.

Fire flickered in the hearth of his Damaski home, reaching out to him, then rescinding back its warmth. Niwa's cheek lay upon his shoulder. She was young. He was young. Her hand smoothed over his chest.

"Remember your promise, General!" The yell diminished to a hushed whisper. Would the gods still release him from his oath to them if this promise that he had dreamt about for almost thirty years was to the woman? What was it they wanted from him? A weight set in his stomach. His promise had been to live for Pharaoh. Had he interpreted the dream wrong all this time? Would he ever return to his wife? How long would he have with her? A year, as she had suggested?

The flame grew in its light, and he turned to Niwa. Her eyes aged before him as his gaze fell upon her. Her eyes, still as green as ever, stared at him over the linen sheet of their bed. He pulled it away to reveal her perfect nose and lips. He leaned to kiss them.

"How much longer can you stay, my love?"

He kissed her once more. "I have stayed a decan with you and our son; this has been time I wish I could extend, time I will treasure always. I may be able to stay a while longer until my men start to question my absence. Imhotep and Mai provide a response for me." He brushed the stray pieces of hair from her face. He wrapped her up in his arms, pressing her against his chest, cherishing her warmth, her scent, her touch . . .

Her hands ran the length of his back as she whispered into his neck, giving him kisses in between her words: "I wish you to stay. When can you stay here forever?" Her question had always been the same, every time he had returned.

He wished he had an answer, a date, a time—something. He wished he could say, "*Now.*"

"I will come to you at every chance, at every opportunity, until I can stay."

She shook her head and rose to her feet. Her hands ran over her face. "You cannot play with my heart like this, Paaten. For years, I sat wondering if you were going to come back. I was with a child, all alone in a foreign land, wishing for you to return. I thought in vain each day would be the day you would return, yet wondered if you would never return, if you were killed, if you were dead. Even now, I wonder if this will be the last time I see you."

Paaten stood along with her, guiding her hands toward his chest. "I have instructed Mai and Imhotep that if I should be killed, they are to bring you a hidden message, a papyrus with blood on it, nothing more."

She pulled away and turned to grab her long Canaanite tunic. She glanced at him before she lifted it over her head to pull it on.

He grabbed his shendyt, wrapped it about his waist in her silence, and drew near to her.

She walked to the bedroom's chest, her fingertips massaging her neck. "And what if they are killed too? Who else knows of me?"

She bent over the chest, pulled out the honey lard, and placed it near the bath well before she turned to him for an answer.

"I will make sure, as General, they are not in the same battles. At least one will live to send word."

She shook her head with a press of her lips.

He closed his eyes, anticipating the coming outburst.

"I know what I promised you, Paaten." A grimace overcame her face. "I did not think it would last this long."

His chest swelled, and his throat burned. He was causing her pain; he caused her tears. He had told her he would never harm her, yet here he was, standing before her having trapped her in this oath.

How much longer?

"How much longer?" was always his question to the gods, but they would only send him the dream with its endlessly repeated refrain: "*Remember your promise, General!*"

He had thought it would have been sooner too. He had been sure the woman Pharaoh would be Queen Tiye, but her health had failed while Akhenaten sat on the throne. Paaten had been appointed General eleven years prior and Commander when he had returned from the land of Hatti five years earlier than that. The memory of torture in the land of Hatti and the whip's sting upon his back became fresh in his memory. The crack of the whip replaced the crackling of the fire in the background.

Niwa's yells came back to him as he tried to push away the temporary relapse to the past. "I want you here. This is your home! This is your home!" She jammed a finger toward the ground with each cry. "Where is your home, Paaten?!"

The torturers' prompt from his youth elicited the habitual response he had ingrained in himself to speak. "Egypt is my home!"

He shook his head at his outburst. Lips pressed thin, he closed his eyes. A defeated breath escaped through his nostrils. Every time he had yelled

"*Egypt is my home!*" while being tortured and whipped as a prisoner of war at the Hittite Governor Matiya's estate came rushing forth in a pounding attack against his heart. Hatred swarmed through his body, taking his legs out from underneath him. He fell to his knees before his wife. Except, this time, there was no whip to force him to his knees as he valiantly defended his honor in the workers' camp of a Hittite governor.

"Yes, of course. Egypt." Niwa's voice cracked as she turned away from him.

His hands curled to fists. "I am sorry, Niwa. I told you about my stay in the land of Hatti. It was an instinctual response." His voice bore a weight only his heart could fathom. He hung his head, knowing the damage those four words had done to his already hurting wife.

She remained silent and kept her back to him as she prepared their son's bath. "Niwa, I do not want to remember when I was forced to say that. My back still bears the scars of the whip that urged me to denounce Egypt and say my home was in the land of Hatti."

Silence. She still worked to prepare the bath.

He stood, grabbed her waist, and spun her toward him. He pulled her into his chest. "Look at me, Niwa."

She stood rigidly, eyes averted, arms by her side.

"Please."

At the plea, her glistening gaze slowly made its way to meet his.

"*You* are my home, Niwa." He lowered his forehead to hers. "*You* are my home," he repeated in a whisper. "I will always return home." He cupped her cheek and nudged her nose with his, hoping her forgiveness would come.

Silence.

Stillness.

He moved a lock of hair behind her ear. "You have my heart. Wherever you are, you are my home."

"You only say such things," she whispered while a tear escaped her eye.

He wiped it away with his thumb, as he had done every time before. "No. If you truly believe that, I have not loved you as I should have." He searched her soul through her eyes. "I know this life is unfair. I have prayed many times to be released from my oaths to the gods and to Pharaoh, but every time I plan to leave, I am haunted with dreams. They will not release me."

"They are but dreams."

He caressed her cheek, letting his fingers graze the edge of her brown locks that framed her face. "You know the dreams of which I speak. You told me you have them too. They are compelling, are they not?"

She closed her eyes and nodded. "I feel as if we are together, as if you were here only yesterday, when indeed a year has passed." Her hand slid around his neck. "They are so real . . . so compelling."

"I have kept every promise to you, my love." He lowered his lips to hers. "I will keep every promise. I will return to you."

HE SMILED IN HIS SLEEP AS HE RELIVED HIS TIME with Niwa from twelve years ago. Home. He was so close.

CHAPTER 19
ESCAPE FROM SORROW

NEFE STARED AT THE SLABS OF MUSCLE IN PAATEN'S back as she rested her head in the crook of her arm. *How can a man that big and that strong fail to save my mother from murder? He even scaled a cliff with me on his back in the middle of a storm. Yet he did not save my mother.*

She rubbed her bottom lip as she thought. *I wonder if he betrayed Mother too, like Jabari? He could have beaten down the door to the council room. He could have saved her. But why protect me, then?*

She squinted in the early morning sun, trying to make out the shadows cast in haphazard lines down his back. Were they ridges? Were her eyes playing tricks on her? She reached out to touch one and pulled back when he stirred in his sleep at her light touch. They were scars.

How did he get these scars?

A breeze whipped into the cavern and down her

bare legs, causing them to shiver. Her dress had been torn all the way up to her thighs for linen bandages, and she had elected to sleep atop her blanket instead of under it.

Aitye's dress had been torn as well. Nefe rolled from her side to her back and peered over to Aitye, whose head rested on Atinuk's arm. His leather tunic still blocked the sea winds from their heads, so he lay next to Aitye in nothing but a loincloth.

She glanced to Paaten. *Nothing but a loincloth either.*

We are dressed like poor servants. I am a Daughter of the King, and I have been reduced to rags.

She sat up and crawled over to Paaten's sling. She dug out some more almonds and ate some breakfast, not because food had any appeal, but because her stomach gurgled and she needed something to ease her hunger pains.

Her eyes traced the rock ceiling of their cave. *I am going to travel to Re here. The sea will rise up and take my bones away from this place. My ba and ka will roam forever in restlessness.* She shook her head. *At least if I had been murdered in Egypt, my afterlife would not be in question.*

"What was she thinking?" she murmured regarding her mother. "Tell Paaten to take me to Canaan? Foolish Mother. I will never reach the afterlife there."

Paaten stirred in his sleep at her whisper. "And how can Egypt's lightest sleeper not know there is a murder afoot in the palace he is supposed to be guarding?" She stuck out her tongue at him and wished to spit at him too.

She rested her head against the side of the cave and took a deep breath. She popped another tasteless almond in her mouth. *I wish I were home. I want Ankhesenpaaten with me.*

Her head rolled to the side, and she looked out to the sea. The slight sea breeze chilled her face and arms. She pulled her knees close to her chest as she grabbed her blanket from her sleeping spot. She wrapped it over her legs and brought the edge of the blanket up to her chin.

She snuck another almond to her mouth. The dry pulp formed a flavorless glob of mush she had to swallow. It was the same with the beans and the dates. Food had lost its taste to her. It was now just a necessity to survive in this dark, horrible world outside the palace.

As she chewed, she again looked out to the sea. That woman from the Per-Amun port haunted her thoughts in the quiet moments. "My father tainted the throne," she whispered, repeating the woman's accusations. "My mother and my father deserved to have their hearts devoured by Ammit."

What did they do?

How did it come to this?

She slipped another almond into her mouth.

"I just wish it was before the plague. Everything was happy then," she whispered. A small tear formed in her eye, and she brushed it away with the blanket. "Everyone was alive then."

As she peered into the glimmering haze of sunlight reflecting off the waves, visions of her family appeared. She saw her sisters, Kiya, and Aitye sitting with her mother in the courtyard. "Father, Mother, what did you do to bring me to this: no family and running for my life?"

The breeze, though, brought forth from her memory Ankhesenpaaten's haunting screams from within the tunnel.

She shuddered just as Aitye's presence beside her made her heart race and her body jump.

Aitye pressed a finger to her lips as she rested into her place beside her. "The men still sleep," she said and leaned her head against the rock.

Nefe glanced at Aitye's bandaged feet and hands before looking out to the sea once more to continue reliving her childhood.

"I see your tears, my Princess," Aitye whispered.

Nefe clamped down on her teeth. *Do not speak to me, you who Mother said was a better mother than she. Mother never said that. You liar . . . or Paaten . . . whoever said it, lies.*

"I miss her too."

"You miss nothing," Nefe muttered. "You are selfish." She heard Aitye chuckle and turned her head to look at her. "Why are you laughing?"

"Perhaps I am selfish, and perhaps you think I miss nothing. But you are the one being selfish."

Nefe's jaw fell as the indignation burned within her. "No, I am not. You and he and he"—she pointed to Paaten and Atinuk—"you all did nothing."

Both men stirred at the slight outburst but did not wake.

Aitye's smile fell, and she sighed. "We all did the best we could. We all fell short." She shook her head. "I know you wish Ankhesenpaaten were here with you, but she is not. I know you wish your Mother here, but she is not. You have lost so much, your majesty. You have lost *so* much. But the three of us, we are all you have left."

"Do not remind me," Nefe said as she slipped another almond in her mouth and pushed the blanket from her body. She was no longer cold.

"You have to speak to us. You withhold—"

"I do not have to do anything. I am the King's Daughter."

Aitye licked her lip, as if hesitating to speak. "Nefe—"

It was the second time Aitye had called her that, but this time there was a finality to it. Nefe shuddered at the unraveling of one of the last threads that held to her past.

"—you *were* the King's Daughter. Now, you are Nefe, a young woman who is loved by your family, now past, and by me, who still lives. You are protected by Paaten and Atinuk. They would die for you, as would I."

"You lie. You did not die for my mother, to whom you had given a life oath."

The tension in Aitye's shoulders dissipated. "You wish I had died, and your mother had lived. You see me with Atinuk and wish your sister were in his place. You see the four of us alive and wish Ankhesenpaaten and your mother had lived instead."

YES! The resounding answer pounded in her throat, but her teeth were too tightly clamped for it to release.

"I understand that." Aitye reached over and fed the fading fire a strip of reed. She sat back, and they listened to the sound of the waves and the crackle of the small fire in silence for a moment.

Nefe focused her gaze on the tiny fire under the cooking pot of beans. The last two months had passed as if she had been dreaming. She thought she would wake up, but that relief from the nightmare never came. Even with the storm, it seemed that if only she could be swept away in the sea, drown, or fall from the cliff, she would finally wake up. But a part of her knew: this was no dream. She was alone.

Aitye's whisper broke her trance upon the small flame and the sound of the breaking waves against the rock below. "When my mother passed, I had lost everyone who had ever cared for me."

Nefe swallowed the lump in her throat. She did not want to think about this right now. She did not want to feel. She just wanted to wake up. She gritted her teeth.

Do not speak. Do not talk. Everything you say only makes this more real.

But Aitye did not obey her unspoken commands. "I was alone in a palace, and I was a steward to a new young queen about my age." She drew a deep breath to soothe the old wound. "You will never feel complete again, but you will come to appreciate and love the people around you, as I did your mother; as I do you."

"You did not keep your oath to her," Nefe's words choked as she sniffled. "You are the reason why Mother is dead and Ankhesenpaaten turned back."

"You can blame me, but it does not change what happened."

"I know that," Nefe spat, sucking back her tears. She suppressed her cries to uphold some of her royal dignity, whatever was left of it.

"I held your mother when she cried after the plague took everyone," Aitye whispered, as if she sensed what Nefe was trying to do. "I saw her at her worst, Nefe. With her, I did not feel so alone, even though I was beneath her."

"I am alone."

"You are not alone, Nefe."

"Everyone I love is gone."

"But not everyone who loves you. I held you as a baby, as your mother bore you. I was there. I saw you; I watched you grow. Queen Kiya and I were there for you when your mother could not be, when she chose to push you away to keep you safe—" Aitye stopped speaking.

"Everyone says that. What was so bad? What did they do? Why am I fleeing? Why did they kill her? Why do they curse the hearts of my mother and father?" Nefe turned to Aitye as tears fell in long streams down her cheeks. "Why?"

Aitye lowered her head and wiped the tears that formed in her own eyes. "Your father, he . . . he turned Egypt into . . . " She rubbed her neck.

"What? Just tell me." The command fell from her lips, but her heart feared the answers.

She released a heavy sigh. "He lost himself; he became confused. He ordered the death and torture of the Egyptian people for worshipping the gods Egypt has always worshiped since Egypt became Egypt."

"That is not true." Her stomach hardened and twisted at the blatant lie.

"Nefe, you said you wanted the truth. This is it. Your father put Egypt in a difficult place. He put your mother in a difficult place. The economy suffered; the people were dying of starvation in the streets while food was left to spoil in the sun."

"They were offerings to the Aten." Nefe gritted her teeth, unsure of how much of this so-called truth she could bear.

"Pawah came to your mother and told her to take poison to your father, or else a rebellion would kill you all. She—"

"She did not kill my father," Nefe said. Her eyes shut tight and she shook her head, covering her ears. "My father traveled to the Aten in his sleep."

Aitye licked her lip and only said, "Because of the circumstances she had been dealt, she had to made hard decisions. Some were bad; some led to her murder."

"I do not want to hear any more." The dryness in Nefe's mouth would not let her swallow the thick lump at the back of her throat.

Aitye brushed away an escaped tear. She paused for a moment to release a shaky breath. "Nefe, there is so much that you do not know, and I hope you never find out. Once you grieve and you still want to know, I will tell you, but the past cannot be changed."

"I know that. It does not mean I cannot wish for the past." Nefe stared at the cavern wall across from them. She wished Aitye would close her mouth again.

"Knowing the past and accepting the past are two different things." Aitye placed a hand on Nefe's leg. "You cannot move past this until you accept what has happened. Your mother never could do that. She carried so much on her shoulders; the weight of your father's decisions and her own were so much for her to bear. It broke her. She did not realize she was broken until the moment Jabari came to her room on the night she was murdered." Aitye shook her head in sorrow.

Nefe wanted to leap from the cave. She did not want to hear what Aitye said. What if everything that she said had happened was true? It would mean she was truly alone. Everything in her life was gone. She was starting over, and her mind and her heart could not accept it. She wanted to scream. She wanted to break down. She wanted to curl into a ball. She wanted to hit something. Yet, she stayed still. Perfectly still.

"She felt alone, Nefe. She wanted peace, but it never came to her because she could not accept what had happened." Aitye touched Nefe's cheek to turn her face to her. "I do not want to see her daughter fall victim to the same fate."

Paaten was right. Let me remember them the way I need to remember them. I never want to know what happened. I will just know it was bad, and I had to leave.

The seaside cave seemed to collapse in on her in that moment. Aitye's words caused her to release an ugly cry; her angry cage of emotions ripped open. She fought to find air to breathe. Her royal visage of stone hiding the depth of her sorrow shattered in an instant, with a grimace springing to life on her face. The future scared her. The future held so many unknowns. It wrapped her in a cocoon and dangled her over a lake of uncertainty, ready to release her and to laugh as she fell. She envisioned drowning after ultimately failing to survive in its pool of mockery and pain.

Aitye pulled Nefe's head to her shoulder and wrapped her arms about her.

Nefe shrank back, but Aitye whispered, "Please do not push me away."

Nefe relented and pressed herself into Aitye's warm embrace. It did not fill the void in her chest, but at least Aitye was there with her.

CHAPTER 20
ESCAPE FROM THE CAVE

PAATEN PULLED ON THE ROPE KNOT AT HIS WAIST that sat above the fold of his loincloth. It would hold. He looked at Atinuk, who sat next to him and pulled on the rope knot at his waist as well. Their legs dangled from the cave opening.

"Paaten, we can wait a few more days." Atinuk squinted at the morning sun's reflection on the water.

"We are out of food." Paaten watched the serene sea and wondered why the gods made the storms come when they were almost at dock. Were they trying to test his strength and will, to see if he was worthy enough to be released from his oath and return to his wife? He glanced at Nefe over his shoulder. "We have been here for a decan. We can no longer survive here."

Atinuk looked at his hands and then at Paaten's hands.

Paaten did the same. His hands had scabbed over;

some areas had lost their scabs, and shiny pink, fresh, and tender skin took its place. The white flesh peeled around each sore. Their nail beds, at least, were pink and healthy. He curled one hand into a fist and winced, anticipating the pain of breaking open the wounds again. He took the last linen of his shendyt and wrapped his hands, leaving some for Atinuk. Paaten peered down out of the cave and then up. *Down seems farther away, at least.*

He released a long breath as he readied himself to climb despite the anticipated pain. He reached over and grabbed a rock outside of the cave as his foot slipped into a locked position. Swinging out of the cave, he took hold of the cliffside. The skin of his hand stretched and, judging from the pain, split. *Cursed storm.* He looked down to find another hold for his foot.

If I fall, Atinuk will not be able to hold my weight. We will both plummet to our deaths.

As if reading his mind, Atinuk called out, "Do not fall, Paaten. I do not want to die today."

"Egyptian men do not fall, Canaanite." He found a foothold and pushed up, grabbing another part of the cliffside.

And so I ascend.

The sun blazed overhead, and the scorching rock blistered his hands. Finally, he rolled onto the flat land atop the cliff and right into a thick ruddy brush.

Lying there a moment to let his hands and feet throb, he listened for the sounds of an army

nearby. No one approached him yet. The smell of
campfire was nowhere near him. The odor of dirty,
fighting men did not exist. *Perhaps the army moved
north.*

A weight fell into his stomach.

What if we were blown too far north?

He pushed the thought away. *One obstacle at a time;
I cannot change what I cannot change.* Once the sun had
moved past the pinnacle in the sky, he unwrapped
one hand and examined the damage. He pursed his
lips.

*Not horrible. Not as bad as I had envisioned. At least,
no splitting.*

He rose slightly so that his eyes skimmed the top
of the brush. Faint war cries screamed in the
distance. The slight vibration in the rock beneath
him signaled a battle had begun. However, there was
nothing except thick ruddy and desert-green brush as
far as his eyes could see. *Are we closer to Kubna than
anticipated?*

"Is it safe to bring them up?" he asked himself.
War can turn in an instant. He glanced toward the sun.
With his hands the way they were, it would take a
half a day to pull the rest of them to the top. He
sighed. "Nor can I let them stay there. They will
starve."

He tugged twice on the rope and waited for
Atinuk to make the climb, keeping the rope taut.

He finally made it, and then he threw one end of
the rope down. Nefe came up next, then the travel

sling, and lastly, Aitye, who held Atinuk's leather tunic.

The war cries drew near as the sun held low in the western sky. Atinuk peered over the ruddy brush as he slipped his leather tunic on. "It seems the Hittites have gained land."

Aitye's words came muffled behind Atinuk and Paaten as she pulled off what remained of her linen dress. "I thought Pharaoh's Army would have been more equipped to hold them off."

"Surely by now they have received word about the death of Pharaoh and her General. Perhaps their morale is not what it should be to fight with vigor." Atinuk returned his gaze to Paaten.

"Perhaps." Paaten felt the last part of his service to Pharaoh's Army wither and die within him. *The last failure.* He had left Egypt weak and vulnerable. His men needed him. He shook it away. "Horemheb will make an excellent General, and Ay will no longer be distracted with the safety of his daughter. They will lead them and do what I could not."

"Because his daughter is dead now." Nefe stood up, already clad in her long Canaanite tunic dress, headdress, shoes, and belt.

Paaten wished he could cut out his tongue. After thinking Atinuk a fool in the cave for not having the foresight to avoid mentioning Ankhesenpaaten's absence, he had fallen into the same blunder. "Yes, my Princess. I am sorry to have brought it up; it was a lapse of judgment."

He reached out for her hand. "Please sit down; do not draw attention."

She yanked away out of his reach. "Is that what my family is . . . was to you? Distractions?"

"Please lower your voice and sit down." Paaten's sympathy teetered on edge. The battle was not far from them. She could be hit by a wayward arrow. She could be spotted and draw either the army or scouts. His stomach plummeted. How would he ensure the silence and loyalty of Egyptian scouts? If they were loyal to Pawah, he would have to kill them. The thought burned his hands. How could he take an Egyptian life? It would be one of his comrades who had only become lost in the infernal abyss Akhenaten had dragged Egypt into.

"Is that what I am to you? A burden? A distraction to keep you from your life?"

"Sit down, Nefe." Paaten rolled to his knees and took hold of her hand.

"Let go of me," Nefe said, trying to pry her hand away. Atinuk swept his arm at her knees, sending her plopping into the ruddy brush. A puff of dust rose into the air.

Paaten stared at Atinuk, who stared back at him with a knowing glance. "We have to move from here. Quickly." Paaten grabbed the sling and hoisted it onto his back. "Quickly, Aitye." He grabbed her arm as she pulled on her Canaanite dress. "Go south," he muttered, and Atinuk pulled up Nefe. They ran along the cliffside, bent at the waist, trying to keep out of sight. Paaten halted the group when he realized the dust from their movements followed them. He hoped the brush would keep the dust near the ground, so he turned to move them inland toward the battle. They were exposed on the nearly flat plain of rock and brush.

He looked behind them, and the dust had disappeared. He surveyed the distance and wished his eyes were young again.

Atinuk yelled just as a spear landed in front of Paaten's feet. Paaten wrenched it from the rock. He hoped it was Egyptian with just a bronze tip. The memory of torture on Hatti land from his youth gripped his stomach as he observed the full bronze spear head. *Hittite.* He hesitated as he spun and looked at Nefe. His heightened heart rate beat in his ears. *If we run, we will be speared in the back. If we stay, they will take us to camp, but we will be alive.*

Atinuk was calling to him. "—Paaten! What to do? Do we run?"

"No." Paaten shook his head, as if sealing his spoken decision. *Should we run? Would they kill all four of us? Would the King's Daughter get away?* He grimaced as he reconsidered his decision. *Time is being lost. Make a decision.*

"Run." He turned to lead them . . . where? Where were they going to run to? An open plain of ruddy brush lay before them. The war cries seemed to be just over the small hill. He looked south and then north. That was when he spotted a band of eight Hittites.

He spun back around. "We will be taken to their camp. Do not speak your name. Do not speak Egyptian. They will kill you. You are my daughter, Aitye. The King's Daughter is your daughter. Atinuk is your husband. We are from Damaski. We did not know there was war."

Nefe's eyes grew wide, but she stayed silent as Paaten wrenched her close. Aitye grabbed Atinuk's arm as the Hittites slowly closed in around them.

Paaten eyed each man, gauging whether or not they thought him an Egyptian in Canaanite clothes, but they seemed to be fooled. He had no kohl around his eyes, and his wig was long gone, replaced by a linen headdress tied with a headband. A month's worth of salt-and-pepper beard graced his chin. He looked at Aitye, afraid she had not had time to put on her headdress, but she had. They looked like Canaanites. He returned his gaze to the Hittite soldier and spoke in Akkadian. "We are not your enemy. We are simply trying to return home amid this battle that has sprung up."

The Hittite scoffed. "Our Governor will decide that." He yanked the spear from Paaten's hands and gestured for them to walk north. "Move."

A pit opened in Paaten's stomach. He had barely escaped the Hittites the last time he was captured.

CHAPTER 21
ESCAPE FROM CAPTURE

TWO HITTITE SOLDIERS FORCED PAATEN AND Atinuk to their knees in front of a large war tent. Swords were held at their necks, while Nefe and Aitye were allowed to kneel alongside them without force. Paaten could sense the lust in the Hittite men as they ran their eyes over Aitye and Nefe.

Paaten's khopesh was hidden under his long Canaanite tunic, and he was not an Egyptian in their eyes. But would they keep him alive long enough for his group to escape? His grip tightened around Nefe's hand. *I must live. I refuse to let the King's Daughter be a bed slave to some Hittite.*

An old Hittite man still clad in leather-and-bronze armor was carried before them on a litter. A sword of iron rested across his thighs. Heavily adorned fingers with rings of silver and gold tapped its handle. His litter was placed on the ground, and the four servants who carried him knelt with their foreheads to the ground at each of the litter's four corners. Two men about the age of Atinuk stood beside him, clad in the same uniform as the old man. Paaten noticed a similarity in their faces. *Father and sons.* His gaze fell to the iron. He knew who the old man was before he even spoke.

Governor Pulli—one of the men who forced Niwa to bed all those years before I knew her.

He felt the cold bronze of his khopesh against his leg as it lay hidden under his long Canaanite tunic.

"I am Governor Pulli, warlord to King Suppiluliuma I." He looked at them down the bridge of his nose as he spoke in Akkadian. "These are my sons, Kalli and Zuzulli."

Paaten bit the insides of his cheeks, restraining every urge to slay the man where he sat. He also wondered if his dialect of Akkadian would tell them he was not from Berytus.

Pulli pointed a bony finger toward Paaten. "You are the oldest of this odd clan. Who are you and where do you travel?"

Paaten dipped his chin at the sliver of civility the old man presented to him. His mind quickly raced on how to respond. If he said Aitye was his daughter, Atinuk his son-in-law and Nefe his granddaughter, they might slay Atinuk and himself, or they might let them go. Should he tell them they were going to Damaski? That was the dialect of Akkadian he spoke, as he recalled. What if they followed them there? Would Niwa and their son be safe from them?

"My name is Danel," he said, hoping his lack of a full beard would not give him away. He saw Atinuk peer at him from the corner of his eye. "This is my daughter Pigat, and her husband, Keret." Paaten gestured to Aitye and Atinuk and then to Nefe. "This is my daughter's daughter, Donatiya." He hoped he had remembered the last two names correctly from his estate in Damaski.

"Assu." Pulli eyed him as he spoke the informal Hittite greeting.

Paaten decided to feign ignorance of the Hittite language, wondering if Pulli was testing him to see if they were Hittite sympathizers or Damaski spies. Damaski loyalties had been split since his capture almost thirty years ago. If the Hittites believed they were sympathizers, they would probably probe them with questions for which he would not know the answers. If he acted neutral, then perhaps they could still be allowed to leave. And if worse came to worse, knowing their language in secret might prove useful.

"Assu?" Paaten asked and knitted his brows in confusion, tilting his head.

Pulli dismissed it with a simple wave of his fingers through the air. "Where do you travel, Danel?" He spoke in the Akkadian tongue.

Paaten gave a small nod of his head in gratitude for being allowed to continue. It appeared the Hittites were believing his story thus far.

"My daughter wanted to see Berytus and the sea.

243

We were unaware of the fighting here and began to return home."

"Where is your home, Danel?"

The question made him grit his teeth and caused his heart to wrench. He had been asked such a question for the greater part of a year he spent as a prisoner of war on the estate of Governor Matiya. Matiya had tried his best to convert him to a Hittite soldier for his estate, but at every instance of the question, Paaten had yelled with a resounding ferocity: *"Egypt is my home!"*

The same words flew up from the depths of his belly but hit the back of his lips. He swallowed the conditioned response. "Damaski." His face held no expression.

Pulli nodded and then snapped his fingers. The swords were removed from their necks, and Atinuk and Paaten were yanked to their feet. Paaten helped Aitye and Nefe stand, guiding Aitye to Atinuk and holding Nefe's shoulder under his firm hand. He feared the worst. In the moment, he regretted his tale, wondering what the old governor would demand in return for safe travel through this land now under the temporary control of the Hittites.

Pulli again pointed a bony finger, but this time it was at Nefe. "My youngest son needs a wife."

Paaten's grip upon Nefe hardened. "She is betrothed to a man in Damaski already."

"Why is her husband not here?"

"He is still in his father's home, as they have not . . ." Paaten forgot the custom. His mind blanked.

Pulli glanced at Atinuk and Aitye.

Atinuk spoke. "They have not known each other in bed, but she is betrothed. Damaski customs dictate that she is already married."

Pulli chuckled. "Then again, I ask you, where is her husband?"

"He is in his father's home, per the Damaski customs."

"In the land of Hatti, you take what you conquer." He ran his eyes up and down Nefe's body and then did the same to Aitye. "Leave your women, and you may go."

"Leave my daughter and granddaughter?" Paaten asked, taking note of the four Hittite soldiers standing nearby with their weapons already drawn.

"Yes, you and your son-in-law may return to Damaski to have another wife and another grandchild."

"If we refuse?" Atinuk said, his hand firmly pulling Aitye close to him.

"Then I will kill you and take your women."

Paaten sneered at him. "Which son will take Pigat and which will take Donatiya?"

"The younger for my youngest, Zuzulli; the older for my oldest, Kalli." He leaned back in his seat. "But not that it matters to you."

"Will you treat them well?" Paaten asked, garnering the stare of Atinuk.

"Like goddesses." The old man scoffed and narrowed his eyes.

Paaten knew Nefe and Aitye did not understand what was happening. They did not know what had been said. All they knew was that these were Hittites, and he was about to leave them.

How could he tell them he would come back at night to get them? How could he remind them again not to speak and to keep their identities secret? The soldiers would surely hear the long Egyptian whisper.

He glanced at Atinuk, and he gave a slight nod of the head. He was in agreement.

Paaten stooped down and turned Nefe to face him. He ran a hand over her cheek and looked into her fearful brown eyes. He spoke in Akkadian to maintain the facade: "They will take care of you. You will live a good life. I will tell your betrothed you were killed in the fighting. I will love you and miss you always."

He pulled her into an embrace and whispered in Egyptian in her ear. "Trust me." He released her, seeing Atinuk had done the same with Aitye. The Hittites seemed not to notice the short whisper. He guided Nefe to Aitye, and Atinuk hugged the both of them in his role of father and husband.

"You make a wise decision, Danel." Pulli ran a hand down the length of his long, white braided lock of hair laid over his shoulder.

Atinuk guided the two women to walk toward the

Hittites. Nefe kept her eyes on Paaten. He pressed his lips together trying to remind her to say nothing.

They stood before Pulli, and he snapped his fingers again. Two soldiers grabbed them by the arms and jolted them toward the grand war tent behind Pulli.

The women's cries carried back to Paaten.

If those sons violate them, they will die by my hand.

"You are free to go." Pulli waved them off. "But only you, Keret. I have need for a laborer, and Danel seems strong and heartily built. It also seems he has had a long and satisfying life. It will end in the land of Hatti."

Atinuk looked back at him. "That was not the deal."

Pulli chuckled. "I changed the deal, Keret, and, besides, Danel seems to have a bit of warrior blood in him. Perhaps he descends from Damaski's militia. I cannot have him coming back here to exact his revenge on me for taking his daughter and granddaughter."

"But I am free to go?" Atinuk asked.

"Yes, I do not see you as a threat, but know this: If you try to come back during the night, I will first slice the throat of your daughter in front of Danel, and then when you are subdued, I will slice the throat of your wife while you watch."

Paaten growled. "Go, Keret." If both of them were bound, there might be no escape. At least, his khopesh lay hidden under his Canaanite tunic. Atinuk had no weapon.

But Atinuk hesitated.

Pulli saw it and added to the wound. "Danel's travel sling will remain here. Take yourself and go, Keret."

"How will I return to Damaski? I have no supplies."

"Here is a bow and one arrow." Pulli gave a snap, and a bow and an arrow were given to Atinuk. "Do not miss your prey, hunter, and that will give you one meal." He chuckled, and his men joined in on the small ridicule.

Atinuk's jawline grew taut as his eyes darted among the warlord and his two sons.

"Go, Keret." Paaten spoke through his teeth, knowing Atinuk was considering which one to kill. But killing one right then would accomplish nothing except getting them all killed. They were outnumbered and in the middle of the Hittite camp.

Atinuk looked at Paaten before throwing his gaze to Pulli. He dipped his chin. "You are most generous, Governor." He turned and left with an escort, pushing his way through the soldiers.

Paaten's sling was stripped from his person, and a Hittite soldier struggled to carry it to Pulli. He finally set it on the ground in front of the governor and flipped open the top.

Pulli hummed with greed. "Gold, I see." He flicked his gaze to Paaten. "Tie him with the others to take back to Hattusha for the King to grant this spoil to me."

At swordpoint, they prodded Paaten to walk.

"And take this sling to my tent."

The Hittite soldier flipped the top closed and brought it into the sprawling tent where they had taken Nefe and Aitye; Paaten was prodded to the side of the tent. There he saw two Egyptians and two Berytians tied to a stake in the ground.

Paaten hoped Atinuk would not get himself killed in whatever action he was going to take. He was forced to his knees and bound to the stake.

"Stay here, Canaanite." The Hittite spat on Paaten's arm as he spoke in the Hittite language. "The next transport will be here in the morning to take you and these filthy desert dwellers to Hattusha."

Paaten again feigned ignorance of the enemy's tongue. At his lack of response, the Hittite soldier pushed him in his head before leaving them. He studied the two Egyptians: one, a Captain of the Troop, and the other, a Greatest of Two Hundred Fifty. Perhaps together, these two comrades might aid escape for all involved. But for that to happen, he would have to reveal himself; he would have to reveal why he was there . . .

He hoped Nefe would keep her mouth shut. There would be nothing more pleasurable for a Hittite warlord than to exchange royal blood for royal blood in vengeance for the death of the Hittite Prince Zannanza.

The Captain studied his face. "General?"

The Greatest of Two Hundred Fifty looked up, his eyes wide in recognition of their leader.

Paaten looked at the Berytians to see if they either were ignorant of the Egyptian language or feigned ignorance, as he had done. He nodded. They appeared not to understand, so he turned his attention to the Egyptians.

"What are you doing here? Dressed like that? Has Egypt fallen?"

He shook his head and glanced over his shoulder to make sure the Hittite soldiers could not hear their whispers. "Pharaoh was murdered by the hand of Pawah."

Their gazes fell, and their hands curled into fists.

"He said no more blood," the Captain murmured.

Paaten closed his eyes. How blind had he been? How had Pawah ingratiated himself as a savior to seemingly all of Egypt? How had Pawah accomplished all of this right under his nose? His failure smacked him in the face, and he sat back on his heels.

"I promised Pharaoh I would protect her daughter and take her away from Egypt. Thus, here we are." He shook his head. "Cursed storm wrecked our barge. We thought Berytus was under Egyptian control."

"Where is Pharaoh's daughter?" one asked, while the other stated, "It was and will be again."

Paaten gestured his head toward the tent. "Pharaoh's daughter is in the tent of the Hittite, along with Pharaoh's steward."

The Egyptian officers looked at each other. "Pawah is no savior if he murdered Pharaoh Neferneferuaten. We will give our lives helping you and the King's Daughter to escape. If we are to go to Hattusha, we will never return to Egypt."

Paaten nodded. "I spent two years in Hittite captivity, and I would have surely perished there if a governor's wife had not had a lapse in judgment. If you die among the Hittites, whether here or in the land of Hatti, it will be a hard death. You will lose your ba, and your ka will break. The Hittites are a foul people. They will most likely burn your body, regardless."

"We have accepted as much. If we die, at least our deaths will help the King's Daughter to escape."

"May Amun-Re see your sacrifice. May Anhur bring you back to Egypt."

"We will not rest until the King's Daughter is safely out of the Hittite camp."

"You are honorable men. When you return, you are ordered to silence. Never shall Pawah know . . . never shall anyone know that she and I live."

"As long as I, Ebana, Captain of the Troop, live, this secret shall never part my lips."

"And this also holds true for me, Senenmut, Greatest of Two Hundred Fifty."

Paaten noticed Ebana twitch; had he done a disservice to the King's Daughter by revealing her identity? Was this man a faithful follower of Pharaoh's murderer? "Even if Pawah—"

"Pawah will never know. He saved our families under the reigns of Akhenaten and Smenkare. We are through with him." Senenmut eyed Ebana.

"Yes, his heart shall weigh heavy on the scales of Ma'at," Ebana responded. "Now, how to break these bonds?"

Paaten sat back on his heels. "Have patience. We will wait until nightfall. My khopesh lies beneath my tunic. The dark will cover us, and the war camp noise will keep our movements unnoticed."

"The troops have already returned from their day of fighting." Senenmut nodded toward the south at the massive numbers of men coming over the rock plain. The sun cast its long shadows from the west, nearly sunk behind the sea's horizon.

"It shall not be long until we make our escape," Paaten whispered and prayed the two sons of the governor would wait until nightfall before taking their new mistresses.

CHAPTER 22
ESCAPE FROM LUST

Nefe's wrists burned from the rope that bound them behind her back. The linen in her mouth gave her the urge to vomit. A gruff hand squeezed her arm, locking her in a firm grip right underneath her armpit. She looked to Aitye, likewise bound and gagged. Her gaze fell to Paaten who was led off, bound as well.

Trust him? He is captured. How will he save us? We are in the middle of a Hittite camp!

Her eyes darted through the soldiers, frantically searching for Atinuk, but he was nowhere to be seen. A scream for Aitye slammed behind closed lips, pressed into a tight thin line as Paaten's words came back to her: *Do not speak.*

Aitye found her gaze, and she gave Nefe a slight reassuring nod as Aitye was dragged off to an adjoining room. The Hittite soldier lifted up a drape meant as a doorway and entered into a large room cut in half by a translucent veil.

"*Pennatuk para.*" He let her stand alone on her own two feet.

The Hittite was speaking to her, but she did not understand. He released her arm and motioned inside. She bit her lip and stood still. His tone grew gruff as he seemed to repeat himself.

"*Pennatuk para.*"

What does he want me to do? What is he saying? The man's stench repulsed her, but she dared not open her mouth to wretch.

"*Pennatuk para.*" His yell broke through her disgust, and she followed the long point of his finger toward the room behind the veil.

Have I been traded to be some Hittite's wife or . . . mistress? Her eyes darted. Her breathing shallowed. Her thoughts muted. She froze.

Aitye grunted from the other room and released a muffled cry.

Do not speak—Paaten's words made her teeth clamp down hard against the gag in her mouth.

No, Aitye. I cannot lose you too.

"*Pennatuk para!*" the Hittite barked at her. She shrank back with tears in her eyes as she looked up at the imposing man. Her body trembled. She had been taught all of her life that Hittites were the enemy. They were big, dirty, hairy, despicable enemies. She never understood why her mother wanted to marry one—especially now, as she stared at the big, dirty, hairy, despicable man in front of her.

Think! she yelled at herself. *Think of something, Nefeneferuaten Tasherit. Think of how to get out of here.*

The Hittite once again gripped her arm under the armpit and shoved her inside, sending her tumbling into the ground. She saw him reaching down for her. Scampering up, her dress tripped her and ripped, sending her face-first into the dirt. The Hittite yanked her up, and Nefe yipped in pain at the jolt in her shoulder. The linen gag crawled down her throat.

He dragged her and dropped her into a pile of cushions on the floor behind the veil. The gag dislodged. A sweeping gulp of air filled her chest and she repressed the urge to scream out.

The Hittite squatted next to her and watched her for a moment before chuckling with a demeaning glare. "*Guen-marlanttuk.*"

He wiped her face with the linen gag and then stuffed it back into her mouth. He ran his eyes over her body and muttered, "*Tuk appiskia ukila.*" Then he peered over his shoulder before sliding those beady eyes toward her once again. A greedy hand slid up her leg.

His touch sent her body into an instant recoil. The slide of his hand against her leg turned into a hard grip just above her knee.

An involuntary yelp came from her blocked throat as she sent a hard kick to his chest, knocking the Hittite backward. With a slight brush of his hand against his leather tunic where she had kicked him, he shook his head. *"Guen-marlanttuk,"* he whispered with a cruel undertone. He slid a dagger from the sheath on his belt.

Her eyes grew wide. *Help!* she wanted to call out, but all she could do was whimper and squirm amid the cushions, trying to get away from him.

He crawled slowly toward her, as if to scare her more. She stopped moving when he knelt over her and held the blade to her neck. He mumbled softly with lust-filled eyes, *"Lē pennatuk."*

Her lip trembled along with her shaky breath as the cool edge of bronze rested against her skin. Tears came from the corners of her eyes as his hand again touched her legs. *Help me. Someone. Please.* She kept her eyes open, watching him sink a row of teeth into his bottom lip as he peered down her body.

Swish.

The drape opened, and he stood up sharply at the sound, quickly sheathing his dagger.

A simply clad man walked in, most likely a servant, and began scolding the Hittite soldier. *"Lē appisktuk guen."*

The Hittite stood and rolled his head to pop his neck.

"Hanti tiyamu guen-Akkad appiskimi daukila?"

He shoved a hand toward Nefe.

The servant pointed toward the draped door with stern face and said nothing more.

"Ah," the Hittite sighed with a grunt, but he did

what he was told. The servant looked at Nefe before tying her feet together and leaving her alone.

Nefe's gaze fell to the adjacent room. Was Aitye there? Was she alive? Nefe tried to hear her moving or perhaps see a shadow falling on the curtain. She opened her mouth wider around the gag to whisper to her. She needed to know something, anything . . . but Paaten's warning firmly held her tongue: *Do not speak Egyptian. They will kill you.*

She whimpered and waited.

Paaten said to trust him, but he failed my mother. He can fail me too.

She rolled over to her stomach and tried to push up, but the cushions only made her sink and fall face-first once again. *I will get out of here. I will not be a victim. I will not die like my mother.*

She focused on the corner of the tent.

I will get out.

CHAPTER 23
ESCAPE FROM THE HITTITES

NIGHT ARRIVED. THEY SAT IN THE SHADOWS, IN the chilly night, with no fire nearby. Two guards stood at the entrance of the alleyway between the tents. More men sat eating their rations around fire pits that surrounded the governor's large war tent complex. The fog came in from the sea and lay thick in the camp. The fires were blurs, and the men appeared as dark spirits in the smoke of the firelit fog.

"They are distracted by food, their guard is down, and we are in the shadows. Our goddess of the mists, Tefnut, and our god of air, Shu, have been good to us," Paaten whispered.

"Now is the time, General." Ebana peered over his shoulder to make sure the guards stayed where they were. "They are on our side; they grant their blessing."

Paaten cut himself loose with one quick upward

thrust of his hands, catching the rope between his wrists on the hooked blade of his khopesh. He freed Ebana of his bindings, and Senenmut next. The Berytians offered their bound hands to Paaten.

Ebana whispered to him, "They cannot be trusted. They do not wish Egyptians well since Akhenaten did not come to their aid when Kubna fell to the Hittites."

Paaten considered Ebana's warning, then spoke in Akkadian to the Berytians. "If I release you, will you do as I command?"

They both nodded.

"You are to be silent and to not slip away until we leave. My daughter and granddaughter are within the tent. These Egyptians are going to help me get them out. Either stay silent and out of my way, or you will be struck down. The only way we will all make it through the camp alive is if you obey my order."

They both nodded again. Paaten made sure no one watched them as he lifted the khopesh from the ground and cut their bindings. "Stay here. Say nothing. Act as if you are still bound."

Paaten quickly covered his khopesh with the length of his tunic as one of the two Berytians eyed him.

"Where did you get that weapon, Canaanite, if you are not Egyptian?"

"I traded for it a long time ago, Berytian. Now, silence." Paaten noticed one of the guards approaching to bring them a dinner of sorts. The guard slopped the beans and bread before them. A woman's muffled scream came from within the tent.

Paaten made a conscious effort to keep his heartbeat steady. He had to be calm. He could not panic. He could not let the anger take hold of him. He had to be quick, with a clear mind.

The guard bent down in front of Paaten and chuckled before speaking in the Hittite tongue. "I bet your daughter and granddaughter are having a better time than you, Canaanite."

Paaten gripped his khopesh.

"You stupid Canaanite. All this time living so close to the land of Hatti, and you never learned to speak our language." The man spat at Paaten's chest.

"You will die for that," Paaten spoke back in the Hittite tongue. While the guard was caught off-guard at the response, Paaten swung his khopesh with all of his might, removing the guard's head from his shoulders. Ebana caught the body before it hit the ground. He stripped the dagger from the guard's belt and handed it to Senenmut. Ebana and Senenmut raided the guard's weaponry in silence while Paaten used the hook of his blade to slash through the side of the tent. The first guard would come looking for his comrade, but Ebana and Senenmut would take care of him. Getting out of the camp would be the difficult task. He stepped inside. The room was empty, but a translucent linen veil divided the tent into two areas. Muffled screams came from the other side of the veil. Paaten slipped to the veil's side and drew a finger to move it out of his sightline just in time to see one of the governor's sons throw Aitye to the ground full of colored, plush cushions.

Kalli.

Her hands were bound, and a linen gag was stuffed in her mouth. She tried to scramble away, but Kalli caught her ankle and pulled her close to him, locking one leg under his arm. He backhanded her face.

"Be still, woman. I have fought enough already." She squirmed and kicked him, but he caught her foot and squeezed until she whimpered. "Be. Still." The command came through clenched teeth.

Paaten snuck into the room and saw the son's dagger lying atop his armor. He grabbed it with a quick motion, careful not to make a sound. Kalli's long Hittite braid drew his eye. Aitye glanced at Paaten.

Aitye! You give me away.

Dropping his khopesh, Paaten bounded toward Kalli and snatched the base of his braid just as he turned to see who entered his room. Paaten slid the dagger across Kalli's neck, spraying blood over the cushioned floor. The Hittite fell from Paaten's grip, gurgling. His hands firmly wrapped about his neck, Kalli rolled to his back and stared up at his attacker.

Paaten watched the life leave Kalli's dark eyes as Aitye drew her legs to her chest and turned away from the dying man. Paaten listened for any approaching footsteps and any other muffled screams. There were none, so he stepped over Kalli and knelt down to Aitye.

"Where is Nefe?" he whispered as he pulled the linen from her mouth and began to untie her.

Aitye's chest rose and fell in a quick pulse. Tears streamed down her face.

He forced himself to ignore her tears in the moment. "Aitye, where is Nefe?" Paaten whispered again as the rope fell from her wrists. She pointed to the room next to that one.

"Find your tunic; put it on. Stay here. I will be back."

Paaten stood, nicked the bottom of the tent wall with his khopesh, and peered in. The room looked empty, so he slashed through and stepped inside. Nefe was huddled in the corner, leaning against the room post: her arms tied behind her; a gag in her mouth, her legs bound at the ankles. At least she was clothed. At the sight of him, her vacant stare filled with hope.

It appeared no man had touched her. *Praise be to Amun-Re.* The tension he had held in his shoulders from the moment he heard the scream now faded. He looked around the room to make sure no one was there as he walked over to her. He yanked her up, pulled the gag from her mouth, cut her ropes, and shuffled her out the way he came. But as he was leaving, Zuzulli drew back the room's entry drape.

"You there, what are you doing with my woman?" He snapped with a shrill pop of his hand. Three of his guards came at once and entered the room. "You dare steal from Zuzulli, son of Governor Pulli? You shall be beheaded for your crime!"

Paaten shoved Nefe into Aitye's arms and readied to fight the three of them. He raised the dagger in one hand and the khopesh in the other. They closed in on him, but he shut one off, circling to his back. Their swords could outmatch his short dagger, but he was deadly with his khopesh. There was one disadvantage, though: the khopesh was not a thrusting weapon like the sword could be. He had to get close enough to swing and slash.

One attacked, but he ducked and spun into the man, landing his dagger in his chest. Another impending attack tickled his back. He spun just in time to catch the man's grip at the hilt of the blade, dropping his khopesh. The cushions on the floor of the tent prevented the clang of the weapon as it dropped. Paaten kneed him in the stomach and used the man's hard grip upon his weapon to fend off the strike of the third man.

Out of the corner of his eye, he saw Ebana sneak through the adjoining room and motion silently to Aitye and Nefe, who followed him out. *At least if I die, she will be safe. Please, Amun-Re, let that be the case. I must fight to give them enough time to escape the camp.*

He sunk his dagger into his captive's back, wrenched the sword from his hand, and yanked his dagger from the deadly wound.

Two men down.

He spun the dagger in his hand as he picked up his khopesh. Zuzulli stood watching and spoke to his last guard. "Do not let him best you, Tuwattaziti."

Zuzulli had swished his cloak back and held his own sword in his hand. "You will pay for the deaths you caused tonight, Canaanite. I will make sure you have a long death, one you will beg me for."

Paaten smirked. He had heard that many times before from his Hittite captors in his youth. "I will surely kill you before that," he muttered under his breath just as Tuwattaziti attacked. This man struck harder than Paaten and rivaled his size and strength. His blade clashed with Paaten's as he blocked Paaten's upward attack of the dagger. *Quick, too. Do not underestimate your opponent*, Paaten told himself and pushed the man from the blade lock.

He glanced at Zuzulli, who had taken a step forward. He knew the man's pride kept him from calling additional soldiers. He would only do that if it were the last option he had to save his life. Paaten had to kill him next, and fast, before he could sound an alarm.

At least that gives Nefe and Aitye more time to get away.

They circled each other until Tuwattaziti stood in front of Zuzulli. Tuwattaziti lunged, but Paaten parried the strike with his khopesh. In a fluid response, he struck Tuwattaziti with his dagger, stabbing the guard's arm before spinning away, leaving his side vulnerable to Zuzulli. The swoosh of air that precedes a strike sounded as Zuzulli's blade came for his head. Paaten ducked, and the ring of bronze slicing through the air reverberated in his ear. Paaten rose again to block Zuzulli's second strike with his dagger; the dagger's blade locked with the hilt of the sword.

Tuwattaziti bounded for him again, and Paaten swung his khopesh, clashing bronze against bronze. He pushed Zuzulli away and swung his khopesh at Tuwattaziti's midsection, but the hooked blade barely missed its target, leaving Tuwattaziti's split tunic as its only trophy.

The two men lunged for Paaten at the same time. He swung his khopesh and locked their two blades in its hook, giving him the opportunity to thrust the dagger at Zuzulli's throat. It missed. Zuzulli jumped back and kicked Paaten in his open side, sending him into the back of the tent. "I am young, and I am fierce, old man," he taunted and chuckled. "I shall have fun dispatching y—"

Paaten threw his dagger, and it hit him square in the face. Zuzulli fell to his knees and then to his side with a thud.

Tuwattaziti's head snapped to his lord. "You fight like a coward, Canaanite."

Paaten stood on his feet and swung his khopesh in a show of dominance. "A coward? Perhaps. But I am alive, and he is dead."

"I shall bring your head to the—"

Paaten lunged, but Tuwattaziti blocked the

khopesh hook from taking off his arm. Instead of countering with a thrust of his sword, he used his weight and rushed Paaten with his shoulder, sending them both to the floor. The big Hittite knocked the breath from Paaten's chest as he fell atop him. Paaten wished for his bronze armor as he anticipated the punch to his ribs. A painful moan escaped him upon contact. He sent a fist into the side of Tuwattaziti's head, knocking the brute off of him.

Paaten reached for his dagger in Zuzulli's face, but his fingers just brushed the handle as Tuwattaziti landed a punch of his own. Paaten's lip sprayed blood as he sent his elbow into Tuwattaziti's nose. The stars from the night had fallen into the room as Paaten shook his head and stood up, dazed from Tuwattaziti's hit.

What was I doing? Zuzulli's lifeless body lay in front of him. *Dagger. Dagger. Get the dagger.*

He bent down to grab it, but Tuwattaziti tackled him; they fell through the draped wall and into the adjoining room.

The rip of fabric seared Paaten's ears as he wrestled with Tuwattaziti under the heavy drapes.

"You boys, stop destroying my war tent!" Pulli's gruff old voice called. "They are only Canaanite women; surely they are not that hard to subdue!"

Paaten's hands wrapped around Tuwattaziti's throat, and he squeezed. His knees pinned his attacker's arms by his side. He held on until the man no longer moved. He pulled the dagger from

Tuwattaziti's belt and sliced through the drape, leaving him to stand before Governor Pulli.

"You?"

But before he could yell out, Paaten leapt for him, stabbing him in the chest. "You will die as your sons," Paaten spoke in the Hittite tongue. "You will never again take another woman by force." He lifted Pulli by his neck, pulled the dagger out, and stabbed him again, twisting the blade at the hilt. "That is for Niwa, you filth."

"Niwa?" he croaked as his fingertips just barely brushed the handle of his iron blade.

A small movement out of the corner of his eye drew his attention. Two servant boys sat frozen. They watched with bloodless faces.

"Say nothing, and I will spare you."

They nodded with jaws agape, staring at their Hittite warlord gasping for air and clawing at Paaten in vain.

Paaten leaned into Pulli's face, lifting him higher so the iron weapon was no threat. "How does it feel to be helpless as another takes what they want from you?" He left the dagger in his chest, hoping to extend his suffering. They locked eyes before Pulli's gaze retreated within himself in search of the woman who had written his death sentence. One hand plopped on Paaten's shoulders and the other gripped the handle of the dagger in his chest. His gaze returned to the present.

"Niwa."

The old governor's memory had not forsaken him, and Paaten grinned in smug victory as he twisted the handle of the blade once more. "Yes, for Niwa."

An ugly grimace sprang upon Pulli's face as a cry came out in a harrowing breath. His nails dug into Paaten's tunic, and tears of pain pierced his eyes.

"This is a justified kill," Paaten muttered. As soon as he had said it, something behind him moved, and as he turned to look, Tuwattaziti lunged for him with another dagger raised. Rage filled the whites of his bloodshot eyes.

Time ground to a halt in the one moment he had left. His life flashed before his eyes. Niwa and his son smiled at him as they stood in front of their estate in Damaski, waiting for him. They each held smiles on their faces and ran to him, welcoming him home. His son buried his face into his neck as he took Niwa in arm and placed his lips to hers . . . *I must return home. The dreams will not end like this.* He had no time to pull the dagger from Pulli's chest and use it to defend himself, so he raised his hand to block the force of the blow, knowing the strike would leave him severely wounded and vulnerable at the next attack.

But Tuwattaziti's face contorted. He stumbled, and the dagger slipped from his hand as its downward fatal strike was rendered harmless. The brute crumpled to the ground at Paaten's feet, knocking his shoulder against Paaten's on the way down; an arrow was neatly lodged in his back at the base of his neck.

An arrow? Paaten peered over his shoulder. Atinuk stood in the first room with a bow and a newly acquired Hittite quiver of arrows strapped to his back. He scanned the two Governor's sons and peered at the Governor with the dagger in his chest. "Are you done? Let's go. You made me kill a man, and I am tired of saving you." He shook his head and turned to leave.

Paaten smirked with a snort; he did not think the man had it in him to sneak back into camp with a single arrow to save them. But he had been surprised before.

He dropped Pulli into his bed of cushions, leaving him to gasp for his last painful breaths. "Like father, like son," he muttered, recalling Kalli's gurgling. But before Paaten stepped from the room, he spotted his heavy travel sling lying in the corner of the tent and noted one servant boy had slipped out. Their time was now considerably shortened. He snatched his sling and picked up his khopesh in the next room before he left in the shadows.

He stepped out of the tent and found the Berytians had run off. Ebana and Senenmut were with Atinuk, Aitye and Nefe at the end of the alleyway. Paaten ran to catch up with them, jumping over the five soldiers' bodies that littered the path to them.

Atinuk tapped Ebana's shoulder once Paaten caught up, and they silently headed east toward the lands of Canaan. They slipped into the thickening fog, keeping a light touch of each other so they would not lose one another amid the growing chaos and rumors of the Governor's death in the night.

"There!" a Hittite yelled. Paaten froze and saw the dark silhouettes of soldiers running toward the west. "Escaped Berytians! The others must be close!" The Hittite soldiers all ran west past Paaten and the others in the low-visibility fog. "They run toward the sea. They run toward Berytus."

Stupid Berytians. I told them to stay with us. At least their lives will provide us an easy escape. Paaten pulled Nefe along behind him as they slunk to the edge of camp. Atinuk swiped some more arrows for his stolen quiver on his way out.

When they cleared the Hittites and the land began to rise toward the heavens, Ebana and Senenmut dipped their chins to Paaten. "May Amun-Re bless you in your oath to our late Pharaoh."

They knelt before Nefe and bowed their heads. "May Amun-Re bless you, Daughter of the King." They stood up and disappeared into the fog to go around the Hittite camp toward the Egyptian line.

Paaten smiled, knowing in his heart they would keep their word. *Tefnut and Shu, this would not have been possible without you. Thank you for your aid—for saving us.*

Perhaps the gods did want him to make it back to Niwa. Perhaps they had released him of his oath so he could return to his wife forever. That thought brought peace to his ka as he guided the group to ascend the mountain pass. He squinted in the moonlit fog, trying to make out the path or even differentiate between rock and tree. *Curse my age. I wish I had my young eyes again.*

NEFE WATCHED EBANA AND SENENMUT RUN OFF into the fog. Part of her desired to go with them. There were still people in Egypt who were loyal to her and her mother. They had risked their lives to save her, had they not? Why was she running to Canaan? Away from her homeland? All because Atinuk said he had a shared land for them?

Must be the same blind trust that allowed my mother to be killed. At the end of all of this, it will have been for naught. Death probably awaits us in Damaski too.

Paaten tugged on her long sleeve. "King's Daughter, we must continue."

She took a step on the inclined land and followed Paaten's footsteps in front of her. *Not that I care.* She shrugged. *Not that I care.*

Aitye walked beside her and gripped her hand. "One moment, Paaten," Aitye said as she cupped Nefe's cheeks and kissed her on her forehead. Tears filled her eyes. "I am so glad you are safe. I could not lose you too."

Aitye had reached into her chest and squeezed her heart. Nefe said nothing and did nothing, except turn away. If she did not start walking, she would crumple to the ground. If she spoke, a cry would fall out of her mouth. Aitye's muffled screams filled her mind. She had cowered next to the post envisioning the horrors befalling Aitye in the next room— knowing it would soon happen to her. Her mind had taken her to the tunnel filled with Ankhesenpaaten's screams.

It seemed tonight was another night that had happened all too quickly. She had tried to escape on her own and failed. Her eyes fell on Paaten's feet. He had saved her. Yet, here she was again running for her life with him, along with Aitye and Atinuk. Atinuk had come back for them, though. He could have left them.

"We need to put as much distance as we can between the Hittite camp and our location," Paaten warned in a gentle goading.

"Agreed," Atinuk said behind her.

Walk! she wanted to scream, but she could not bring herself to look at Aitye.

Paaten walked up the mountain pass, and Nefe followed. Aitye tried to grab her hand as she passed her, but Nefe yanked her hand away.

It is better like this, Aitye. Neither of us has to hurt when one of us is killed. I cannot be alone again. Not like that.

CHAPTER 24
ESCAPE FROM THE FOG

THE FOG ONLY GREW THICKER. "PAATEN, ARE YOU sure this is the way?" Atinuk's whisper came.

Paaten squinted as he looked up into the black fog. Only a sliver of moonlight fell through in an eerie haze of light. Without the stars, he could not tell if he was headed in the right direction, and his vision failed him at night. Surely, they were in Canaan lands by now. They had walked a great distance; perhaps aimlessly, but he knew he had to get them away from the Hittites.

He adjusted his sling on his shoulder. "We will make camp here," he said over his shoulder, but he turned and searched the land in front of him once more.

"Where is it?" he muttered to himself as he squinted and strained to hear rushing water. *The river past the river in the valley will lead us to Damaski. We should at least hear the first river by now.*

An unsettling thought gnawed at his stomach. What if he had made them lost in this fog? What if they had been going north into the land of Hatti?

Goddess Tefnut, please show me the valley. Please lift the fog, and let me see the valley.

Aitye touched his elbow, and he jumped. "We are to make camp here as you said?" she asked him. "We cannot do much more tonight."

He looked out into the dense fog. "We cannot. I just hope we are deep enough within the mountain pass to avoid the Hittites and Egyptians. Let us hope they war with each other by the sea and do not venture here."

The air was crisper in the pass; the breeze whipped through the peaks. Although he was glad his long tunic covered his legs and arms, the wind still pierced him. A shiver made his muscles tighten. He turned to his small clan as the women sat on the ground. Nefe's teeth chattered. Aitye sat next to her, rubbing her arms. Atinuk caught his gaze.

"We will not survive the cold here, Paaten. Not like this in the mountains."

"I know," he muttered and again looked for anything that was familiar. His army had traveled through the pass before from Berytus to Damaski. They had traveled from Kubna to Damaski, around the mountains to Damaski. He knew the land, but in the fog, with no stars to guide him, he was lost. "There is a cave somewhere. I have stayed there before."

Atinuk sighed. "We need to make a fire. I will find some wood."

Paaten's chin dropped to his chest. They had used all the reed sandals during their stay in the cliff cave. *Wasted resources for a temporary comfort.*

Paaten shook his head. "No, do not leave without a means to find your way back." Paaten dropped his sling and pulled out the long, blood-stained rope. He handed one end to Atinuk. "In case you cannot see in the fog to return."

Atinuk grinned.

"What?"

"You do trust me." Atinuk wrapped his waist with the rope and knotted it.

Paaten kept a stony visage, but a temporary chuckle in his heart returned. "I trust no one."

"Of course, Paaten." Atinuk began to walk away.

"You only came back to the Hittite camp to save Aitye," Paaten spoke in Akkadian.

Atinuk waved him off. "I came back for all of you."

"With one arrow," Paaten goaded.

Atinuk peered over his shoulder. "I got more."

"Well, now go get some wood."

Atinuk chuckled. "I know you care about me," he muttered as he walked off. Paaten tied his end of the rope around his waist and rummaged through the travel sling. He pulled out the blankets, the bow drill, and the cooking pot. He sighed, placing the bronze pot against his head. The reason they had left the cave while still not completely healed: no food.

"We need food."

Aitye got up and grabbed the rope. "I will tell him." She disappeared into the fog as Paaten handed Nefe her blanket. She wrapped it around her shoulders and drew her legs to her chest.

Paaten began to arrange some nearby stones into a circle. Paaten shook his head. *We have no water either.* They did have the wine from his sling, but that was it. He glanced to Nefe, who stared at him.

"Do you wish to speak to me, Daughter of the King?" he asked as he pulled up the dry grass around the stones and laid the pieces within the ring.

She nodded but remained mute.

"What do you wish to say?" Paaten sat back on his heels. He thought about starting the fire, even though he knew the grass would burn quickly. The fire would hopefully fend off any animals that might attack in the night, but it might also draw the eye of any passing soldier. He would have to make a fire—they would not survive without it.

He grabbed the bow drill and began attempting to start the fire. At least there would be some warmth for the princess.

"I did not think you would save me," she whispered as he successfully got an ember glowing a few moments later.

Paaten blew on the small ember with a gentle

breath and then raised his head to look at her, surprised at her statement.

"I tried to get away, but the servant caught me. He bound my legs." Nefe pulled the blanket tighter. "I heard Aitye's muffled screaming, and I knew I would be next. There was nothing I could do."

"I am sorry, Daughter of—"

"No, you do not understand."

Paaten closed his mouth and returned to nurturing the flame before the breeze blew it out.

"I thought you would fail, like you failed my mother. I never heard my mother scream, but I did hear Ankhesenpaaten's screams in the tunnel. Her screams haunt my dreams—they haunt me while I am awake."

"You have been through many hardships, my princess." Paaten added more grass to the dying flame and bent down to give it more air.

She nodded. "I know you see me as a burden, but I want to thank you for saving me."

Paaten again lifted his head. "I do not see you as a burden."

"Then what do you see me as?"

He leaned over and grasped her hand. Locking eyes with her, he said, "I see you as the daughter to my friend, Pharaoh Neferneferuaten. You bear her name; you have her resemblance. I see you in part as my redemption for failing her. I see you in part as a young woman who has lost too much too soon. You are someone I wish to comfort, but I do not know how."

The fire flickered. Paaten averted his eyes and released her to throw more grass on the small smoking sliver of fire.

"I do not think I can be comforted. I feel lost inside; there is a void—an emptiness. My family is gone." Nefe closed her eyes, but no tears fell. "Aitye told me there is a difference between knowing and accepting. I know they are gone, but I cannot accept it."

"In time, you will." He chewed his lip as he stared at Nefe. He debated telling Nefe of accepting his life: time without Niwa and his son. He had known what he had to do for the gods and Pharaoh, and in accepting that, he would miss out on years of his life with them. But if the plague had taken them or if Niwa had married Washuba or another, he did not want Nefe's sympathy. She already had too many tribulations to work through without fearing for the stability of her protector. If Niwa lived and was still his, he would ask her to adopt Nefe.

"It is hard to believe it." Nefe pulled the blanket near her ears.

Paaten reached over and laid a heavy hand on Nefe's shoulder once more. "You are young. You have your whole life ahead of you. I know we will never replace your family, but our clan right here, we look out for each other."

She stared at him before furrowing her brow. "But you said you do not trust Atinuk."

"Eh," Paaten shrugged with a smirk and shook her shoulder. "Any man who willingly returns to a Hittite camp with a single arrow to help save someone is worth trusting." He eyed the fog where Aitye disappeared. "A foolish, but . . . honorable man." His hand left her shoulder, and he continued his attempt to keep the fire going. "One arrow," he chuckled. *Yet, that one arrow saved my life.*

CHAPTER 25
ESCAPE FROM PAST DEEDS

ATINUK HEARD SOMETHING MOVE BEHIND HIM. Footsteps, maybe. The rope tugged lightly around his waist. *Is it an animal? A bear, a wolf, a striped hyena? Those little devils only come out at night.*

He dropped his gathered wood, pulled an arrow from his quiver, and rested it against the nocking point of his bow. He turned around and lifted his bow, not yet drawing the arrow back. But the footsteps sounded familiar, so he lowered his bow.

"Atinuk?" a familiar low voice called.

His heart fell, as did his shoulders. "Aitye, what are you doing? I almost shot an arrow at you." He quickly returned his arrow to the quiver and his bow across his shoulder.

"I am sorry, Atinuk. I told Paaten I would tell you that we need food." She emerged from the fog; the moonlight outlined her silhouette.

"I do not know how I will hunt in this." He

looked around. "And I cannot make out the plants in this moonlight; I do not want to chance foraging a poisonous plant."

"We may have to go hungry tonight, then. At least we ate this morning." She followed the rope straight to him and rested her forehead on his chest, pressing her hands on his waist.

His heart skipped a beat as he swallowed the immediate lump in his throat at her bold actions. "Yes, and hopefully we will eat again tomorrow," he whispered.

Is she making her feelings toward me clear, or is she simply cold? He wrapped his arms about her shivering body.

He placed his chin on the top of her head. "Forgive me, Aitye. I should never have left you there in the Hittite camp."

"They were going to kill you, Atinuk." Her hands slid to his back and pulled him close. Her cheek pressed against his chest.

Did she fear for my life, as I feared for hers?

"No, I was a coward."

"You came back to rescue all of us. A coward would have stayed away. Only a fool would have tried to fight all of those Hittites there as we stood."

He ran his hands down her back as she looked up to him. He paused, trying to read her face from the shadows that fell from the moonlight. *Does she not want me to rub her back? Is she simply cold?*

"Did . . . did they hurt you?" He took a chance

and lowered his forehead to hers. She did not pull away.

"Almost." Tears formed in her eyes and glistened in the soft light.

He shifted on his feet. *What to say? I was almost too late once again, but when I arrived, she was dressed and wiping her tears while holding Nefe.* "When did Paaten—"

"He saved me before the Hittite could . . . " Her voice trailed off. "Paaten did not stare at my nakedness."

Atinuk winced. They had stripped her. "Forgive me, Aitye. I should have come sooner. I was waiting for nightfall."

"You came when you could, and I am grateful."

"I am glad Paaten saved you when I was too late. I am thankful for him." He sighed. "Even though he still does not trust me and thinks I wish harm upon him and Nefe, I am glad he is here with us. Although it was his foolish idea to sail north—"

She placed a finger on his lips. "He did what he thought was best. How could we have known about the storm or the Hittites in Berytus?" Her finger dropped, and her body shivered in his embrace. He tightened his arms about her. "We could have been caught and killed if we had disembarked at Azzati, too. We will never know, but what I do know, right now, is that I am safe and in the arms of someone I have come to care for."

His heart leapt, and warmth radiated through his

core. Atinuk smiled at the declaration, and in the heady rush that overcame his will, he lowered his lips toward hers. But before they touched, Aitye whispered, "Even though I think you have not told me everything."

He stopped in his advance and pulled back. "I have not." He kissed her forehead and decided he would tell her what pertained to her. "I hope it does not change the way you feel about me."

"You defended me from the Cypriotes at Per-Amun, you pulled me from the waters, you bandaged my wounds, you saved us from the Hittites, and you comforted me in my sorrow. What have you done that would overshadow all of these things?" Her whisper warmed his neck.

He took a deep breath and kissed her forehead once more in case she decided what he had done nullified the past months with him. "I spent a long time in the palace after the plague took Tadukhipa. Pawah tasked me to watch the stewards of Pharaoh and his Queen, to log everyone's comings and goings, and report back to him."

He paused, hoping she would not think ill of him, but she said nothing. "I saw you about six years ago. I" —he stuttered as a sheepish grin hid in the shadows of the moonlight— "I thought you were beautiful. I watched you often." He averted his eyes. "I learned a lot about you."

She shifted her weight on her feet, and her

shoulders rose to hide her neck. "What did you learn?"

"It was my task to watch you and the others," he said, buffering his response.

Her question came again. "What did you learn?"

He did not want to tell her what he had learned about her through unconventional means, but he knew the time was coming. "I did not think it was possible to see a life with someone you have never spoken to, but . . . " His words seemed jumbled as they came off his tongue. "I watched you for years, which I know is odd to say." He hesitated and paused, searching her eyes in the moonlight for any indication of anger.

"It is, but it was your task to do so?"

"Yes," he whispered.

"Then tell me, what did you learn?" She searched him for truth.

"I learned you are loyal, dedicated, and understanding; you ran the other stewards with a firm-but-gentle hand. I never saw you with a husband or children, but I did see you with the royal daughters."

"And that is why you care for me?"

He hesitated, putting off the answer to her question. "Pawah, or, rather, his followers, approached you several times to turn you against your Pharaoh. You would not give her up, even to gain your freedom." He rubbed the outside of her arms and smiled out of half his mouth. "So loyal, so pure."

Her gaze fell to his half-smile before it faded. She lifted her face and studied him. There was another question hidden in her eyes: *What else are you not telling me?*

He chewed his lip and decided to come out with it. There was no holding back—not if he wanted any kind of a relationship with her. The truth, he figured, was better than a lie.

"I heard you pray to Hathor for the children one day. I heard you pray for Meritaten when she was Queen. I heard your prayers, Aitye. Your unbelievably selfless prayers." He knew her next question before she asked.

"You watched me while I was in the stewards' chambers? While I prayed?" Her voice shook with uncertainty.

"No, I listened. At night, I was supposed to listen to conversations and report back to Pawah anything I had found out of the ordinary or any points of frustration with Pharaoh. I assume he wanted to know whom he could persuade to be a follower." He rubbed her arms as her hands dropped by her sides. "I know I have done wrong."

"Is there anything else?" Her tone was as cold as the air. Her body stood as rigidly as the trees that surrounded them.

He dropped his hands as well. "No." A weight fell

LAUREN LEE MEREWETHER

to the pit of his stomach. *Am I losing her? Is she rescinding her care for me?*

She grabbed the rope at his waist and spun around to walk away.

No! I cannot lose her.

He pleaded. "Please, Aitye."

She stopped, her shoulders rising with each breath.

"Aitye, I knew I loved you the moment I heard your prayer for your mother's ka. You had prayed the same prayer many times before, but there was the one time when I realized my feelings for you. I sat in the corridor, as I had every night for several years, where the women's voices in the steward's chambers traveled over the stone." He stood behind her and whispered, "I knew your voice."

She peered at him over her shoulder.

"You told Pawah all of my private conversations with the other stewards; you told him of my prayers, my most personal—" She held her breath as she struggled to find the right words. "You let Pawah use my words to kill Pharaoh."

"No," he whispered and guided her to face him again. "I never told him anything. I said the stewards of the Queen were loyal, which they were. All of them, and I am sure it was because of your example."

She stood; her teeth chattered. "You heard all of my innermost . . . " She shook her head and crossed her arms over her chest, taking a step backward.

He stepped closer to her and again grasped the

286

sides of her arms. "You never wanted anyone to hear, but I did. I heard. I heard all the prayers from all the stewards. I heard all the conversations. You were the only one who was truly pure and selfless, unwavering, genuine." He leaned forward, rubbing her arms again. "Queen, Pharaoh, Egypt, all were lucky to have you as the royal steward. You took on their burdens as if they were your own and prayed for them. I heard the fervor, Aitye."

"But those—" She closed her eyes and shook her head. "Those prayers were mine."

"I am sorry." He lowered his forehead to hers. "I am sorry," he whispered again. "Forgive me. I never thought I would speak to you, let alone be with you. I never let myself see a future with you because I was loyal to a woman who no longer lived among us. I knew even if I were to succeed in providing for the daughters of Nefertiti, you would never be . . . " He was mumbling, speaking to the wind. He stopped talking and shifted his weight on his feet. What he had done was a violation of her and of her faith, and he doubted she would easily forgive him, let alone want to be with him. He hung his head.

But she finished his statement. "You never thought I would be with you on the barge to a future you had planned for Royal Wife Kiya or the daughters of Pharaoh."

He stood before her, pleading a silent forgiveness with a gentle nod of his head.

At least, she understands.

She bit her lip and looked up to the starless sky. The glisten was still in her eyes. "I know why you did it, and I know you thought you would never speak to me." Her gaze fell to him.

He cupped her cheek. The need to strip himself bare before her urged him to speak once more. "But now that you are here with me and we have had these months together, I see that future with you; I *want* that future with you."

Silence.

A vacant stare.

Her arms, still crossed over her chest, readjusted in the cold.

He needed her to say something, anything.

Her jaw twitched before she asked, "If the Hittites had let me go with you but kept Nefe and Paaten, would you have gone back to save them?"

He had asked himself that question too as he sat waiting for nightfall. Though, the question coming from her caught him off guard. Perhaps she wanted to see if he was true to his word or if he valued her life over theirs. Either way, he answered the question with what he had decided earlier in the day. "I would have made sure you were safely tucked away in one of these caves with food, fire and instructions on how to get to Damaski if I had not returned by morning. Then I would have gone back."

She stared at him in the dim moonlight. A slow smile crept across her lips. "I feel vulnerable with you, Atinuk." Her arms stayed crossed across her chest. "You have heard every inner struggle and strife; I kept nothing from the gods—"

"All I know, Aitye, is that you were genuine, real. More real than any of the others." His fingertips brushed her arms. "I do not remember specific prayers, except the ones I already mentioned to you; I just know you never lied about who you were or what you felt. You never prayed for yourself."

After a moment, she lifted a hand to smooth his cheek. "Prayers were not needed for me. I was but a servant."

He covered her hand with his. "A servant who is a queen in another land."

She chuckled. "I do not descend from royalty."

"No . . . but I shall treat you as such," he whispered, locking eyes with her.

He turned his face to her hand and placed a small kiss on her palm.

Her arms uncrossed as she stepped near to him once more, and he again pulled her into an embrace. His chest expanded to accommodate a heavy sigh of relief, and he finally tasted her lips.

CHAPTER 26
ESCAPE FROM THE MOUNTAIN

Niwa's faded jade eyes watched as he knelt before his seven-year-old son and enfolded him in his large arms. Paaten's cheek brushed the hair on his son's head as he squeezed him. A searing pain stabbed his chest as he glanced to his wife. He turned his head and kissed his son on his temple. His eyes burned as he saw a tear run down Niwa's cheek. His son's small hands wrapped around his large back, barely touching his shoulder blades.

"I love you, Father."

His heart ripped open, and the urge to vomit rendered him mute. The only thing he could do was keep his progeny in his embrace. "I love you too, Paebel," he finally whispered.

Niwa stepped forward and placed a hand on Paaten's shoulder.

"We will be here when you return," she

whispered in an unwavering voice, yet her chin trembled.

My wife is so brave and strong, he thought, seeing her resolve to stand tall and keep firm for their son.

He gave Paebel one last kiss and stood to embrace Niwa once more. His lungs filled with the scent of her honey, oil and wine. "Do not allow any inside. The illness is making my men sick and the enemy as well. It is sweeping through the lands; there is talk of plague. Do not take in any more women from the land of Hatti. Do not let Washuba come back until the illness is gone. I have seen it take my men quickly."

"But Paaten, there are many poor women in the land of Hatti. They need this sanctuary. Washuba is their savior. I cannot deny them—"

"Please, Niwa." He held her head in his hands. "Please." He knew he asked for selfish reasons, and he knew she was more selfless than he. "My heart cannot bear the thought of losing you and Paebel to this illness."

"Paaten, you know the life I lived before you came into it. Those women are still living that life. When you left me, I had to find meaning. I had to find something to pass the days, and that was when I knew why you had saved me. I knew then what my purpose was: I have to help these women and their children. The plague will not keep them safe from the Hittite men who wish them harm."

He lowered his forehead to hers and smiled amid tears of his own. He would not change her mind; his request was selfish. She had found a calling—a way to make her suffering worthwhile. He had made her promise to find happiness in Damaski. Saving other women who were in her former plight was her happiness. His son took pride in helping her. How could he ask her again to stop?

"You are a warrior," he whispered, wiping away her tear. "You are stronger than I am."

She wiped his tears with her thumbs. "I will keep Paebel safe. He is your heir. If I am to die, he will inherit everything and live a good life."

"I do not want to lose you," he whispered again and brushed his lips against hers. His General's collar and armor lay by the door of their home. He dreaded putting them on and leaving once more.

"You will never lose me." Her warm breath rested on his lips. He took a deep breath and gave her one last kiss. He pulled Paebel close to them as he ran his fingers through Niwa's long brown locks, letting his lips linger on hers.

"When the Pharaoh of Egypt is a woman, I will return to you forever."

"I hope that day is soon," she whispered and gave him one more soulful kiss. "Until you return again, my love." She cupped his face and then gestured to his Egyptian uniform.

He stooped down to pick up his armor. He slid

it over his head and then tied his collar around his neck. Niwa's hands came to rest on his chest. "I hope you will not be away too long this time. We have been lucky to see you three times in the past four years."

"I hope Pharaoh's Army will be able to return here once the illness is gone." He gave a weak smile; every time he came home, he almost did not return. *Let Pharaoh's Army be*, he would tell himself, but he knew they would come looking for him and kill him for desertion, along with his Hittite family. He ran his hand through Paebel's hair before cupping his cheek. "Take care of your mother for me."

He nodded at his father, tears in his eyes.

Anhur, Pakhet, Hathor, Horus—let my son not hold my absence against me. Let him know why I must leave. Keep him safe from the plague. He turned his gaze to Niwa. *Keep them safe from this plague.*

Imhotep stood outside the home, having knocked already once that morning; he knocked a second time, goading Paaten to make haste. He had probably run out of answers to give the men on their General's whereabouts.

Paaten pressed his mouth upon hers for the last time while Paebel hugged his waist.

A knock came again. And again. And again.

PAATEN'S EYES FLICKERED OPEN. *THAT WAS THE LAST time I saw them.*

A knock came again.

Am I still dreaming? He looked up at the growing sun in the east. *Have I overslept?*

A knock came again.

"Who is there?" he asked in a groggy, gruff tone. His thick tongue ran across his dry lips and mouth. He sat up and saw a man standing over his travel sling.

Paaten's hand gripped his khopesh as he jumped up. "Who are you?" He glanced around to see if there were other strangers present.

He shook his head to get his bearings. This man was dressed as a Hittite, but not as a soldier: a simple tunic, leather curled-toe shoes, a long leather robe, a leather conical hat, and a long thin braid of gray-black hair falling from the back of his head.

The man slowly stood, raising his hands to show he was weaponless. "I mean you no harm," he spoke in a broken Akkadian.

"What are you doing here?"

"You all looked dead, Canaanite." He shrugged and pointed to the fire that had gone out during the night. "I was simply looking for supplies."

Paaten eyed the man. He had seen his face before, except it had aged. "Washuba?"

The man dropped his hands and angled his face at Paaten. His lips pursed, and his brow furrowed. "How do you know me, Canaanite?"

Paaten chuckled and let his khopesh fall. "Washuba. Do you travel to Damaski?"

Washuba narrowed his eyes and ran his gaze over the length of Paaten. "Again I ask you: How do you know me, Canaanite?"

"I am no Canaanite, you Hittite fool." Paaten laughed, but then a sudden dread came over him. Had this man married his wife? Did this man know if his wife and son were still alive? He stopped laughing in an instant.

His three companions stirred on the ground; Atinuk awoke, disoriented.

"Who is a fool?" Washuba's hand went to his belt.

"Washuba." Paaten held up his hand to halt him, knowing he had no weapon, and even if he did, he was not going to use it. The Washuba he knew had left the Hittite army long ago; he had deserted, abhorring the fighting and the killing. He found the little house Paaten had built for Niwa and took refuge in it until Pigat found him there. It was then that Niwa and Washuba decided to enter the smuggling trade—except they were smuggling poor, abused women out of the land of Hatti and into her estate at Damaski.

Paaten eyed the now-older gentleman and his plump belly. *Is this man married to my Niwa? Did this man bury my Niwa and Paebel?*

Atinuk jumped to his feet, distracting Paaten from his recounting and his fears. Atinuk grabbed his bow and threw his quiver over his shoulder. "Are we under attack?" he asked, looking around.

"Doubtful; this man does not fight." Paaten gestured toward Washuba and sat back down. He stretched out his legs to thaw the prior night's cold from them. He winced. His blanket provided almost no warmth, or at least, it felt like it did nothing.

Washuba again eyed Paaten, and, after taking note of his size, his eyes widened in recognition. "Paaten?"

A smirk popped onto Paaten's face.

Washuba snorted and let his hand fall from his belt.

Aitye and Nefe awoke and sat up straight at the presence of a Hittite in their camp.

"Have they come for us?" Aitye's voice shook as she grabbed Nefe to shield her from Washuba.

"No," Paaten answered in Egyptian, and then spoke to Washuba in Akkadian, "You have not returned to your life as a soldier, have you?"

Washuba used both hands to wave off the notion. "I shall never return to that life."

Paaten stared at him, recalling Niwa's description of Washuba on that day he had come back to her and found out what they had been doing for the women in Hatti. She had said Washuba made her laugh and had never killed a soul. There had been a gleam in her eye. Paaten swallowed. *I have made my wife cry more times than not, and I have killed many men.*

His stare turned vacant as he revisited his mind's

imaginings of Niwa with Washuba. She had said she did not love him, but Paaten had been gone for nine years. *A lot can change in that time.*

Atinuk glanced back and forth between the Hittite and Paaten. "How do you know this Hittite?"

The question seemed to replay in Paaten's ears as he turned his attention to the present. "He—" Paaten cut himself off. What would he tell them? They were a four-day walk from his home. He had not told any of them about his life in Damaski. He glanced at Nefe, Aitye, and, lastly, at Atinuk. They had trusted him, and yet he had withheld this secret from them.

"He is an old friend," Washuba said, patting Paaten on the shoulder. He looked around. "I see you have no food."

Paaten ignored his statement, focusing instead on the threat of the night prior. "Have you seen the Hittite army?"

"Yes, they are acting foolishly. Their formations are embarrassing. It is as if Governor Pulli's age finally caught up to him." Washuba chuckled and shook his head.

Paaten stilled as Atinuk opened his mouth to speak. Paaten cut him off, not wanting Washuba to know he had killed the Hittite Governor and his two sons; Washuba knew Paaten was in Pharaoh's Army, but he did not like to talk of the killing. "I see; so there are no soldiers coming up the mountain pass?"

"No," Washuba chuckled. "No, they are down there by the sea acting like fools."

"Good. Let us keep some distance in between us and them just to be sure we do not have to run into them again."

"Paaten, we have gone a full day and night without food. We need to eat. At least, Aitye and Nefe do." Atinuk gestured toward the women.

"I have food," Washuba offered. "My cart is a little ways off, down the pass. I will bring it up. I have some travelers with me." He looked at Paaten and then threw a wary eye at Atinuk.

"He is trustworthy," Paaten said. Then he switched to the Hittite tongue. "He loves this one," Paaten said, nodding his head toward Aitye.

Washuba chuckled, responding in the Hittite language as well. "Your Hittite is rusty, friend." He patted Paaten's shoulder again. "Come with me. We have much to discuss."

Paaten stood and told Atinuk in Egyptian, "Stay with the women. I will return with Washuba and his cart of food."

Atinuk only eyed Paaten. "I did not realize you spoke Hittite."

"I was held captive there for two years. I know a little." Paaten shrugged and left with Washuba.

When they were a ways off, Washuba scoffed. "You should work on your Hittite. It is not very good anymore."

Paaten pursed his lips at the jab. "The only thing I can say perfectly is: I will never hurt the woman who saved me." His mouth turned up into a small half-grin at the memory. He peered at Washuba. He remained afraid to ask if his family still lived, but he desperately needed to know the answer.

"Yes, but you hurt her quite a bit," Washuba said as he moseyed along the trail. He looked off at the fog-covered sea in the west.

Paaten's half-grin fell flat. "I know I did."

"No, you do not know." He thrust his hand into Paaten's chest, stopping him in his tracks. "We thought you were dead, Paaten."

Paaten's heart lifted. "We? Are Niwa and Paebel alive?"

Washuba nodded once. He looked back at the sea and the terrain around them, as if he debated telling him something. His gaze finally came to rest on Paaten. "She mourned you, friend. Three years went by, five, six, seven. No word from Mai or Imhotep. Nothing." He shook his head. "She kept having dreams of you with her. Then she accepted your death. Then she told herself that you were alive. Then she accepted your death, but then she again told herself you were alive. When the woman Pharaoh took the throne three years ago, she thought you would return any day, but you did not. The last I know, she had accepted your death."

"She accepted it?" Paaten swallowed the lump in his throat. "Has she . . . has she then married another?"

"You worry about this now? Where was your worry nine years ago or even five years ago?"

The hard edge to Washuba's voice and the lack of an answer to his question made Paaten think the worst. He stared at Washuba. Had this man married her? Had there been someone else?

Washuba rubbed a circle on his chest to calm himself. "I held her as she cried, Paaten."

Paaten held his breath as he listened. Had Washuba stolen his wife?

"She is such a strong woman of both will and character. She was faithful to you." He scoffed. "You who turned her—"

"Was?" His voice was weak, as were his knees.

He shook his head. "She still is."

"So she has not married another?"

"No."

He closed his eyes and hung his head in relief. "I have been faithful to her as well."

Washuba brushed off his statement. "She is a beautiful, rich woman with a husband most believe to be dead. She has had many opportunities. Many suitors come to her, but each time, she always tells them her husband is away. She told me about your agreement in your marriage, should she want out."

"And?" Paaten asked, taking note of his fidgeting hands.

"I tried to persuade her to do so."

Paaten took a step back. "Why would you do that, my friend? Why would you persuade her to tell the city I have died when there was no word?"

He dropped his hands to his sides and

straightened his back. "Because I loved her, Paaten." His confession came out bold and without shame.

Paaten blinked a few times, trying to understand the statement from his so-called friend.

"I wanted a life with her." He crossed his arms over his chest and shook his head viciously. "You did not see her. You were not there. She wept in my arms many times. She stood tall and strong, but, behind closed doors, she wept. Your son watched his mother mourn his father time and time again, and after every instance she convinced herself you were still alive."

Paaten shifted on his feet as his thoughts drifted to the ruined letters in his travel sling. "I could not send Mai or Imhotep with a message. I had no way to get a message to her." The stabbing pain in his chest caused a wave of nausea to pass over his stomach. He had not been good to Niwa, and she hurt because of him. *After I promised to never hurt her.* "Egypt is fragile; the throne is . . ." His voice trailed off. "I know there is no excuse."

Washuba began to walk again. "Well, you are alive, and she has been faithful to you . . . " His voice trailed off, and he stopped and turned to face Paaten. "You did your best for her, and I honor you for that."

Paaten took note of the break in his voice and the momentary aversion of his eyes. "There is something you are not telling me."

Washuba winced. "Well, I suppose I should just come out with it—I kissed her, and she let me." Washuba lifted his chin. "You should know." He let out a deep breath, as if the burden on his chest was somehow lifted.

Paaten stood frozen. All of the moments envisioning his wife with another man hit him. He had written off Washuba for the most part after she told him she did not love Washuba, but now he firmly placed Washuba's face onto the faceless man in his imaginings. He closed his eyes and rubbed his brow. His other hand curled into a fist. War waged within him. He had caused her to fall into the arms of another man. He had hurt her. He had left her wondering if he was alive. Washuba kissed her. Washuba was her comfort in his stead. Washuba was there when he was not. Washuba kissed her . . . and she let him.

"How . . . " His words would not come. There was not even a question associated with the word he spoke. But one question swelled within him: Did it end with a kiss? But he feared the answer and whether or not he could refrain from killing the man after his response.

Washuba sighed and crossed his arms again. He kicked a small stone with his leather-covered toe. "I thought you were dead, Paaten. I loved her, and she was hurting. I could not bear to see her in pain. I thought if she could see a life with someone else—me —then she would not hurt as much."

Paaten's question still remained unspoken.

"I owe you the truth, at least," Washuba continued. "I have tried to be an honorable man my entire life, and I am sorry I dishonored you and your wife. I should have stayed away until I knew for certain you were dead." He looked up to the heavens, glanced at the mountaintop, and pursed his lips. "I loved her so much. I know there is no excuse."

A swirl of rage coursed within Paaten, but instead of taking action, he took a shaky breath. "You loved her, or you love her?"

"I will always love her, Paaten. She gave meaning to my meaningless life, but I have found another wife whom I love. We built a house on your land, and we live there together."

Paaten's hand dropped from his brow to his jaw. They locked eyes.

"It was only a kiss—nothing more. When she realized what we were doing . . . she stopped it. She confined herself to her room. After the winter, I left for the land of Hatti in search of more women who wanted sanctuary in Canaan. When I returned, she acted as if nothing had happened between us."

Paaten's muscles loosened, and his spine slumped. "How long ago?"

"Three, almost four years. On that trip I found the woman who would become my wife. We married two years ago." Washuba drew a deep breath and uncrossed his arms.

Paaten nodded and pressed his mouth into a flat smile. "I am happy for you."

Washuba nodded.

Silence.

They stood staring at each other for a long time until Washuba's question came: "Are we at peace, you and I?"

Paaten gritted his teeth and rubbed his jaw. He stared at Washuba for a while longer before nodding.

Washuba averted his eyes. "Good. I am glad." He turned to walk toward his cart, and Paaten followed. "And you should also know your land is now a shared land of sorts."

Paaten nodded, hearing him but not listening. Except . . . two words stuck in the back of his mind. "Shared land?" he repeated.

"Niwa began calling her land 'the shared land' about a year or so after the last time you left."

"Well, perhaps she wanted to call it that because of all the Hittite women who lived on her land and in the house I built."

Washuba chuckled. "There are several more houses on your land now, Paaten, but that is not what I reference."

"What are you saying then, Washuba? Be plain."

"Over the years, there have been a few who claim to be descendants of Danel, but there was one whom Niwa took into her house with your son. They stayed in there for almost a full day. I was not there; this had come from Donatiya . . . you remember Pigat's daughter?"

"Yes," Paaten nodded and urged him on with a gesture of his hand.

"Donatiya said he had come, stayed, and left. Ever since, Niwa has called her land a 'shared land.'"

"So did he take his inheritance?"

"I do not know. He left before I returned. I think the plague got him, for he never came back."

"Do you know his name?"

"Niwa never said." He shook his head. "She said she would take care of it when he returned."

"What does that mean?" Paaten's head inclined at the accusatory tone in his voice.

"I do not know."

"What are you implying?"

"Niwa became a different person over the years. Rougher. Firmer. More aggressive. She had to. She had no man in Canaan to defend her; she had to be assertive to defend your land against the thieves and against the men in Damaski who wanted Danel's land for themselves. The servants, Pigat and Keret, and your son are with her at all times to defend against accusations of infidelity. The people are ruthless, Paaten. They have made her . . . more callous."

Washuba shook his head. "She said she would take care of it . . . " His voice trailed off. "He was not the first man to come claiming relationship to Danel. Those men never returned either."

Paaten's eyes narrowed at the man who had held his wife in her sorrow and at the implied impugnment of her honor. "Are you saying she killed them?"

"No. Niwa would never kill anyone," Washuba

scoffed, but then he lowered his head. "But she had admirers in Damaski who would do anything for a chance to gain her favor. She is a rich woman and probably one of the most powerful women in Damaski. The other rich women have their husbands to speak for them. She speaks for herself, and the city elders listen. It is quite uncommon for—"

"Do not speak about my wife in this way, Washuba. You already dishonor her with your kiss and now with your words?" Paaten shoved him on the arm. "You think she ordered their murder?"

He lifted his hands in innocence. "All I am saying is that when I returned, she began referring to her land as a shared land, and she said she would *take care* of the man claiming to be a descendant of Danel."

"But he never came back?" he asked Washuba.

"No."

Paaten glanced over his shoulder and looked up the pass at the three shadowy figures in the rising sun. He hummed in thought.

"Shared land," he whispered under his breath.

CHAPTER 27
ESCAPE FROM DOUBT

"His name is Washuba." Atinuk peered down the mountain pass as he wrapped a blanket around Aitye's shoulders.

"What does he want?" Aitye asked, following Atinuk's line of sight.

Nefe's stomach rumbled, and she pressed her hands against her belly. *Atinuk said this Washuba has food.* She stared at Paaten and Washuba, who were walking up the hill. A donkey-pulled cart rolled behind them. Two women walked beside the cart, one on each side of it.

"He said he is a friend to Paaten," Atinuk said and shook his head. "I do not know him."

Nefe noticed the women's hands and faces were wrapped in linens underneath their headscarves. "Why do they wear bandages?"

Atinuk shrugged as he wrapped Paaten's blanket around Nefe's shoulders. He plopped down beside

Aitye and grabbed her hand. "We will see what he wants when they arrive."

Nefe looked down at her own hands, remembering the constant truth she had told herself since she left the palace: *I am alone.*

She curled them into fists. *It is better this way. I cannot hurt if I do not love anyone.*

Aitye wrapped an arm around Nefe and whispered in her ear, "Are you well?"

"Hungry." Nefe slid her shoulders out from Aitye's embrace.

"What is wrong? Have I wronged you in some way?" Aitye asked, removing her arm.

Nefe kept her mouth shut and stared at Paaten and Washuba, who drew near.

"Nefe?"

She pulled her blanket tighter over her shoulders and clamped down hard on her teeth. *Leave me alone. Can you not see it is for the best?*

Paaten stepped in front of them with his hands on his hips. "This is Washuba; he brings food for us. This is Katita and Arala. They have decided to leave the land of Hatti and seek refuge in Damaski. Let us welcome them as travel companions."

Nefe stared at the women's bandages. *Hittites. Disgusting—Paaten is friends with our enemies.* "Why are they wrapped?"

Paaten looked back at them and then at Washuba. "They are pretending to be lepers." He turned his face to Nefe. "That way, no one bothers them."

Washuba said, "*Semitekussâituk.*"

The women pulled the bandages from their faces, revealing their youth: one, older than Nefe and the other, about the age of Aitye.

Nefe muttered, "That would have saved us from the Hittite army."

Paaten shook his head. "The Hittite army would have killed us; we were too close to them to be allowed to live with leprosy."

Nefe shook her head. *They would not have bothered us.*

Atinuk looked up at Paaten. "Should we go further up the mountain pass before we eat? Are we in danger of either army finding us?"

"No, they are trying to establish order after Pulli's age caught up with him." Paaten turned to acknowledge Washuba as a signal to Atinuk not to speak of the slayings. "It should be fine if we eat first." He looked at Nefe and Aitye. "Unless you are able to go farther?"

Nefe shook her head just as her stomach grumbled again.

Washuba chuckled and went to his cart. He pulled out some fish from a barrel of salt. He spoke to Paaten, who stooped at the fire pit and began to build up the fire: "*Tarnatuk pahhur ak, arama.*"

Nefe watched Paaten chuckle in response with a vacancy in her eyes. *I do not want fish. I would rather not eat. Nothing sounds appetizing. It would be tasteless on my tongue anyway.*

Aitye's stare burned the side of her face. Nefe glanced at her. "What?"

Aitye held her gaze for a moment before looking away. She stood up and took the fish from Washuba while Atinuk fetched the cooking pot and the cutting knife from Paaten's travel sling.

The two Hittite women came and sat next to Nefe. They glanced around. Washuba spoke gently to them and motioned to Nefe. "*Happarzi lāmanas.*"

"*Assu.* I am Katita," one woman spoke in Akkadian to Nefe.

"I am Arala," the other said.

"Nefe." She shut her mouth to keep from saying her full name and title. She turned away from them; they stank like the Hittites they were. She barely understood the blabbering of the inferior Akkadian language and nothing of the savage language of the Hittites. She did not care to learn, either. She would speak Egyptian, and those who served her would translate. Her nose turned up, and she jutted her chin. She refused to smell her own stench that traveled up her nostrils.

"Are you from Damaski?" one spoke in broken Akkadian.

Nefe ignored her and pulled the blanket tighter over her shoulders.

They whispered to each other in Hittite while Nefe looked away. The other asked, "Do you live in Damaski?"

Nefe glanced at them. "No." She spoke in Egyptian. "Leave me alone."

She stood up and walked off into the woods. She rounded a large tree and collapsed against its trunk out of sight. Her lip trembled. Her mind was blank. Her world was collapsing once again around her. She squeezed her eyes shut and focused on the bird calls on the air. *Nothing is the same. Nothing will be the same. What is the point of going on? I do not want this life. I want my old life back. I want my sister. I want my mother. I want my father! I want Pawah to die for what he did.*

Her breath hitched in her chest, and she realized she struggled for air. Her fingers dug at the linen tunic covering her heart. She stopped breathing until the moment the dark circle rounded her vision, and she took a sweeping breath.

It is all too much.

Her eyes opened once the smell of fish floated to her and the light murmur of conversation was close behind.

"The fish are ready," came a whisper on the side of the tree trunk.

Nefe leaned over and saw Aitye sitting there.

"Leave me alone, Aitye," Nefe mumbled and sat back.

"I cannot do that, Nefe." Aitye crawled around and sat next to her. She leaned her head back into the trunk.

"How long have you been sitting here?" Nefe turned her head away and crossed her arms.

"Does it matter?"

Aitye's soft voice reminded her of Ankhesenpaaten's when she would comfort her. Nefe closed her eyes, pushing away the memory. It was too painful.

"I know you are hurting."

Nefe bit her tongue.

"Give this new life a chance. We have not even made it to Damaski yet. We—"

"I do not want this life. You would not understand. You have someone. Atinuk cares for you. He saved you. I have no one. My sisters are all traveled to the Aten. My mother and father are gone. I am alone."

"You are making yourself alone. You have me and—"

"You have Atinuk. I am nothing to you. I am a burden to you. Just leave me alone."

"That is not true, Nefe." Aitye took her hand. "I love you. It will be easier once we settle into a new life. I promise you."

"People make a lot of promises." Nefe yanked her hand away. "They fail; people journey on to wait for us in the afterlife; it is easier not to expect too much from people and their promises. It is easier not to . . . " Her voice trailed off.

"Easier not to love? To say nothing? To keep to yourself? Not to share in the joys and sorrows of life? To—"

"You know nothing!" Tears burned Nefe's eyes as the truth in Aitye's words seared her soul.

"I know loneliness is a long, sad lie."

Nefe gritted her teeth to hold herself together while Aitye continued to speak.

"You are never alone, but one day, if you push away all those who love you, you will never know what life could have offered you." Aitye shook her head. "What a horrible life."

Nefe drew her legs to her chest and wrapped her arms about them. She hid her face in between her knees. "When Paaten and you travel to the afterlife, who will I have then? Who will be there for me? Is it not better to be prepared than to be suddenly alone?"

"Nefe, there are many people in Damaski. I am sure there are people there your age. You are no longer the King's Daughter. You could be married and have children. You could have many friends."

Marriage?

Nefe had never considered it. She was to be a celibate priestess of Isis if Tut did not take her for a wife as well. But as the image of Aitye and Atinuk holding hands passed through her memory, she considered marriage. She was of age.

Aitye was still speaking. "The possibilities are endless, but you have to accept your past and let it go."

What ridiculousness! She spouted, "How can I let go of my family?"

Aitye sighed and looked off into the sparse

313

mountain woods. She was silent for a long time, and Nefe's heart sank. *Aitye cannot help me.*

"Consider this," Aitye began, and Nefe perked up, hoping there was something Aitye could say to make her see the hope in a future in Canaan. "The tree. It starts as a seed. It grows roots and then sprouts. It pushes through the dirt and grows strong and tall, but it always keeps its roots, for without them, it withers and dies. But if it never emerges from the dirt, it never lives either."

Nefe squeezed her arms around her legs. "What are you saying, Aitye?"

"You have to push up from the dirt, Nefe." Aitye draped an arm over Nefe's shoulders. Her warmth caused the tension in Nefe's shoulders to fade.

"My family and my past are my roots," Nefe whispered but shook her head at a sad realization. "I will never see them again."

"Just as we do not see the tree's roots, but they will give you the strength to rise from the ground so that you can stand tall and grow." Aitye squeezed her arm around Nefe.

As Nefe stared at a tall tree in the distance, she pressed her lips into a soft smile. A softness pressed against her soul. *Maybe there is life in Damaski.* In the moment, the air seemed fresher, and the morning sun seemed to fall perfectly through the trees. She had not felt this much at peace since the last night she laid her head down in the palace.

"And growing tall means you need to eat; the fish is ready." Aitye still peered at her.

Nefe's smile faded. "I know what you are saying, Aitye. I just need some more time."

Aitye rubbed Nefe's back. "Trees do not grow tall overnight, but when you are ready, there are those of us who are here for you. You are never alone, even if you think you are."

A tear rolled down Nefe's cheek as Aitye guided her head into her shoulder, wrapping an arm about her.

CHAPTER 28
ESCAPE FROM DISTRUST

Atinuk dropped the dead ibex by the fire; its glassy amber eyes stared up at Paaten, and a single arrow perfectly pierced its heart. Atinuk wiped the sweat from his brow. "That is heavy." He looked at Aitye and Nefe, who sat huddled under their blanket by the fire in the setting sun. The two Hittite women sat across from them. Washuba pointed to himself. "Man," he said in Akkadian and then repeated in Hittite. Paaten said it in Egyptian. Then all four women repeated "man" in Akkadian, or at least attempted to.

Atinuk drew in a deep breath. "Rest assured, they have the rest of their lives to learn," he chuckled in Akkadian and plopped down next to Paaten. They pulled their knives out of the travel sling and began to work on skinning the ibex while listening to Washuba's lesson. "How did you learn to speak so many languages?" he asked Paaten.

"My father studied in the temples of Thoth even though he was in Pharaoh's Army. He loved languages. He taught me, ensuring I could at least speak Akkadian and understand Hittite and Nobiin. He said knowing their language may save my life one day should I be fighting abroad and need to get home. He was right." He paused from his task and looked to the west in memory of his father. "He was right."

Atinuk nodded and pursed his lips as he cut.

"I only knew the Mitanni tongue," Atinuk offered to continue the conversation, "but Akkadian is pretty close to it . . . " Atinuk bobbed his head. "Somewhat. Not really. It took me years to learn Akkadian. Almost a decade to learn Egyptian."

"You still have not learned Egyptian." Paaten chuckled.

"I speak it well enough for you to understand me, O great General."

Paaten laughed at Atinuk's inflated confidence and at Nefe's disgusted face as Washuba pointed at her. Paaten called out, "Woman," to help Aitye and Nefe understand what Washuba was pointing at. At the translation, Nefe's shoulders dropped, and her brow smoothed. She repeated the word with a small chuckle.

The two men worked a few moments in silence listening to the lessons until Paaten asked, "So this shared land in Damaski—where is it?"

Atinuk sat back on his heel and rested his wrist

on his other knee. He twirled the knife with his hand and swallowed. He scanned their small group: Washuba, the two Hittite women, Nefe and Aitye, and lastly, Paaten.

He picked up the ibex's leg and continued to skin it. "I would rather not talk about it, as you wield a knife in your hand."

"Why, Atinuk?" Paaten set to work again. "Do you not trust me?"

Atinuk scoffed. "You speak of trust. Yet you still do not trust me."

Paaten shook his head. "You are right. I do not trust you."

"Why?"

"Answer my question first."

"We are no longer on your barge, Paaten. You answer my question first."

Paaten stared at him, acknowledging the courage to speak such a thing. He smiled. "Fine, I will speak first." He twirled the knife and stabbed it into the dirt as a sign of peace between them. He leaned back against the tree trunk. "You keep something from me. Still. I no longer doubt you want safety for Aitye and the King's Daughter. I have trusted you since before the storm in that regard, but there is something you withhold from me. What is it?"

Atinuk sighed in relief and smiled. "So all that time you spent telling me—"

"I was entertaining myself."

Atinuk peered at him through slitted eyes and then shook his head. "You had me fooled."

Paaten chuckled. "It would not have been entertaining if I had not."

"Of course." He returned to the chore of preparing dinner.

Paaten waited for a response to his original question, but none came. He began again. "Tomorrow we will set foot on my land, and I want to know if I am introducing a threat to my family. What are you not tel—"

"Niwa knows I am no threat."

Hearing Atinuk speak his wife's name made him pause for a moment, even though he had tentatively anticipated it. "So you are the one who claims to be Danel's great-grandson?"

"I *am* his great-grandson. I proved it to your wife. I can prove it to you. I can prove it to the city elders. She begged me not to go to them, though. In doing so, I would take the land from her and those women." He spoke in a low voice and gestured toward the two Hittite refugees. He stopped and wiped his brow yet again. "I told her that I had a woman I needed to take from Egypt. As long as I had land to pass to my children from her, I would not go to the city elders."

Paaten nodded along. He had already assumed as much from what Atinuk had revealed in the beginning and from what he had learned from Washuba a few days earlier.

"She adopted me as her son that day."

Paaten stopped nodding. His eyes grew big. "What?"

"I never told you." His back slumped. "Part of me needed to see if you were in fact as faithful as Niwa described you; I needed to see if you were honorable and worthy of my great-grandfather's wealth." He too stabbed the dirt with his knife and leaned back against a rock. He stared at the fire.

Paaten stared at him. This man was his adopted son, all this time? "Are you saying you are my son?"

"It was what Niwa and I agreed to." Atinuk faced Paaten. The shadows of the fire fell across his face. "I also feared for my life in the beginning. I thought you would kill me to keep the land for your children."

Paaten scoffed. "That would never be justified in the eyes of Ma'at."

"I know that now. I know you do not kill for personal gain, but how was I to know that then? Pawah told me nothing but lies, and I saw firsthand the corruption that tore down the house of Egypt." He shrugged. "So my great-grandfather's inheritance will be split among me and your children."

Paaten noticed he kept mentioning "children" instead of son or child. *Surely, he knows Niwa is past the age of bearing children by now. I will have no more children with her. Maybe he does not know the Akkadian word for a single child.*

"I am not a greedy man." Atinuk shook his head. "I do not need that much land or wealth. I could not leave her with nothing, especially when my great-grandfather married her for the sole reason of giving her his wealth when he perished."

"When did you see my wife? I thought you said you saw Royal Wife Kiya before she passed. The plague took her not even two seasons after I returned to Egypt."

"I arrived after you left Damaski. I made my way to Egypt, and by the time I got to Aketaten, she was sick and dying." He fidgeted his fingers. "I was too late."

He imagined Niwa and Paebel sick and dying when he returned home, and a sense of dread filled him. The fear had been the same for the past nine years, but he had learned to push past it and not to substitute assumption for truth. He noticed Atinuk's slouched shoulders. "I am sorry you could not be with her." Paaten took a deep breath and narrowed his eyes in focused thought. "I truly am."

"You only say these things now because you know I can strip you from your land."

Paaten rolled his head over his shoulder and stared at him with an expressionless stare of disbelief. *He cannot be serious.*

Atinuk smirked. "You are right. There is no fun in goading someone if they know it." He rubbed his hands on his thighs and stretched his legs out. "No, I have been watching you for a long time. It was my job to watch Pharaoh, his Queen, and their stewards. You were around the Queen and Pharaoh Neferneferuaten quite a lot near the end, but you never seemed to falter in your dedication and duty, both to the throne and to your wife." He glanced back at Paaten. "I think you are as faithful as Niwa described and worthy to share in my inheritance."

Paaten's chest swelled with gratitude. "Thank you for not leaving my wife and child in poverty."

Atinuk stared curiously at Paaten and blinked. He pursed his lips. He opened his mouth to speak but then grinned as a light lit in his eyes. "I could not leave them like that. I could not strip them from their livelihood. I am not a greedy man, as I have said." Atinuk rested his head against the rock and closed his eyes. "I just need meat and wine."

Paaten picked up his knife, chalking up the confusion over "children" and "child" to Atinuk's imperfect grasp of Akkadian linguistics, and restarted the chore of preparing dinner. "Greedy men need meat and wine instead of beans and beer," Paaten chuckled.

"Speaks the beast of a man," Atinuk mocked, taking one last moment to rest before he lifted the ibex's leg once again to continue skinning the animal.

CHAPTER 29
ESCAPE FROM ANGER

HE SAW HER IN THE DISTANCE. HER LONG BROWN hair flowed in the soft breeze under her linen headdress. She walked the long estate that Danel and he had made sure would sustain her and keep her safe. Washuba led the donkey-pulled cart full of the supplies. The four women and Atinuk walked beside him. As Paaten's feet took him to his now-shared estate, his mind raced. What would he say to her? After nine years?

His fears of her dying in the plague subsided as she stood alive in front of him. The urge to wrap her in his arms and lay upon her lips twenty-nine years of passion was stilled only by the presence of Nefe, Aitye and Atinuk.

His gaze fell upon her emerald eyes. Silver teased her faded tresses, and the slight wrinkle of age accompanied her brow, but she still was the most beautiful woman he had ever laid eyes on. His heart thumped within his chest as she looked him up and down. Washuba and Atinuk stood speaking, but Paaten was not listening to them.

Paaten said nothing, for his heart beat too loudly in his ears. Washuba escorted the Hittite women to the old house Paaten had built for Niwa.

Niwa had her eyes locked on him, not acknowledging the others for a moment. Did she recognize him in Canaanite clothes? It had been almost three decades since she had seen him dressed like that.

"Welcome," she said, turning her head to Aitye and Nefe. "Atinuk, so this is your Tadukhipa?" she asked as she looked at Aitye. "And her daughter?" Her gaze fell to Nefe, but her brow knitted in confusion, assumedly at Nefe's age. She spoke in perfect Akkadian.

Atinuk's chin dipped. "No," he whispered. "Tadukhipa was among those taken in the plague."

She looked at Paaten with a hateful glower and said before Atinuk could continue, "Is this your wife and daughter then, Canaanite?"

Paaten shook his head. That hate. It ripped open all his old wounds of battle and laid him bare on a bed of fire.

"No, Niwa." Atinuk again drew her gaze. "Tadukhipa had asked me to look after her sister wife's daughters as her last request. This is Nefe, the only remaining daughter. This is Aitye, her sister wife's steward; this is the woman I have come to love since Tadukhipa's passing."

Niwa smiled with a wince and rubbed his arm. "I am sorry, Atinuk. You are a good man for honoring her wishes. I wish you could have had your life with your Tadukhipa, but I am so happy for you in finding love once more."

Atinuk nodded. "I will take them to my home, Niwa, as I planned to take Tadukhipa, if you allow it."

She smiled at him with pressed lips. "Your house is built next to mine, as we agreed. It has remained empty for most of your absence. It is empty now."

Paaten took a small step toward her, but she snapped her head to him. Her eyes held a rage that fueled their bright-green color. "I see you, Paaten." Her eyes ran down to his toes and back up to his head. Her jaw grew taut, and she swallowed.

"Take your Egyptian women, if Atinuk changes his mind about them, and find a cave to sleep in."

"Niwa, that is not fair," he said at her indication of his unfaithfulness.

She thrust a finger in his face. "You do not get to speak of fairness." Then she spun around and headed for her home.

He watched her walk away from him, as he had done to her all those years ago, but she did not look back as she went into the home.

Nefe whispered to Aitye, "She said something about 'women.'"

Aitye pulled on his sleeve. "I heard something

about a cave. What did she say? Does she not want us here?"

Paaten was not listening. His mind had turned to that day he had first decided to leave her to go back to Egypt. His heart wrenched, ripped, and tore, once again. "Atinuk," he said. "Please take Nefe and Aitye to your home. I need to speak with Niwa."

With a long stride, he stalked up to his house while Danel's words pounded in his ears: *Do not leave her at all. She may not be the same woman when you return.*

He knocked on the door, and Paebel answered it. He looked almost like Paaten, except he had shimmering hazel eyes. He stood a hair shorter, but his physique comprised the same broad shoulders and thick legs. The same defined chin adorned his face. Paaten's heart fell into his stomach. His son was a young man at sixteen years of age. Hair graced his lip and jaw. The next breath stung him. *Nine years since I have seen my son.*

Paebel studied his face.

"Son." Paaten swallowed. He reached out and put a hand on his shoulder.

A wave of recognition crossed Paebel's face. "Everyone said you were dead, but I knew you lived," Paebel said and dropped his head. He rammed his body into Paaten's, arms open wide around his father. "Are . . . are you here to stay?"

The same seven-year-old boy from his memory appeared in his arms when he had to kneel to hold him. He had missed Paebel's transition to manhood, but no longer would he miss out on his life. The realization of finally being home took root in his heart, and he squeezed his son, pressing his chin against the top of his full head of hair.

"Yes," the answer finally came. "Yes."

Paebel let out a captive breath and then pulled away from his father with eyes alit and a wide smile. He turned and yelled into the house. "Mother! Father is home. He is here. He has returned. He is alive! Just as you said; just as I told you!" Paebel rushed toward the room, but Paaten caught his arm.

"I have hurt your mother. Let me go to her alone."

Paebel looked at the slightly ajar door. Then he nodded and gave his father one more hug and pat on the shoulder. "I am glad you are home at last, Father."

Paaten placed a light hand on Paebel's cheek. "Thank you for taking care of the estate in my absence. We shall work together now, my son . . . my grown son." Pride filled his eyes at Paebel's manly build and his care of his mother.

Paebel nodded. "I understood your duty to your gods in keeping your oath, Father." He glanced to the slightly opened door. "Mother does too. She told us of you every day. It was as if you were here with us." His eyes held the same pride for his father, a man of his word. "Now, you can be."

His son's acceptance of his long absence caused Paaten to lift a prayer of gratitude to the gods, but Paebel's mention of "us" made him question who "us" was as Paebel walked out of the house, leaving Paaten and Niwa alone.

Paaten pushed open the door and saw Niwa in a chair by the fire; her headdress lay beside it in a heap. *It has been nine years. How can Paebel be so happy to see me, yet Niwa pushes me away?* His thoughts drifted to Washuba's confession. *Maybe she does not want me to find out, but I do not hold it against her.* His thoughts focused on the promises he made to her. He had kept every one.

"Paebel built this for me," she said, running her hand along the smoothed wood of the armrest.

Paaten knelt before her. He grabbed her skirt and wrenched it into balls within his fists. "I—" he began.

"Did you think, after all these years, I would fall into your arms? And we could be the happy family that *I* have always wanted?" She grabbed his hand and pushed it off of her skirt. "No! *My* children and I are a happy family without *you*! I have shed too many tears for you. I have no more to shed!"

Children? Paaten opened his mouth to speak, but Niwa spoke first again.

"Of all the men who came and forced me to bed, none of them hurt me as much as you."

Her words stabbed him in his heart. "Niwa?" He shot up, hating being compared to men such as Pulli.

"The only good things I have regarding you are the children you left me with. I love them. They have my heart, for it will never be yours again."

"Niwa," he whispered and stood her up with him.

She let him guide her from the chair, which was an action that contradicted her words. *She is angry. I understand, but maybe she still loves me.*

"I—"

She cut him off again. "I see you bring Egyptian women here. To throw in my face? To show me that you chose them over me and your children all this time? Your home has always been Egypt. You have been with Egyptian women. You chose Egypt over me." Her green eyes flamed. "I mourned you, Paaten, time and time again. I thought if you were alive, surely, surely, you would have sent a message to me. But I can see you were too busy with your Egyptian women. I thought if you were alive, you would have tried to contact me."

Tears glistened in her eyes. "I thought surely, when we received word that the female Pharaoh took the throne, he would keep his promise. He would come back; he would return to us. But I waited years for you, Paaten. Nothing."

A grimace fell on her lips.

"Then those dreams . . . they haunted me with my memories. They were so real. It was like you were here yesterday, but I knew my Paaten would never go more than a year without at least a message of some kind. So you must have been killed."

Tears ran down her cheeks.

"But I will cry no more for you. You have toyed with me long enough. You left me to fend for myself with no word from you. I hate you!" She unsuccessfully attempted to shove him away. "Leave."

Paaten grasped her hand and ran his fingers along her wrist. "After all the times you told me to stay?"

"And you left. You denied me."

"You agreed to this life. I told you I would come back to you as much as I could. I had written you many letters"—he pulled out the mess of papyruses in his belt—"but Mai journeyed to Re, and Imhotep became maimed, and I could not go myself. I did not trust any other to deliver my letters and read them to you. We were caught in a storm at Berytus on our way here; it ruined them. I am sorry, Niwa. I tried as much as I could to bring them to you."

He stopped to gather his thoughts while she took the papyruses with their smeared ink. Her shoulders lowered as she turned a now-dried papyrus over in her hands.

"That Egyptian woman out there is the daughter of Pharaoh. My dream came true, Niwa. Pharaoh was killed. I promised her I would save her daughters and take them away from Egypt, but only one decided to come with me. I am released of that oath to the gods, now. I never chose Egypt over you."

"Yes, you did," her soft whisper came.

He ignored her. "I had the same dreams. I did not know if you and Paebel were taken in the plague. Every night I wondered, but I would not let myself mourn you. I told myself you were alive and that I would not believe otherwise until I came and saw for myself. And now that I have come, I am here forever."

She closed her eyes and fell to her knees, letting the letters fall to the ground. "I can only mourn you so many times, Paaten. I cannot do it again."

He knelt beside her and grabbed one of her hands, now limp. Their gazes locked, but she turned her head, as if refusing him. "You do not have to, Niwa. I am here. I am here to stay."

She closed her eyes and shook her head. "I waited so long to hear those words. I thought they would bring me joy, but all I can think of is . . . "

She took a deep breath and chewed her lip, pushing back tears as she hesitated.

"I was unfaithful to you, Paaten," she blurted out.

He caressed her cheek. "I know of Washuba's kiss."

She snapped her head toward him, and a pink hue came over her cheeks. "It was more than a kiss."

"But he said—"

"It was a kiss, nothing more, but to me, it was. I wished to be with him. I wanted to be with him. Day after day, I considered taking ram's blood and showing it to the city elders, claiming I had received word of your death."

Even though her words pained him, Paaten fell to his bottom beside her and pulled her close. "Why did you not?"

"Washuba . . . after all he has done for me and the women who live here, I still see a Hittite man. He kissed me, a married woman. It seemed he had no regard for my marriage, even though we had received no word of your passing. I did not know if he would keep his promises to me as you had." She scoffed. "Yet I longed for his touch and his embrace, as I longed for yours."

He could understand; he had fought the same urges. "I still long for yours, Niwa."

She dropped her head with a sad smile. "I also think it was because I was ashamed of my feelings toward Washuba. I needed you, and you were not here. Everyone except our children told me that I should consider you dead after the fifth year." Her arms crossed. "Perhaps it was the fear of confirming that I would never see you again. I could have a certain future with Washuba versus an uncertain future with your memory. I accepted your death, but I never truly believed it."

"Then you never accepted it, my love." He grasped her hand. "Otherwise, you would have married Washuba; you would not have thought twice about taking ram's blood to the city elders. You would not have felt ashamed."

She rested her head on his shoulder and squeezed his hand as his arm wrapped about her. "I knew I had not received papyrus with blood. I never heard word that Pharaoh had a new General. I had dreams of you; if your gods are real, why would they keep sending me dreams if you were gone? I told the children these things, and they held me to my resolve.

Paebel said his father would keep his word, and you have proved him right . . . " Her voice trailed off as she nestled into his embrace. "I feel so safe here in your arms, just as safe as I did so long ago. I had forgotten how it felt."

He refreshed his memory of her honey, oil and wine scent. She had said "children" again. Had he another child? Was she speaking of the Hittite women's children? She considered them all her family. He pushed past the thought.

"We have the rest of our lives together to remember and to live like we did for those few months. Do you remember them? I dream of that time always. When I chased you in the garden after you splashed my legs with water from the irrigation channel?"

She smiled. "I loved you so much then, Paaten. I thought we would grow old together."

"We can now. I made you that promise."

"But we are already old," she chuckled and stroked her faded brown hair streaked with strands of silver.

He shook his head. "Older, but not old." He leaned his forehead to hers. "My heart was and is always with you, Niwa. There was never an Egyptian woman; there was never any other woman." After a moment, he chuckled with a grin. "Even Atinuk can attest to that. He spied on me for eight years to see if I was worthy enough of his ancestor's wealth."

She pressed her lips into a soft smile. "I do not

need his attestation." Her smile faded, and she whispered, "I am sorry I lashed out at you."

He shook his head and stroked her arm. "I am sorry nine years separated us. No more. If you are willing, I want to earn your desire and love again."

She closed her eyes, pushing out tears. Bringing his hand to her cheek, she implored, "Do not leave again."

"I have promised."

"I know—deep inside, I know—but there is a part of me that is still scared. I still long for your touch, Paaten." She leaned into his arms. "Your embrace. I cherished those dreams even though they broke my heart."

He cupped her cheek and smoothed away a few stray wisps of her hair. "They will not be dreams anymore, Niwa." He pulled her into his lap, letting her rest her head on his chest. He took a deep breath as the fire warmed him. "You once told me that you wanted a life with me, no matter how little time it might be."

He caressed her hand in his.

"Is that still true?"

She lifted her head and gazed into his eyes. "Yes," she whispered, barely audible. "Always."

A smile grew upon his face as she leaned toward him. His hands ran through her hair and grasped the base of her neck as he emblazoned his seal of dedication upon her lips. "I have missed you, Niwa."

CHAPTER 30
ESCAPE FROM THE PAST

NEFE SAT ON A LARGE STONE OUTSIDE OF ATINUK'S house. Her spine slumped, and she looked toward the river and the mountains beyond. She was alive and in Damaski. She was safe. Her gaze fell to the women and servants working their gardens.

"A new life?" She shook her head. "There is nothing for me here."

"I do not see it that way." Aitye's voice startled her. She came to sit on the rock beside her.

"I do," Nefe muttered. "Paaten only came here for his *Hittite* wife, as it turns out." She reflected on what Atinuk had told them only moments earlier before she had stormed out of the house. "It was never to keep me safe."

Aitye chuckled.

"What?" Nefe peered at her.

"His wife has been here for almost thirty years. I think he has always wanted to keep the royal family safe. Why do you think he stayed away from her so long?"

Nefe did not have an answer, nor did she want to think on such things. "Because she is a Hittite . . . ?"

The question soured her tongue. *The Hittites are the enemy. That was what everyone always said; that is what I knew as truth from an early age.*

She wondered how the General of Pharaoh's Armies had had a Hittite family and a Canaanite land full of Hittite refugees all this time and no one knew about it. *Had I known about it when we left Aketaten, I would have called him a traitor.* She rubbed her neck. *But now . . . I do not know what to think.*

"He still loves her. He still stayed away from her to serve your family." Aitye followed her stare out at the women in the fields.

Nefe thought about what she said. *I guess love that survives that much absence is true even if it is with a Hittite woman.* She scanned all of the women there. There were all seemingly Hittites with their lighter skin and brown locks. She saw Arala and Katita emerging from the little house in the distance. They were smiling. *A new life for them. A new life for me. I will have to relearn everything I know—even how I am supposed to feel about Hittites.* If she were to be completely honest with herself, Arala and Katita did not seem as bad as she had been led to expect. They were friendly during the last few days on the mountain pass to Damaski; they were nothing like the horrid Hittite soldiers she had encountered at Berytus. She pushed that memory away. She had been told all Hittites were like *them*, but it seemed not to be so. Washuba was funny. He had made her chuckle and smile in the Akkadian lessons he taught her while in the pass.

Aitye cut into her thoughts. "You are here in Damaski, and you have your whole life ahead of—"

"You keep saying that," Nefe cut her off. "I see nothing. We made it here. So what? Now what?"

"Life is only beginning, Nefe."

Nefe crossed her arms. "It does not seem as great as you made it sound in the mountain pass. There is nothing for me here."

Aitye pulled both of Nefe's hands into her lap and took a deep breath. "I am asking you to do what your mother wanted and start over. Her last words to Paaten were to remember his promise to take you to a new life. She was killed knowing that you would be given this chance. Live a life that makes you happy."

Nefe averted her gaze as she thought of her poor mother while Aitye continued speaking: "She gave you this life; you cannot do that if—"

"I know."

Aitye pressed her lips into a sad grin. "Knowing and accepting are—"

"—two different things." Nefe shook her head. "But what shall I do here, Aitye? Pull weeds?" Nefe gestured toward the women tending the estate's gardens. "I will be the best weed puller in Damaski—"

"Stop it. You know how to weave and play the lute

and the harp. You sing praises to the Aten—I am sure there will be a young man who loves your voice. That is, if you want to marry, and if not, there are many women on this estate who remain unmarried. They seem to have full lives."

"Yes, full lives pulling weeds. I am a Daughter of the King. Everything I know is in Egypt. All of my lessons, all of the temple rituals—everything I know means nothing here. What am I to do here in Damaski?"

"Learn." Aitye squeezed her hands with an urging in her voice. "Explore. Start with learning Akkadian? Do you want to be a merchant woman? Do you want to be a wife? What do you want to be?"

Nefe shrugged. "I can ask you the same. Are you going to marry Atinuk?"

"The future is unknown." Aitye grinned.

Seeing Aitye's smile from a sideways glance, Nefe shook her head, thinking the opposite. "And that scares me."

Aitye lifted Nefe's chin to face her. "It should not. I am going to start by learning Akkadian, and you should as well. Few people speak Egyptian here. It will be lonely if you cannot communicate with anyone else."

Aitye rubbed her back as a young man walked by them with a bag of feed thrown over his shoulder. He glanced at Nefe and then stopped. "Are you the Egyptians?"

"You speak our language?" Nefe's jaw fell at the man's choppy speaking, but she was still amazed anyone in Damaski would see they were Egyptian and could speak their language, especially on a farm estate such as this.

He stared at Nefe, eyes entranced. "Not much."

"How do you know the Egyptian tongue?" His height and build reminded her of someone.

He chewed his lip and lowered the bag of feed to the ground. "Could you say again slower?"

"How do you understand me?" Nefe slowly asked, taking note of the fine black hair over his lip and chin. *He has a handsome face too.* Her thought drifted to Aitye's talk of marriage, but she pushed away the notion. *But he is familiar to me.*

He stumbled through his words. "My father and a city elder taught me. Damaski is a tributary to Egypt, and I want to be a city elder one day." He said a few phrases incorrectly, but Nefe could understand what he was saying.

"Who is your father, that he knows Egyptian?"

He pointed to his house. "My father is your General Paaten."

Nefe averted her eyes. *That is why I thought he looked familiar. He is half Hittite . . . but maybe that is not so bad.* She stole a glance at him. *Yes, not so bad.*

"Paaten has a son?" Aitye asked as Atinuk walked toward them.

"Yes. I am Paebel." He smiled and glanced between Nefe and Aitye.

Nefe pressed her lips into a grin while her cheeks burned red.

A smile popped onto Aitye's face, and she placed a hand on Nefe's back, slightly pushing her to sit up straight. "I am Aitye, and this is Nefe." She pointed to Atinuk as he approached. "This is Atinuk."

Paebel waved, but his gaze ended on Nefe. "*Sulmu*," he greeted them.

Nefe kept her eyes averted while Atinuk spoke in remembrance of Paebel upon his first visit to the estate.

I have never spoken to another man my age who was not related to me, she realized. *Someone I am*—she gulped—*attracted to.*

She wanted to look up but could not bring herself to do it. *I can be married now, as Aitye says. That thought is frightening. What would I even say to him? He is probably already married. Look at him. Yes, must be.*

At the lack of further conversation after Atinuk had said his piece, Paebel waved again. "Enjoy Damaski," he stammered. He stooped to pick up the bag of feed.

Aitye jumped from the rock. "I can take that feed to the stables," she offered.

"It is heavy; I can do it." Paebel lifted it with one hand to hoist it onto his shoulder.

"I can." Atinuk stepped forward with Aitye and took the feed bag from him, not allowing Aitye to take it. "The donkeys are kept back there?" Atinuk asked, pointing to the stables barely visible at the back of the houses.

"Yes. Thank you." Paebel's arms fell to his side.

"Aitye, you do not need to come," Atinuk told her. "Sit, rest."

Aitye narrowed her eyes at him. "I want to see the stables," she said with a pointed tone in her voice.

Nefe's eyes grew wide as Aitye's intentions dawned on her. She glanced at Aitye and shook her head. *Do not leave me, Aitye!*

Aitye only smiled in response. "Why do you not sit with Nefe, Paebel? She is wondering where she will fit in on this land. Perhaps you can help her see a future here." Aitye watched Paebel do as she wished and stared at Nefe before she turned to accompany Atinuk to the stables.

Paebel walked up to Nefe and sat down. Nefe kept her eyes averted.

The silence between them only intensified the sound of the river in the distance, until Paebel finally spoke: "Have I said something to upset you?"

Nefe shook her head.

"Why do you not look at me?"

Nefe swallowed the lump in her throat. *Because I think you are handsome, and I do not know what to say to you.* She shrugged. "You are Paaten's son."

"I am," he chuckled, but then a hesitancy formed in his voice. "Does that concern yo—"

"Do you have a wife?" Nefe's eyes grew big as she stared at her hands. That question flew out of her mouth uncontrollably. Her ears tickled with a tingling burn at her blunder. She froze, not believing those words had left her lips.

"No." His lips spread over his face in a slow-building smile. "Women in Damaski are . . . greedy," he said after searching for the word. He spoke slowly with the wrong phrases still, but Nefe was able to understand what he was saying. "They want the wealth of the land, but they care not for my mother since she is from the land of Hatti. I am sixteen years old, and I should have a wife, but . . . " His voice trailed off. "I never met anyone who I thought would understand my heritage, being both Hittite and Egyptian."

Nefe lifted her face to him. *The mixed heritage makes his face beautiful to look at. His eyes are a rare blend of brown and green.*

"I am fourteen."

"And you do not have a husband?"

She shook her head.

"Egyptians are usually married by fourteen, unless I have misunderstood." He rubbed his neck and hung his head at Nefe's blank stare.

Is he implying that something is wrong with me?

"That did not . . . my question is not . . . I am not saying . . . I . . . Can I begin again?"

Nefe laughed at his burbling and nodded.

He awkwardly grinned and readjusted his seat upon the rock, squaring his shoulders to her. "Why

342

are you not married?" He paused, and then shook his head. "Again, that is not what I wish to say."

She laughed again, but stopped short. It felt good to laugh. She had not truly laughed in a long time. She laughed about thinking about laughing. Tears formed in her eyes. *It feels good to laugh.* She stopped again and beamed at Paebel.

His smile faded when he saw her tears. "No, do not cry. I do not mean to hurt you."

Nefe gave a slight shake of her head. "These tears are not for you." She wiped her eyes and chuckled once more. "Speak in Akkadian. It will come easier for you."

"Do you understand Akkadian?"

"Not much. Less than you know Egyptian." She smiled, but he held a sly grin before he rattled off in his native tongue.

"I think you are beautiful and cannot imagine why no man has taken you for a wife yet. The men you knew in Egypt must be stupid as well as blind."

Nefe bit her lip.

Curse me for not learning more Akkadian on the barge.

She replayed what he said in her mind, but he spoke so fast. "I understood something about men and Egypt."

"Close," he chuckled.

"Well," she said, looking to the stables, "Aitye told me I should start my life here by learning Akkadian."

She lowered her chin as she debated asking for help. But she would rather learn with him than with

Atinuk or Paaten. "Will you teach me?" She quickly added, "Then I will understand what you said."

"If you teach me more Egyptian," he proposed.

A light grew in her eyes.

A friend with whom I can share my knowledge of Egypt.

Before she could respond, a young girl appeared next to Paebel and pulled the sleeve of his tunic.

Paebel and Nefe jumped. She had not been paying attention to their surroundings, and the girl seemed to spring up from nowhere.

She mumbled something in Akkadian to Paebel while she glanced at Nefe.

Paebel responded and then looked to Nefe.

"This is my sister, Panna." He rubbed her dark, long curls. She pushed his hand away and narrowed her eyes at him.

"She is eight years old. I told her you are Egyptian, and she asks if you have any sisters?"

Nefe's smile fell, and she sat back.

"Sisters?" It was more a whisper to herself than a response.

Paaten had a whole family here; he had a whole second life. Nefe looked at the mountains and sighed. *My second life will be here as well, I suppose.*

"What is wrong, Nefe?" He reached out and grazed her hand.

His touch drew her attention. "I have no family, not anymore," she whispered, unable to look at him.

How could she laugh in one moment and feel such sorrow in the next?

His hand slipped into hers, causing her gaze to lift to him.

"You can be a part of this family. Everyone on this estate is a family."

She studied his face. He took after his father, and Panna looked like her mother.

Panna swung her shoulders and spoke too quickly for Nefe to understand.

Paebel smirked. "She asks if you will be her sister."

Nefe laughed, but a small sting pierced her heart as she answered, "Yes, I can be your sister."

The door from Niwa's house swung open. Paaten stepped through and looked around. His gaze fell on Paebel and then on Panna. Niwa appeared behind him and whispered in his ear.

"Panna?" he mouthed and came to her, kneeling in front of her. "Panna." His eyes ran over her and a bittersweet smile gripped his mouth. "You are beautiful," he whispered.

Panna eyed him with a strong tilt of her head.

Niwa knelt down as well. "This is your father, Panna. He has come home now."

Panna hesitantly took a step forward and then fell into Paaten's arms. He swallowed her whole body in his large embrace as she whispered, "Mother and Paebel told me all about you."

Nefe watched him; her own father had never

embraced her like Paaten did Panna. Yet, she felt a warmth grow in her cold core as she observed Paaten and the tears that fell from his eyes.

Throughout all these years, Paaten served Pharaoh, and he saved me. He gave up his own family for me and my family. The realization filled the vacancy in her heart. She scanned his wife, his son and his daughter. All at once, her shoulders felt at ease for the first time since the last night she had laid her head down in the palace. "Thank you, Paaten," she whispered to herself, inaudibly, "for saving me."

She saw Aitye out of the corner of her eye and glanced at her. Aitye stood next to a tree and looked up at its branches before returning her gaze.

Egypt will be my roots as I start my life in Damaski. I will grow tall and strong with my protector, Paaten, my comforter, Aitye, and my new friend, Paebel.

Nefe's face turned to the west, and she thought of her loved ones who were safely tucked away in their tombs. Then she looked toward Egypt. She could only hope Ankhesenpaaten still lived, and perhaps one day, she could see her again. But today and tomorrow, she would live free in the land of Damaski.

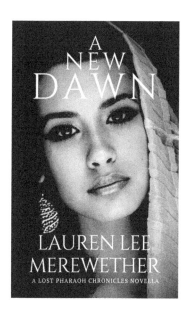

THE STORY CONTINUES

See what becomes of Ankhesenpaaten in the remaining volumes of *The Lost Pharaoh Chronicles* and the final complement, ***Nefertiti's Legacy***.

Continue the story with books three and four, ***Scarab in the Storm*** and ***Silence in the Stone***.

A LOOK INTO THE PAST

King's Daughter and the main series, *The Lost Pharaoh Chronicles*, take place during the 18th Dynasty of the New Kingdom. *King's Daughter* specifically begins at the end of Pharaoh Neferneferuaten's reign. This story is an offshoot of Lauren's highly rated and highly acclaimed debut series, *The Lost Pharaoh Chronicles*. Continue the series with book three: *Scarab in the Storm*.

This complement story is a part of a complement collection that is mostly fictionalized, but based on historical fact of that period. The following are a few examples:

One of the main characters, Nefe, is the daughter of Nefertiti and Akhenaten. Her historical name is Neferneferuaten Tasherit, where Tasherit means "The Younger." She was named after her mother once Akhenaten renamed her Neferneferuaten-Nefertiti. She was born in about year seven of her father's reign, around two years after her sister Ankhesenpaaten. In *Secrets in the Sand* and *King's Daughter*, her mother Nefertiti was Pharaoh Neferneferuaten, but some associate this Pharaoh with one of her daughters: Meritaten, Ankhesenpaaten, or Neferneferuaten Tasherit. A new theory suggests Pharaoh Neferneferuaten was the name under which two Queen Pharaohs, Meritaten and Neferneferuaten Tasherit, ruled. Whoever was Pharaoh, Neferneferuaten Tasherit disappears from the historical record. At the time of *King's Daughter,* she is fourteen years old. The author wanted to portray Nefe as a princess who had lost her family, her perception of her parents, her way of life, her home and her sister, who left her for someone else. Some may only see Nefe as a spoiled, royal child, but the author wrote her as a misguided, scared, and sheltered teenage princess trying to cope and progress through the stages of grief alone in an unfamiliar environment.

Another one of the main characters, Paaten, is based on the historical general of Pharaoh Akhenaten's armies, Paatenemheb. His tomb (TA24) was found empty in Aketaten. Some believe he is the same as Pharaoh Horemheb, a later Pharaoh, but most Egyptologists disregard that theory. His tomb was most likely emptied well before the Ptolemaic times when the southern tombs of Aketaten were used as storehouses; however, the author took liberties and decided since both of these two historical figures (Neferneferuaten Tasherit and Paatenemheb) were lost to time, she would write their story for them.

During the reign of Akhenaten and the subsequent Pharaohs, the military became lax and corrupt. In the story, Paaten takes a barge for their escape—one that a Cypriote says the King of Cyprus built. From the Amarna Letters, Akhenaten requested Egypt's naval ships to be built by the Cypriote King Alashiya. By the time of Pharaoh Horemheb, the seafaring ships are depicted with rails.

The Amarna letters also mention that Egypt lost the vassal state of Byblos (Kubna) during the reign of Akhenaten. The author took liberties to assume it was taken by the Hittites, but it could have been acquired by other Canaanite city-states that were attacking, since Egypt failed to intervene during the period. Additionally, the author assumed its southern sister port city of Beirut (Berytus) was also lost during the period of Neferneferuaten, but there is a lack of historical data on this topic.

The cliffs that Paaten, Atinuk and Aitye climbed during the storm at Berytus are referencing the cliffs on the Mediterranean coast of Beirut. [As a side note, this area includes the freestanding rock formations that are said to be the remains of the Greek mythological creature, Cetus, killed by the eyes of Medusa.]

Between Beirut and Damascus there is a

mountain range, Mount Lebanon, with forested areas and the Bekaa valley to the east. This is the location of the "mountain pass" the band of refugees takes from Berytus to Damaski in the story.

Additionally, Nefe does not understand what the Hittite soldier, the Hittite servant or Washuba are saying in the Hittite tongue. Using an online Hittite lexicon dictionary, the author attempted to write their complex language. Here are the rough translations of what the Hittite soldier and servant are saying in the order the phrases appear in the book:

- *Assu* is the informal greeting such as "hello"
- *Pennatuk para* means "you move (forward)"
- *Guen-marlanttuk* means "you (are a) foolish woman"
- *Tuk appiskia ukila* means "I take you for myself"
- *Lē pennatuk* means "do not move"
- *Lē appisktuk guen* means "Do not take the woman"
- *Hatti tiyamu guen-Akkad appiskimi daukila* means "You accuse me of taking the Akkadian woman for myself"
- *Semitekussāituk* means "You show them"
- *Tarnatuk pahhur ak, arama* means "You let (the) fire die, my friend"

- *Happarzi lāmanas* means "You (plural) trade names" ["Introduce yourself"]

The phrase "in peace" was the standard Egyptian greeting and farewell. The author could only find the words used similarly to the English "hello" in the Akkadian and Hittite languages, and instead of writing "hello," she used the words "assu" in Hittite and "sulmu" in Akkadian.

The following are other notes from the author's research from the time period:

- The author used "Pharaoh" as a title in the story due to the mainstream convention of Pharaoh meaning "king" or "ruler." Pharaoh is actually a Greek word for the Egyptian word(s) "pero" or "per-a-a," meaning "great house," in reference to the royal palace in Ancient Egypt. The term was used in the time period this series covers; however, it was never used as an official title of the Ancient Egyptian kings.
- Ancient Egyptians called their country *Kemet*, meaning "Black Land," but because the modern term *Egypt* is more prevalent and known in the world today, the author used Egypt when referencing the ancient empire.
- The term "citizen/citizeness" is similar to our modern "Mr." and "Ms."; "Mistress of

the House" is what they called a married woman in charge of her household.

- The body was very important in the Ancient Egyptians' beliefs of the afterlife. During this time period, they believed everyone had a ba, not just the Pharaoh, as in earlier times. The ba and ka would be released after death but would need to journey back to the body every night to rest. Without a body and/or without a name on their grave, the ba and ka would be lost, forever in a state of restlessness. This state is similar to our modern-day "hell." The same state would occur should Ammit devour the person's heart on their journey to the afterlife. Ammit would only devour the heart if it weighed heavy against the feather of Ma'at, meaning the person had committed unjustifiable crimes against the human and divine order, as judged by forty-two gods.

- Ancient Egyptians did not use the words "death" or "died," but for ease of reading this series, the author did use "death" and "died" in some instances. The Egyptians instead used euphemistic phrases such as "went to the fields of Re," "became an Osiris," and "journeyed to the west" to lighten the burden of the word "death."

- Gold was considered in the 18th and 19th

dynasties as the skin of the gods, and some sources say it could never have materialized into a trade commodity due to the symbolic importance placed upon it. Silver, similarly, was considered the bones of the gods, and, to a much lesser extent, bore the same symbolic importance.

The author loved diving deeper into this fascinating culture and hopes you did too. If you enjoyed this story and want to find out what happens with Ankhesenpaaten, continue reading *The Lost Pharaoh Chronicles* with books three and four: *Secrets in the Sand* and *Silence in the Stone*. End the saga with book four's complement, *Nefertiti's Legacy*.

Visit www.LaurenLeeMerewether.com for more information and to stay updated on new releases and new series.

Thank you for reading the second story of the complement collection for my debut series, *The Lost Pharaoh Chronicles*. I hope you enjoyed jumping into another culture and reading about what happens to General Paaten and Neferneferuaten Tasherit (Nefe).

If you enjoyed *King's Daughter*, I would like to ask a big favor: Please share with your friends and family on social media sites like **Facebook** and leave a review on **Amazon, BookBub** and on **Goodreads** if you have accounts there.

I am an independent author; as such, reviews and word of mouth are the best way readers like you can help books like *King's Daughter* and the original series, *The Lost Pharaoh Chronicles,* reach other readers.

Your feedback and support are of the utmost importance to me. If you want to reach out to me and give feedback on this book, offer ideas to improve my future writings, get updates about future books, or just say howdy, please visit me on the web.
www.LaurenLeeMerewether.com
Or email me at
mail@LaurenLeeMerewether.com

ACKNOWLEDGMENTS

First and foremost, I want to thank God for blessing me with the people who support me and the opportunities he gave me to do what I love: telling stories.

Many thanks to my dear husband Mark, who supported my early mornings and late nights of writing this book.

Thank you to my family, production team, beta readers, and launch team members, without whom I would not have been able to make the story the best it could be and successfully get the story to market.

Thank you to the Self-Publishing School Fundamentals of Fiction course, which taught me invaluable lessons on the writing process and how to effectively self-publish, as well as gave me the encouragement I needed.

<u>Finally, but certainly not least, thank you to my readers.</u> Without your support, I would not be able to write. I truly hope this story engages you, inspires you, and gives you a peek into the past.

My hope is that when you finish reading this story, your love of history will have deepened a little more—and, of course, you cannot wait to find out what happens next in the rest of the series and in the last complement story.

ABOUT THE AUTHOR

Lauren Lee Merewether, a historical drama fiction author, loves bringing the world stories forgotten by time, filled with characters who love and lose, fight wrong with right, and feel hope in times of despair.

A lover of ancient history where mysteries still abound, Lauren loves to dive into history and research overlooked, under-appreciated and relatively unknown tidbits of the past and craft for her readers engaging stories.

During the day, Lauren studies the nuances of technology and audit at her job and cares for her family. She saves her nights and early mornings for writing stories.

Get her first multi-award nominated novel, *Blood of Toma,* for **FREE**, say hello, and stay current with Lauren's latest releases at www.LaurenLeeMerewether.com

facebook.com/llmbooks

twitter.com/llmbooks

amazon.com/author/laurenleemerewether

bookbub.com/authors/lauren-lee-merewether

goodreads.com/laurenleemerewether

instagram.com/llmbooks

Scarab in the Storm

(The Lost Pharaoh Chronicles, Book III)

Egypt is divided and conspiracy runs deep—the boy King Tut inherits a nation of chaos, and his wife, Queen Ankhesenamun, is desperate to earn his trust.

Pharaoh Tutankhamun must decide Egypt's path amid political turmoil and corruption while Queen Ankhesenamun struggles to convince Pharaoh that their lives are at stake. With truth shrouded in mystery, doubt attacks the royalty as a power mercilessly pursues the crown. Egypt's fate is determined by Pharaoh's and Queen Ankhesenamun's success or failure in the coming storm.

The Lost Pharaoh Chronicles Complement Collection accompanies the main series.

Visit www.laurenleemerewether.com or Lauren's Amazon Author page to order the collection.

Releasing 2021

Please note the complement collection will contain spoilers if you have not read the series and relevant prequels first.

Nefertiti's Legacy will contain spoilers for entire *The Lost Pharaoh Chronicles* series and the complement *King's Daughter*.

The Lost Pharaoh Chronicles Prequel Collection

Visit www.laurenleemerewether.com or Lauren's Amazon
Author page to order.

Releasing 2019-2021

Discover how Tey came to the house of Ay in ***The Valley
Iris***, why Ay loved Temehu so much in ***Wife of Ay***,
General Paaten's struggle and secret in the land of Hatti in
Paaten's War, how Pawah rose from an impoverished
state to priest in ***The Fifth Prophet***, and the brotherhood
between Thutmose and Amenhotep IV in ***Egypt's
Second Born***.

The Mitanni Princess and ***King's Jubilee*** are available
for free via sign-up on Lauren's website.

*Note: King's Jubilee is the short-story version of Egypt's Second
Born.*

Made in the USA
Las Vegas, NV
24 June 2021